ONE LAST THING

A NOVEL

MELISSA HILL

Completely revised & updated 2nd edition.

Originally published in 2003 as *Something You Should Know*, by Poolbeg Press, Dublin.

NOTE

Note: This book was written, produced and edited in the UK, where some spelling, grammar and word usage will vary from US English.

1

The scales lay menacingly on the bathroom floor, daring Jenny to put herself out of her misery.

She stepped on and felt her throat go dry watching the needle come to a standstill after a long time bobbing back and forth. Then winced at the verdict.

Eleven and a half stone.

Damnit, she really needed to get her act together.

Getting into the shower, she heard Mike whistle from downstairs in the kitchen. She couldn't understand how her fiancé could be so sprightly in the mornings. He never seemed to want to pull the bedcovers over his head and drift back to glorious sleep, shutting out the rest of the world. Whereas she was *definitely* not a morning person.

Pity this exam was so soon she sighed, rinsing the shampoo out of her hair. She would need to study like the clappers today, so the earlier she got started the better. No way she'd nab this promotion if she didn't pass.

Life was so chaotic lately she'd been finding it hard to concentrate, but needed to make up for lost time now and hope that today's cramming would be enough. To be fair, Mike had gone out of his way to ensure that she had a quiet day to herself.

Jenny wrapped her wet hair in a towel before joining her fiancé downstairs in the kitchen.

He put a steaming mug and a plate of warm buttered toast on the table in front of her and kissed her lightly on the forehead.

"Morning sunshine."

She made a face.

He chuckled. "Now I know why I'm marrying you – your morning scowl always brightens up my day."

Biting back a grin, she took a bite of toast, grimaced and then spat it back out onto the plate. "Ugh. What's that?"

"What's what?"

"The toast - what did you put on the toast?"

"Kerrygold," he answered nonchalantly. "Why?"

"Kerrygold...." She trailed off in amazement. "I'm eating Low-Low these days, remember. I *can't* have real butter on my toast or anything else when I'm watching the scales."

"Low-Low, huh?" he said, his eyes twinkling with amusement. "So Leo Burdock's fry chips in Low-Low these days?"

"That's different. Chipper chips don't count..."

"Right," he said, struggling to keep a straight face. "Come on Jen, forget this dieting nonsense – you're perfect the way you are." He reached across the breakfast bar and planted another kiss on the top of her head.

"Nope, I'm determined, *really* determined to fit into that wedding dress in my wardrobe."

"Really determined, huh?"

"Absolutely."

"Right. So what about the Low-Low thing?"

"What?"

His eyes danced. "You're still eating that toast."

"But that's because – because I'm rushing, so I don't have time to wait for fresh stuff and – ah, stop it ..." Despite herself, Jenny chuckled, until remembering what lay ahead. "I dread hitting the books and look – it's such a nice day too." She looked wistfully out the window at the cloudless spring sky.

"You'll be fine once you get started." Mike pushed his plate away and refilled his teacup. "Anyway, it will be all over soon and then you can forget about it."

"That's the problem though," she mused. "It's *too* soon." She picked up one of the study manuals that lay on the table and stared at it as if willing the info to transport itself from the pages into her memory.

"You'll be grand," he soothed again. "You're already familiar with most of the material. Haven't you been working alongside the mortgage manager for months? You're bound to have picked up on the important stuff.

Just use today's peace and quiet to cram and then tomorrow night we'll go out for a bite and a couple of drinks. What do you think?"

Jenny nodded and they shook on it. He was right. There was no point in fretting about the exam. She should just get stuck in.

"I was thinking," he added. "If you don't mind combining work and play, I might ask the new guy along. I haven't had a chance to get to know him socially yet."

Jenny helped herself to another piece of toast. "Cool," she said. "I'm eager to meet the new whizz kid too. What's he like?"

"I think he's going to be a real asset. He's had plenty of marketing experience and you know how useless I am at that."

She smiled. Mike was an excellent programmer and while his firm provided software for some of Ireland's biggest companies, he was no marketeer. His business needed the right person to promote their stuff within a rapidly saturated Irish market. He and his partners had been trying for some time to find someone who knew the industry from the inside out. Seemed this new guy was a rare breed: a highly proficient programmer and equally adept at sales and marketing.

"He's no fool either," Mike continued. "Took us a while to hammer out a decent contract. Fresh from the States, he didn't want to come in on ground level and commission bonuses like the rest of them. Stephen thought he was a cocky little git."

"Ha. I'll bet he was just disappointed that you weren't employing some ravishing redhead with a cleavage to die for."

He chuckled at her all too accurate assessment of his business partner. "The lads already had a few run-ins as it is. Poor Frank kept calling him Ronan last week – he couldn't get the hang of his name and your man wouldn't stand for it. It's Roan, not Ro-n-an,'" Mike mimicked exaggeratedly.

Jenny's toast stopped halfway to her mouth. "What did you say his name was?"

"I know. Unusual, isn't it? Roan – I've never come across it before. I think he's originally from Kildare somewhere, he said."

Her mouth went dry and for a second she didn't think she would be able to breathe.

It couldn't be *him*, could it?

"I knew a guy from Kildare a few years back when I lived with Karen," she said, trying to keep her voice even, although her hands were shaking. "Roan Williams – I wonder is it the same person?"

Mike didn't seem to notice her discomfort.

"Yeah, Williams, that's his surname all right. Crikey. It's true what they say about it being a small world. Did you know him well?"

Jenny tried to swallow. The toast felt like a lead weight in her mouth. "Not that well," she answered automatically, her mind racing, unable to get to grips with this.

Roan Williams of all people ... working with Mike. Should she just say something? No, not yet. She needed some time to think about this, to process it.

Her fiancé's voice interrupted her thoughts. "Jen, did you hear me? Maybe we should go into the city centre tomorrow night – what do you think?"

She looked at him blankly.

"OK." He held his hands up, chuckling. "You're miles away already so I'll leave you to it. I'm off to battle the traffic and when I get home this evening, I'll pretend to be a first-time buyer and you can tell me everything there is to know about securing a mortgage for the house of my dreams, OK?" He drained his cup and put it in the sink, then gave Jenny a light kiss on the nose.

She instantly felt like a heel. "Sorry, I don't know how you put up with me. I'm just a bit ... distracted."

"Dunno either, but come August I'm stuck with you for good so I suppose I'd better get used to it." She swung at him as he ducked out the doorway, laughing as he went. "Oh, and don't forget," he added, popping his head back around the door. "I'll be back a bit later this evening so don't start on dinner too early."

"Are you sure you don't want me to go? I can always finish up early ..."

"It's grand. I just wish my little sister would get herself a job south of the Liffey and save us the journey. See you later."

Jenny nodded and forced another smile but it was a relief to see him leave. She remained sitting at the kitchen table for a long time after she heard the front door close, her thoughts going a mile a minute.

She shook her head, unable to believe this was happening, to say nothing of the timing.

Just when everything was going so well, fate had to throw one last curveball.

2

Karen checked her watch and quickened her pace as she strode down Grafton Street, cursing under her breath when she read the time.

She was going to be late.

It was almost nine o'clock and she still had to find the place. Pushing her dark hair away from her face, she stopped suddenly when an outfit caught her eye in the window of Pamela Scott - a seventies-print halterneck dress that would be perfect for Jenny's wedding.

Pity she already had her outfit. Ah, she might buy it for herself anyway. With everything that was happening lately, she deserved a treat.

Karen continued quickly towards College Green, and just as she reached the pedestrian crossing at Trinity College, she heard her phone ring from inside her handbag. The lights went green and she struggled to find the device whilst crossing the road. Blasted things....

She'd only just stepped into the doorway of the

Victorian bank building to take the call when the ringing promptly stopped. Typical.

"Shite," she exclaimed, glaring at a passer-by who was staring at her with undisguised interest. She was about to replace the phone in her handbag when it beeped loudly.

A text from Jenny: *CALL ME AS SOON AS YOU GET THIS.*

Sadly her friend would have to wait, Karen thought, rushing up the street. She was *definitely* late now. She raced along and eventually stopped in front of a building with Stevenson & Donnelly Solicitors inscribed on a brass plaque by the doorway. Then pushed the intercom buzzer to gain entry.

Inside, the receptionist smiled at her. "Miss Cassidy? Mr Donnelly is ready for you." She gestured to one of the doorways behind the reception area. "Would you like some coffee?"

"I'd love a cup, thanks." Karen smiled back as she removed her coat and knocked on the heavy wooden door.

"Come in, please."

She was duly greeted with a nod from a serious-looking older man seated behind a large oak desk with heavy books and sheets of paper strewn all over it.

Typical solicitor's practice.

"Karen, hello. It's nice to finally meet you face to face. Please – sit down." The solicitor gestured to the plush leather armchair in front of his desk.

"I'm very sorry I'm late, I couldn't find you at first."

"That's no trouble at all, dear. Did Linda offer you some coffee?"

At that very moment the aforementioned receptionist appeared with a tray, and Karen gratefully accepted a mug of strong coffee and a Rich Tea biscuit.

"Thank you, Linda." The solicitor smiled and then sat back in his chair. "So, let's get down to brass tacks. We discussed the basics over the phone but I just want to run through the broader specifics with you again, to get a better sense of the issue. The property in question - it's located in Harold's Cross, you said?"

Karen nodded. "Yes, a two-bedroom townhouse jointly purchased a couple of years ago."

"And there's a mortgage remaining on the property?"

"Yes. Which is basically the root of the problem. I'm unsure of my rights – legally I mean, because the house was never in my name. I just didn't see any need at the time."

"I see. Both mortgage and property were solely in your partner's name?"

"That's right," she answered solemnly.

"But you contributed financially throughout."

"Oh, absolutely – Shane and I each had separate accounts but we keep – I mean we kept – a joint account for utility bills, heating and whatever."

"Well, that's a start certainly. I assume you have bank statements that verify same? And Mr Quinn does not dispute the fact that you made mortgage contributions?"

"Not as far as I know, he doesn't. It's just ..." Despite herself, Karen was nervous. "From what I've read, it seems that it was always Shane's house, wasn't it – legally I mean and what I paid means nothing?"

"Mr Quinn may have been registered as sole mortgage holder, but in truth, the building society holds full title until the mortgage is fully repaid. Though based on what you've just outlined, any courtroom is likely to rule in favour of the other party."

He was so dispassionate about it all. Didn't he realise how hard it was for her to come here and discuss all of this with a complete stranger? Still, it meant nothing to him, she supposed. He was just doing his job. Sympathy didn't come into it. Karen had sought his advice and here he was advising her. What did she expect; a big hug, soothing words and a box of Kleenex?

"You see," she told him, "I have nowhere else to go so I'm still living there. Mr Quinn has asked – " She frowned. *Asked? That was an understatement.* "that I move out so that it can be sold. But I don't see why I should move out. That's why I'm determined to bring this to court. That house is my home and it's just not fair that he can evict me after ... everything."

She noticed that Donnelly was writing all of this down on a notepad as she spoke. At least she *thought* he was. Maybe he was just doodling; bored by her predicament. Probably used to more exciting stuff.

The solicitor said nothing for a while until he asked, "I assume you've discussed all this with Mr Quinn at some point?"

Karen stiffened. "At this stage, we communicate purely through our solicitors. Mine – the one I had before you I mean – initially hoped we might be able to come to an arrangement. But Mr Quinn and I have quite an ... acrimonious relationship. He won't agree that I'm entitled to anything. Which is why I am here with you today."

She was amazed at how civil she made it all sound.

"I see," Donnelly stated. "Well, as things stand at the moment you may indeed have no option but to take this to the courts. You are quite fortunate that Mr Quinn has let you stay on so far. However, I would imagine – if things are as you say – that he may well be keen to move on and bring matters to a satisfactory conclusion."

Karen was fuming. Why was he taking *his* side? Keen to move on indeed. He made it sound like she was nothing – just a temporary inconvenience. What about *her* feelings? She wanted this sorted out so she could begin to move on too. But she'd be damned if she was going to just roll over and play dead. There was no way anyone was going to throw her out on the street. She had paid her dues too; hadn't Donnelly himself admitted that?

The solicitor noticed her expression and smiled kindly.

"My dear, I know nothing about your personal relationship with Mr Quinn, which has no bearing on this situation regardless. I'm merely discussing legal options with you, but one thing you also need to consider is that the sooner this matter is resolved, the better for both parties."

Karen nodded. This was awful. At least with

marriage, everything was pretty much black and white and you knew your rights.

How did it ever come to this? she wondered, her heart aching afresh. She and Shane had so much fun at the beginning, picking out bits and pieces in DIY and furniture stores, and making that house into a home together.

Stop it, she warned herself then. Don't get maudlin; just concentrate on the task at hand.

"I understand and I'm sorry if I seem a little ... emotional." Her head lowered and she looked up at him through dark eyelashes. "I suppose I just never considered that something like this could happen." She felt a lump form in her throat.

"I appreciate the personal difficulty," he said kindly, "but now you must try to be pragmatic. Please think some more about an agreement with Mr Quinn before you opt for the courts. Because you were never married and the house was never in your name I worry that your claim may be dismissed as frivolous. As for contents ... this is something you may well have to iron out between you. Unless you have retained receipts for each purchase, it is nigh on impossible to ascertain ownership of fixtures, furniture etc." The solicitor leaned forward and regarded her thoughtfully. "Are you absolutely sure that you want to follow through, my dear? I must tell you that I don't believe you can retain even part-ownership of the property. The law is pretty clear in this instance."

Karen wasn't fazed. "You're not the first person, or indeed the first professional to tell me that. But I owe it to myself to follow through, and I'm determined that nobody will take that house from me – not without a fight."

He set down his pen. "All right. I'll press ahead with Mr Quinn's solicitor and be in touch again with next steps."

Karen stood up and went to shake his hand. "Thank you. And thanks also for taking the case. This means a lot to me. I haven't had much luck over the last while."

"You're welcome and rest assured that I'll try my best for you." He smiled and shook her hand warmly. "You have my number– any further queries, please give me a call."

As she left, Donnelly noticed the steely determination in her dark eyes and shook his head as he sat back down behind his desk. It was a common occurrence these days. So many couples buying property outside of marriage without giving a second thought to their legal rights should anything go awry.

Poor girl, she was determined to go as far as she could with this. And despite his intricate knowledge of the law and the futility of such a case, the solicitor hoped that somehow, this lady might emerge victorious.

She deserved to.

3

"Not much of a housekeeper, is she?"

Barbara Quinn looked around the small kitchen and wrinkled her nose in disgust, eyeing used teabags on the table, a smear of butter and scattering of crumbs on the worktop, dried spaghetti on the wall above the cooker and a pile of used dishes in the sink.

"No, tidiness was never Karen's forte," her brother agreed, opening the fridge and stepping back as a strong whiff of something unidentifiable filled his nostrils.

"I wish the estate agent would hurry up. What if she comes back?" Barbara didn't want to stay here any longer than necessary. She was sorry she had come actually; sorry that her curiosity had got the better of her. The place was an absolute dive.

"Relax, she's at work." He looked around the room and frowned. "It *is* an awful mess, isn't it? I suppose I'd better go upstairs and do a bit of tidying up in the bedrooms."

"Don't be long. It's nearly lunchtime and I fancy going into town for a bite once we're finished."

Barbara went into the living room and flopped onto the small two-seater couch among a couple of brightly coloured scatter cushions. This was a nice room. The bay window was a lovely feature and seemed to make the space feel a lot bigger than it was. Despite the mismatched furniture and that gaudy rug.

If she got her hands on it, she'd replace the cheap pine laminate flooring with solid oak, and have the walls repainted a more muted colour - anything but that vulgar terracotta. And purple cushions on a cornflower-yellow couch? That girl hadn't an ounce of taste.

Barbara picked up a magazine from the coffee table and began to flick idly through it. She was studying a page from the fashion section so intently that she didn't hear the key turn in the front door. She did, however, hear it shut and startled by the noise, leapt up from the couch.

"Hello," Jenny greeted, surprised. "I didn't realise there was anyone here. Karen's on her way – she just stopped off at the shop. She gave me the keys." She held them up apologetically.

"He's just upstairs. I'll get him," Barbara mumbled, quickly starting up the steps, but mercifully her brother was already on his way down.

"Jenny, how are you? I haven't seen you since –"

"Fine, thanks," she interjected shortly. "I didn't realise you'd be here today." Before adding pointedly, "I don't think Karen did either."

"Well, we just needed to check out a few things." He nodded at his companion. "You remember Barbara, don't you?"

Jenny turned and studied her with undisguised surprise. Shane's sister – she hadn't recognised her at all. She was certain that her hair had been darker the last time she'd seen her.

"Can we go now, please?" Barbara asked, ignoring Jenny. "I don't think I can stand the stench in here any longer and now my skirt's ruined too. Those cushion covers have obviously never been washed."

Jenny examined the other woman's clothing for signs of spoilage but couldn't see a thing. The cheek of it – Karen would be livid. She was sure that her friend had no idea anyone was here. And if Jenny had known from the outset who was, she wouldn't have been so pleasant when she came in.

"I suppose we'd better go," he muttered. "Nice seeing you again, Jenny."

"No rush. I'm sure Karen would like to see you both before you go," she replied archly, enjoying the sight of the two of them squirming.

"Ah no, sure we'll head away – we have to be somewhere else anyway. Tell her I said – "

The door slammed and they heard a voice call out angrily from the hallway. "You can tell me yourself!"

Karen bustled past, her arms laden down with groceries. She dropped the shopping bags and turned to him, furious. "What the hell is going on? How did you get in?"

"Now hang on just a minute. I have as much right to be here as you do – more actually."

"Well, I've got news for you, Quinn. According to my latest solicitor, I've paid my dues too. Which means," she added, eyes blazing, "that I have every right to tell you to get the hell out of here." She was pleased to see his eyes widen at the mention of a new solicitor. "Why did you have to go behind my back?" she continued. "But that's not your style, is it? You can't be straight up about anything; never could."

"Maybe you'd better leave," Jenny said quietly, feeling that she needed to say something to defuse the situation.

The sister rounded on Karen. "How dare you? You're lucky that he's let you stay here for as long he has. If it was up to me ... " Barbara trailed off, glaring at her. "Though at least it won't be long before we're all rid of you – finally."

"Barbs, there's no need to upset anyone – we're going now ..."

Just then, the doorbell rang, and the Quinns looked decidedly nervous as Karen went to answer.

"Hello, Patrick from Ryan Mitchell Auctioneers," said the affable-looking man standing in the doorway. "I'm here for the valuation."

"Valuation..." Karen whirled around to face them. "You organised a valuation on my house without my permission? How dare you. How *dare* you try to sell this house from under me, you gutless bastard..."

"Erm, maybe now's not a good time ..." the estate agent murmured, mortified.

"You're damn right it's not," Karen growled. "I'm very sorry but it seems that someone has wasted your time. There will be no valuation of this property today - and not for as long as I'm here."

"We'll see how much longer that will be," Barbara hissed, easing out the door past the white-faced agent, who stood back unsure of what to do next. Eventually, he retreated to the safety of his car parked a little way down the road.

When the siblings followed, Jenny closed the door behind them and went back into the living room.

Karen was sitting on the couch and hugging one of the purple and gold Sari cushions she was so fond of, her face red with anger.

"How *dare* he come here behind my back? And worse, I would never have known if I wasn't off today. It mightn't have been the first time either – he could have been here loads of times that I didn't know about." Enraged, she threw the cushion across the room. "Why did he have to go behind my back and why did he bring that botoxed, bleached-blonde bimbo with him?"

Then despite her tears, she grinned, seeing Jenny trying to hide a smile.

"Sure enough the place would have to be in an awful state. I was late for my appointment this morning, so I didn't get a chance to tidy up." She snorted. "Typical."

"*He* had a cheek coming in without telling you, don't forget," Jenny reminded her.

"I know that Jen, it's just that I don't want to give him any excuse to get me out." She sniffed. "But the solicitor I met with this morning reckons that he'll take the case for me."

"I'd forgotten that you were seeing him today. That's great news. What else did he say?"

"I'll tell you over a cuppa and a muffin." Karen stood up, gathered her shopping and went into the kitchen. She put the food in the cupboards and then filled the kettle, absently removing a piece of dried spaghetti that had somehow ended up on the wall above the cooker. Then turned back to Jenny. "First, you tell *me* why you sounded so anxious in that text earlier. And why you're here now, instead of at home studying?"

Jenny glanced down at the floor. "It's nothing really; you've enough on your plate. Tell me what the solicitor said about the case."

Karen picked a chocolate chip from one of the muffins and popped it into her mouth. "Forget that. I know there's something up. Did you and Mike have a fight?"

Jenny sat down at the untidy kitchen table and absently began playing with the sugar bowl. "No. But the thing ... the thing is ... I think Roan's back."

Her friend immediately stopped picking at the muffin.

"Roan Williams? Back here - in Ireland, you mean?"

Jenny nodded, her eyes firmly fixed on the table in front of her.

"But how do you know?" Karen asked. "Have you

seen him, have you heard from him .... what do you mean you *think* he's back?"

"He's back in Dublin and he's taken a job at InTech." Catching her look of disbelief, Jenny continued. "Mike told me his name this morning – you know the way they've been looking for someone to take over the sales and marketing end? Apparently, the new guy is Roan."

"But are you sure? I mean, how do you know it's actually him? Oh," she said, as a thought crossed her mind. "Mike doesn't know, does he? Roan didn't say anything ...."

"I doubt he'd know that Mike had any connection to me. Anyway," she looked away, "it's unlikely he's given me a second thought since."

"Jenny, are you absolutely certain that it's the same Roan? I know it's an unusual name but ..."

"With the same surname and from Kildare too?"

Karen grimaced. She poured boiling water into the teapot and stirred it. Then she looked at Jenny and hesitated a second before speaking. "Look I don't mean to sound flippant, but ... well, that was years ago. His coming home shouldn't mean anything to you at this point."

Tears were streaming down Jenny's face now, and Karen noticed that she was shaking. Perplexed, she went to put a comforting arm around her friend's shoulders.

"You're not still carrying a torch for him, surely? You've got Mike now and he's one of the nicest guys you could meet. You're getting married soon and –"

"It's not that and ... hell, I *know* I should have told you already. To be honest I didn't know where to start..."

"Go on," Karen urged, somewhat perturbed.

Jenny took a mouthful of steaming tea and looked her friend squarely in the eye. The hot liquid burned her throat as she swallowed, but she didn't care.

"It's just ... it's just ... you know pretty much everything about that time. You were there for most of it, after all. But there's something you don't know, one last thing I was afraid to share that could ruin everything..."

THREE YEARS EARLIER

4

Karen groaned when she spied the line of people gathered along the limestone steps in front of the house.

"Damnit. How did they all get here so fast?"

Jenny took out the newspaper and examined the page that they'd defaced circling ads in *Flats to Let*.

"Says here that viewing on this one's from five and it's only, what?" She checked her watch. "Still another hour before the landlord even gets here. Ah, this is hopeless, Karen. Look at all those people ahead – one of them is bound to snap it up."

"But what can we do? We need to find somewhere to live – here, gimme a look at the paper again."

Jenny handed her the crumpled evening newspaper, the ultimate bible for mid-nineties flat-hunters in Dublin – particularly the Rathmines suburb they were in.

It didn't look good. They had been waiting for ages outside another place earlier, and when the landlord finally did show up, he'd told the eagerly awaiting potential tenants that the place had already been let. It was such a waste of time – they could spend days at this. She had to get the bus back home to Kilkenny tonight, and it looked like Karen would be staying on her friend Gerry's couch for a while longer, after yet another luckless session today.

Time was running out.

Since deciding to get a place together Jenny had hoped that they would be able to find somewhere easily. Since her unceremonious return from Australia, she had been keen to get settled in Dublin. She and an ex had planned on backpacking for a year, but she'd returned early after they broke up. While her former employer Alliance Trust Bank couldn't rehire her in her previous role, she was offered a position at one of the Dublin branches, starting soon.

Jenny welcomed the change of scenery. It would feel like a backward step to return home to the small close-knit town in which she and Karen had grown up, so she'd been delighted when her friend suggested they get a place together in the city. For her part, Karen had been living in a houseshare but was keen to move on.

"I'd rather stay in an igloo than remain with those control freaks," she'd told her. "If I leave so much as a wet teabag in the sink, they make me feel like I've committed a mortal sin. And you'd swear that any dirty dishes would up and disappear forever if they didn't get scrubbed right away."

The childhood friends had never lost touch, and since Jenny's return, the bond between them was even stronger. Now that she was back, she was keen to get going with her new life and forget all about Australia – and her ex.

Karen worked for an insurance multinational based nearby and until she and Jenny found a place, she was staying on her friends' couch.

"Hold on a second, here's one," Karen said now. "It's only a phone number, but by the looks of it I'd say it must be close by."

"Let's call and find out. There's no point in staying here." Jenny looked back at the growing number of despondent flat-hunters remaining.

"Hello, I'm enquiring about the place advertised in the paper?" Karen said into the phone. There was a short pause. "It is?" She smiled and gave a thumbs-up. "Leinster Square, yes, I know where that is."

Jenny felt a tingle of anticipation.

"Guess what?" Karen said, hanging up. "It's in the ads today by mistake. The landlord isn't due to show it until next week because it's being redecorated, but he's there now and he says he'll let us have a look."

The girls jumped in a taxi and were outside the house within five minutes.

"It doesn't look bad at all," Jenny said, examining the freshly weeded and well-tended flowerbeds on either side of the path. "And the fact that he's decorating is a good sign too."

Impatient, Karen pressed the buzzer a second time and had just released her finger when a large heavyset man answered the door with a smile.

"Hello, you're the lady I was speaking to on the phone just now, is that right?"

At least he was friendly, which made a change from some of the other landlords they had met so far – all surly individuals who weren't exactly great conversationalists. They had tried to engage in chat with some of them and if they were lucky had got the odd grunt in reply. This man, however, with his thinning hair and bright eyes, had an amiable demeanour.

He opened a dark blue door on the top floor. "This is the flat. As you can see, the furniture is all over the place while it's being painted, but I'm sure you get the general idea. One of the bedrooms is through there, and the other is just over that way, beside the bathroom. Have a good look around now, don't mind me." He made his way back downstairs, leaving the two alone in the living room.

They looked at each other excitedly.

"This is miles better than anything we've seen so far – and a bedroom each? I thought we'd have to share." Jenny went into the tiny bathroom, which was brightly tiled in blue and green. "It's a little over our budget, but I'm sure we could manage. What do you think?"

She had shared a grotty room with others in Sydney

and was desperate for some privacy. But maybe Karen would be happier sharing a bedroom if the rent was cheaper.

Her friend grinned. "Of course, we should take it. Let's go ask when we can move in."

5

A week or so later, Karen watched Jenny try to smooth down her unruly curls. She had to admit, her friend looked very smart, dressed in a burgundy jacket and matching skirt, the rich colour nicely setting off her blonde hair. "Are you nervous?"

"I suppose I am a little bit," Jenny replied, deciding finally to clip her hair back from her face, still frowning at her reflection. "I don't know – do I look untidy? Oh, I wish I had straight hair."

Karen laughed through a mouthful of cornflakes. "You do realise that women all over the world routinely pay a fortune for curls like that? I love the suit – the executive look is really you."

So it should be, Jenny thought. It had cost an absolute fortune in Jigsaw. She wished she could just get today over with.

The first day was always the worst.

. . .

LATER THAT EVENING, Jenny returned in a state completely at odds with the poised professional who'd left earlier that morning. Red-faced and drenched in sweat, her hair had spilt loose from its clip and her curls were matted against her forehead.

"What on earth?" Karen gasped, taking in her wretched appearance. Her first day couldn't have been *that* bad surely?

It was only then that Karen noticed a guy standing behind her friend. Broad and attractive, he wore a dark pinstripe suit and was carrying a nylon laptop bag under his left arm. His hair was cut short and tightly cropped and his eyes were also dark, a deep chocolate brown – striking against his honey-coloured complexion.

There was a hint of dark stubble on his chin and he seemed to Karen like the kind of guy who always had stubble, no matter how often he shaved.

"She's been mugged," he stated. "Got off at the bus stop in front of the shopping centre just now, when a gang of gurriers grabbed her bag. I saw it happen and we both gave chase, but it was too late. She's still a bit shaken." He regarded Jenny with a concerned look.

"Ah no," Karen grimaced, jumping up. "Did they take much? Have you cancelled your cards?"

Jenny nodded. "There wasn't that much cash in my purse, luckily enough."

"Hey, sit down," Karen urged, leading her to the couch. "Will you both have tea? I've just made a fresh pot." She duly poured mugs of strong tea for Jenny and her companion. "Maybe you should ring the guards too – they might be able to get your bag back at least."

"Probably a waste of time," Jenny said despondently. "I'm sure it's a regular occurrence, and since there wasn't much taken they won't bother." She took a sip from her tea, then suddenly remembered her manners. "Oh, sorry – I forgot to introduce you," she spluttered. "Karen, meet Sir Galahad in disguise."

"Roan for short," He duly flashed a brilliant white smile but as they shook hands, Karen noticed that his front teeth were slightly crooked.

"I *really* appreciate you helping me out," Jenny gushed. "You didn't have to get involved at all."

"Of course I did," he insisted gently. "I think it's terrible that no one seems to bat an eyelid when these things happen any more."

Karen watched the exchange between the two with interest. It was obvious that her friend was smitten by her so-called white knight.

Roan gulped tea and looked around the room. "Nice place, much nicer than mine."

"And where might that be?" Karen enquired for Jenny's benefit.

"Along the canal. I share a house with three guys that tell me they're from Monaghan, but with the way they carry on you'd think they were raised in a zoo. Last week I found a plate of something resembling spaghetti bolognese under one of the armchairs - must have been there for weeks."

"I'm trying to place your accent. You're not native to Dublin?"

"No, but not far either. Kildare, but I've been here for a while with college and work." He pointed to the laptop at his feet, before returning his beaming gaze to Jenny's equally smitten face.

"Will you have another cuppa?" Karen asked, feeling like a third wheel.

"I won't thanks. I was actually on my way home when I was waylaid by a damsel in distress." He winked at Jenny who blushed furiously in return. "Feeling any better now?"

"I'm fine. It was the shock that got to me more than anything. Thanks again, I appreciate you coming to the rescue."

"No problem," He gave them both a repeat of his earlier dazzling – albeit crooked – smile on his way out. "Hopefully, we'll run into one another again sometime."

Jenny remained shell-shocked in more ways than one. "Isn't he just *gorgeous*?" she gushed when the door closed and her knight in shining armour had safely retreated.

Drop-dead gorgeous he might be, Karen thought knowingly, but everyone knew you could never trust a guy who looked that good.

6

The following evening, Jenny returned home to the biggest bunch of red roses she'd ever seen.

"Somebody likes you." Karen grinned up at her from the couch.

"You mean those are for *me*?" she gasped. "I thought Shane might have sent them to you."

"Are you nuts? Shane Quinn doesn't know what a rose looks like. Your Sir Galahad, I bet."

Dinner on Friday? Pick you up at eight, said the card.

It seemed that Jenny's luck had suddenly taken a turn for the better.

Roan took her to a restaurant in the city and from the minute they were seated, they chatted together like old friends.

Jenny talked easily about her life and learned in return that his father was a doctor and had hoped his elder son would follow him into the profession. But Roan wasn't keen and instead, his younger brother had taken up the mantle and was studying medicine at Trinity College. While his mother stayed home and made her own career out of looking after the three men in her life.

"She wants me to move home," he confided, "so that she can keep a closer eye on me, probably get me married off even."

Jenny laughed. "Part of the reason I went to Oz was because my mother was so set against it. Sometimes we argue so much I can't believe that we're actually from the same gene pool. My dad though, he's a different story." She smiled fondly at the thought of Jim. "He'd let me get away with murder – even help me commit it. And speaking of which," she added, glancing at the dessert menu. "I'd do time for a slice of that tiramisu."

Roan duly signalled to the waiter and she exhaled, relieved that he was the kind of guy who didn't begrudge every morsel she put into her mouth. Paul, her ex, used to make her feel like The Cookie Monster every time they went out.

"Split this one?" he suggested easily when the bill arrived. "After all, you ate nearly twice as much as I did."

Jenny didn't quite know how to take this. Wasn't he the one supposed to be taking *her* out? Then again hadn't he been chivalrous enough already? And had surely spent a fortune on those roses...

"Of course," she said, taking out her purse.

In the taxi, she smiled when his hand rested on her thigh.

"Fancy heading back to mine?" Roan mumbled, his

breath warm as he nuzzled her neck, making her body tingle from the tips of her toes upwards to the top of her head.

They reached his place and Jenny practically threw the fare at the driver; she was so eager to be alone with him.

But was somewhat taken aback when she saw inside his home. Dirty dishes piled high, coffee mugs and empty food cartons strewn all over would put a teenager's bedroom to shame.

"Sorry about the mess," he grimaced. "It's not normally like this, but one of my flatmates has his brother staying at the moment. He sleeps on the couch and there's not much room for his gear. We usually take it in turns to clean up but ..."

Then Roan flashed that devastating, deep-dimpled smile and took Jenny in his arms, pulling her close and kissing her – gently at first, but becoming more and more intense as his passion deepened. Her breath caught in her throat as he began planting tiny kisses on her neck, right on the sensitive spot just below her ear.

And everything else faded into insignificance.

7

The following weekend, Jenny struggled to figure out the dynamic between the rag-tag group of Karen's friends gathered in the local pub.

She'd immediately warmed to former roommates Gerry and Tessa and had previously met Karen's boyfriend Shane, who was tonight accompanied by his mate Aidan, and a sour-faced girl introduced as his sister.

"Lydia and Shane had a bit of a fling once," Tessa confided with a mischievous whisper, which immediately explained Karen's glower when the latest arrivals appeared.

Jenny gulped. It was *never* a good idea to make an enemy out of Karen. She smiled then as Roan returned with a fresh round of drinks, took the vacant stool beside her and rested a proprietary hand on her knee.

"Roan?" Lydia gasped in surprise. "What are *you* doing here?"

He looked up sharply, and Jenny thought she saw a faint blush appear on his face as he spied the newcomer.

"Where's Siobhan?" the other girl asked, looking over his shoulder. "You two set a date yet?"

Jenny felt her heart thump loudly in her chest. *Set a date?*

"Um, we're not together any more," he muttered uncomfortably.

Lydia's eyes widened with disbelief. "What? The last time I met you guys you'd just proposed."

"Ah, that's it," her brother declared. "I *knew* I had seen you someplace before." Aidan looked at his sibling for assistance but then remembered. "Your ex, Mark – that was it. He was the bloke going out with his sister?"

Jenny tried her best to look nonchalant, but her insides were churning.

"We broke up shortly after that," Roan said quietly. "We're still friends though, no hard feelings."

"After eight years together?" Lydia was incredulous.

"Yep." Roan drained his pint in a single mouthful and stood up. "Anyone for another?" He was obviously keen to change the subject.

Or hide.

"You should have seen Siobhan," Lydia gushed once he'd retreated to the bar. "Stunning. A model you know, always jetting off to London, Milan, places like that. She has such a *fabulous* figure. He must be heartbroken."

"Must be," Jenny muttered.

"They'd been going out forever and everyone

thought they'd be together for good. Still," she added conspiratorially, "Roan always had a wandering eye..."

"Jen, will you come with me to the Ladies'?" Karen suggested shortly. "Need to borrow some lipstick."

Lydia looked disappointed to lose her audience when Jenny duly got up and followed.

"Thanks, that was ... awkward," she said airily, checking her reflection in the bathroom mirror.

Karen looked at her. "I know Lydia's a bit of a wagon, but..."

"But what?"

"... just be careful, OK. That's all I'm saying."

"I don't think that *is* all you're saying, actually," Jenny retorted, realisation dawning when her friend wouldn't meet her eye. "You don't like him at all, do you? I noticed that you haven't exactly been falling all over him but you could speak to him at least."

Karen grimaced. "It's just ... I know you're keen but ... there's something about the guy that I can't quite put my finger on. And I take it this is the first you've heard about any engagement either."

Her friend was famously mistrustful of people, Jenny knew, but that didn't mean hearing this didn't hurt.

But Karen didn't know Roan well enough yet, that was all.

"It's none of my business, is it?" Jenny insisted confidently. "If he says it's over, then it's over. Nothing for me - or more to the point, *you* - to be concerned about."

8

Karen closed a file on her desk and sat back in her chair, trying her utmost to ignore a growing migraine.

She checked her diary and found that she had nothing urgent pencilled in for the afternoon which was a bonus. Then buzzed reception. “I won’t be coming back after lunch. Can you hold any messages until tomorrow?”

She hoped that it sounded as though she would be away somewhere work-related and not at home nursing her aching brain.

Shortly after, she stepped out of the building into the cool, crisp, afternoon. It was heading towards the middle of November, which meant that she would need to start organising the office Christmas party soon. She would also need to cut down on junk food if she was going to fit into any of her party clothes. She was doing way too much pigging out in front of the telly with Shane, she admitted ruefully.

They didn't see too much of Jenny these days. Since their confrontation in the pub, her friend had been spending pretty much all of her free time with Roan.

Karen now wished that she hadn't admitted her misgivings to Jenny that night after Lydia had dropped her bombshell. But what was done was done, and like Shane said, she needed to work on holding her tongue.

And on her trust issues.

Still, while she couldn't put her finger on it, she truly did think something was a bit ... off about the guy. She found it difficult to have a proper conversation with him; it was always small talk and to her mind, he seemed ill at ease and even a bit ... snide sometimes.

Which made Karen suspect that the feeling was mutual.

Feeling a little peckish now, she decided to pop into the shopping centre and grab something to eat on the way home – maybe a salad roll, or something healthy at least. As Karen approached the deli counter in the store, she heard laughter coming from a nearby aisle and a male voice she recognised.

Speak of the devil...

What were Roan and Jenny doing here when by rights they should both be at work too?

But then catching sight of the couple in question, Karen quickly realized her error. Her friend was nowhere to be seen.

Tall and willowy, Roan's companion was pretty with

long, dark, glossy hair. He stood close to her as she picked up items from the dairy cabinet. They looked ... cosy.

Then, evidently realising he was being watched, Roan looked up.

"Karen - hey," he smiled easily.

She didn't smile back. "I thought you'd be at work at this time of day," she said coolly.

"I could say the same for yourself," he quipped.

She looked at him, frowning. The guy didn't even have the decency to look embarrassed.

Yup. Her instincts had been spot-on.

Sir Galahad, my ass.

THAT EVENING, she chopped peppers and onions in preparation for dinner. "I bumped into Roan in the shopping centre earlier," she told Jenny breezily.

"I know." Her friend looked up from the magazine she was reading. "He said that you were acting weird. What's going on? It's painfully obvious that you don't like him but could you not be civil to him – for my sake at least?"

Karen was taken aback. Smart git was obviously covering his tracks.

"I was acting weird for a reason. He was with this girl and they –"

"For goodness sake, it was an old college friend. Is he not allowed to have friends now?" Jenny threw down the magazine and stood up to face her at eye level. "It's not fair. I don't go on like that with you about Shane."

Karen felt annoyance rise from within. Why couldn't Jenny see through this guy?

"You didn't see what I saw. They were joking and laughing and -"

"So, because he's joking and laughing with another girl, he's automatically cheating? That's what you're trying to say, isn't it?"

"Well ...not exactly but – "

"But what?"

"I just don't want you to get hurt. He has a history and ... " Karen trailed off.

"A history? For goodness sake, we've been over this time and time again. OK, he was engaged to somebody and it didn't work out. Is he not allowed to move on? I have a history too. I can't understand what the big deal is."

"Jen, do you truly believe that it's all over between him and the fiancee?"

"Naturally, I believe him. If Shane tells you something, you believe him, don't you?"

"But Shane's different and –"

"Oh come *on*...." Jenny reached for her coat.

"Where are you going?"

"*Out.* Where I can get some peace, and I don't have to listen to you constantly undermining my relationship." She stood in the doorway, eyes flashing.

Karen furiously resumed chopping. "Fine, suit yourself. But you've changed a lot lately, you know. Your world seems to revolve entirely around this guy. You don't ask about stuff that's happening in my life, and you tell me nothing about yours. You don't even come out with the gang any more and –"

"Why would I want to – when all I hear is you badmouthing my boyfriend?" Jenny marched out the door, slamming it loudly behind her.

Karen stood transfixed in surprise. The two of them hardly ever fought; it was a longstanding joke throughout their friendship that it was impossible to argue with Jen.

Shane had warned her not to get involved, but how could Karen sit back and watch her best friend get hurt?

She picked up the knife again and tried not to treat the misfortunate onion like it was Roan Williams's head. The guy evidently had Jenny wrapped around his little finger.

And Karen had no idea what to do about it.

9

Shane's tone was unusually serious when a week later, he and Karen tried in vain to hail a taxi from the city following a trip to the cinema.

"I need to talk to you about something," he mumbled, both hands in his jeans pockets.

She waved furiously at a taxi which sped blithely by. "Can't it wait? I'm trying to nab us a lift here."

"We haven't a hope at this time of evening - might as well start walking." Shane caught her hand and began to steer her towards O'Connell Bridge.

She trundled along reluctantly."I don't fancy walking all the way home though. If we wait long enough, we're bound to ..."

He stopped in the street. "Look, I wasn't going to say anything tonight but ... I have some news."

She paused alongside him, finally conscious of his unease. "Go on."

"Well, you know that I'm not happy at Viking ..."

Karen nodded, staring idly down at the murky waters of the River Liffey. She already knew he wasn't happy at work. Shane had taken an engineering job shortly after his degree and had lately come to the realisation that the firm was too small to secure the kind of contracts he really wanted to work on.

The company had recently tendered for the construction of a new stand at Croke Park. Shane suspected that such a small outfit hadn't a hope against the big boys, and the tender had indeed been awarded to the much bigger engineering firm. It wasn't the first time it had happened – the better-known company nearly always secured the deal.

"The thing is," Shane continued, "Jack – remember he's the architect?" he said referring to his older brother who lived in London. "Well, he knows someone from a big German firm, and apparently they're looking for staff."

"Brilliant. Can he get you an interview?"

He wouldn't meet her eyes. "I've already had the interview, Karen. They sent a rep over last week and ... they've offered me the job."

"That's terrific news! What's the salary like?" she enthused, putting her arms around him. She knew that he had been a little distracted these last few weeks, but typically he wouldn't tell her anything about the job until it was in the bag.

"Incredible. It's a huge multinational, and what they're offering is unreal for someone of my experience. They want me to work on the design team for this massive water treatment plant they're planning. When I was in college, working on something like this was all I dreamed about."

"Great, but I thought we had loads of water-treatment plants around here," she chuckled.

The dreamy look disappeared from his eyes, and his expression again grew serious. "That's what I need to talk to you about. The project ... the company is in Frankfurt."

Her heart sank. "Frankfurt. As in Germany? You mean ... you're telling me that you're thinking of relocating?"

He wouldn't meet her eyes. "I'm not just thinking of it, hon. I've already accepted the job – they want me to start next month."

Karen felt a myriad of emotions as she tried to make sense of what he was telling her – but anger was by far the strongest. "How long have you known about this?"

"For a little while," he said softly, taking her hand in his, "I just couldn't bring myself to tell you before now. And I told you tonight because ... well, I couldn't keep it to myself for much longer."

Shane, her Shane, was packing up and moving to Germany – just like that. How could he make such a major decision without telling her?

"Let's go for a pint and we can discuss it properly," he said.

She looked at him through narrowed eyes. "I don't think there's anything to discuss is there? You're moving to Germany to start a new life. I don't know why you want to talk to *me* about it now – when you seem to have your mind already made up."

"Of course we need to talk about it," he retorted. "Obviously, I've thought about how this might affect you and me and –"

"*Might* affect you and me? Are you mad? Obviously, it will affect you and me," she parotted. "*Obviously,* we're finished."

"Finished? What are you talking about? I thought maybe we could – "

"What – commute? Try a long-distance relationship?" She pulled her coat tightly around her. "Forget it, it would never work."

"What? Do you mean to tell me that you're prepared to give up this relationship – this *good* thing we have going, just because I'm no longer living close by?"

"Hey," she said shortly, "you're the one who's upsetting the apple cart, not me."

He gave her a hurt look. "Karen, you're not even prepared to even consider the possibility that we might be able to do this, are you?"

She rounded on him, eyes flashing. "You have some cheek. Tonight, you tell me out of the blue that you're swanning off to work in Germany – *next month*. You didn't even bother to let me know that something like this was in the pipeline. How did you *expect* me to react?"

Mercifully she managed to flag down a taxi, and she and Shane got into the car. Karen was so angry that she barely remembered telling the driver where they were going.

She truly hadn't expected this. She'd thought that their relationship was going well and assumed that Shane might include, or at least consult her. Here she was thinking they were happy together, and all the while he was making plans without giving her a second thought.

She stole a quick look at him as he sat in silence staring out the window as the taxi sped towards home.

Probably felt guilty for not having told her earlier. Still, it wouldn't have made any difference to his decision – he was going regardless. No point in either of them making promises she was sure they wouldn't be able to keep.

As the taxi crossed the bridge at Portobello, Karen asked the driver to drop her off at her place. Shane, who lived further up the road, looked at her sadly, his face filled with disappointment.

"Can't we even discuss this?"

"There's no point," she said abruptly. "You've made your decision and that's it."

"For goodness sake, Karen – stop being so bloody childish," he said, his voice clipped, as the taxi turned into Leinster Square. "That's not 'it', and of course we need to talk about it."

Karen noticed the driver shift his position so that he could get a better look in his rear-view mirror at the warring couple in the back.

"Shane, good luck in Germany. I hope you have a fantastic life. And *you,*" she snapped at the driver, "mind your own bloody business."

She thrust the fare at the guy and without another word to Shane, slammed the door behind her and stomped up the pathway.

Watching the car move away, Karen battled in equal measure with disappointment and sadness. Stop, she warned herself. No point in getting sentimental. Shane had made his decision – she'd just have to get over it and move on.

Glancing at the upstairs window, she noticed that the living room light was on. It was almost ten – unusual for Jenny to be home at this hour when she usually stayed at Roan's these days.

She bloody well hoped he wasn't in there with her. She was *not* in the mood for making awkward small talk just now.

But when inside the flat Karen pushed open the living room door, the sight that greeted her banished all thoughts of her own situation completely from her mind.

10

"What's wrong?" Karen gathered Jenny in her arms and her friend began to sob afresh. "Hey, you're scaring me. Has something happened between you and Roan?" Seeing Jenny nod but unable to speak for crying, she continued. "Did you two have a fight? What has he done?"

Jenny sat up dishevelled and wiped the tears from her eyes. Her hair hung in strings around her face.

"I went to the doctor today ... *hic* ... and found out ... I found out that I ...." She hiccupped furiously, unable to complete the sentence.

The conclusion hitting her, Karen's heart dropped like a stone as she engulfed her in a fresh hug.

"Oh, honey, I understand – I had a feeling in the last few weeks that something was up, but ..."

Dammit.

"It's my own fault. I thought it would be OK because I'm on the Pill."

"It's OK – I'll be here for you every step of the way," Karen soothed, "You won't be alone. Whatever you need I'm there - I'll even help you break the news to your parents if you like."

Jenny gave her a lopsided smile. "'Somehow, I don't think I'll be telling Mum and Dad about this. I'm not pregnant, Karen. It's nothing like that, thank goodness." Her voice dropped to a low whisper and her cheeks went pink. "I've contracted some kind of ... infection and I must have picked it up from Roan. An STI." She looked away, mortified.

Karen stared, open-mouthed. She tried to say something but for a long moment, words escaped her.

"What?" she whispered eventually. "What kind, I mean? How serious are we talking...."

"The clap, apparently. I've been having a few problems, so I went to get things checked out and the doctor called me back today to give me the results. I didn't think ... I mean, something like this never even crossed my mind – I just feel so ... mortified."

"Oh you poor thing," was all that Karen could manage right then and as she hugged her friend once more, her thoughts descended into fury.

The bastard. The good-for-nothing bastard. She'd *kill* him when she got her hands on him. She *knew* it! Roan had finally tripped himself up. Oh, how she'd love to see him strung up by his –

"I haven't said anything to Roan about it yet. I just don't know what he'd say. God, I feel so ... nasty, so filthy."

"Don't you dare blame yourself for this, Jen– you're not the one that's nasty. That asshole - I knew it." Karen's voice softened when she saw Jenny's hurt expression. "Hey, don't get me wrong; I'm *definitely* not going to say I told you so. But even you have to admit now that he's not to be trusted."

Jenny smiled ruefully. "Hell of a way to find out that your boyfriend's unfaithful isn't it?"

Karen hugged her again. "I swear to God, if I get near him, I'll *murder* him."

Despite herself, Jenny had to laugh. "You know, I've kind of missed having you in my corner." She pushed her hair out of her eyes. "I know it's been hard for you to hold your tongue, but I was too pig-headed to listen. I'm really sorry, Karen."

She sniffed again, and the two of them looked at one other momentarily before they burst out laughing.

"What a pair we are," Karen said, shaking her head, "the two of us discovering on the same day that the men in our lives are complete and utter losers."

Jenny sat up in surprise. "What do you mean – what's Shane done?"

Karen told her about Germany and it was Jenny's turn to be sympathetic.

"But forget me," she continued, waving her own troubles away, "what are you going to do now?"

"Well, I hate the thought of it, but I suppose I'll have to ... confront Roan."

"And?" Karen probed, waiting to hear that she was also going to dump the rat.

"And – I'll tell him exactly where to go, too. I can't believe that I fell for all the lies he must have been telling me. Remember at Christmas, when he was supposed to come home to meet Mum and Dad and he cried off with the flu? I believed him, but that was probably a lie too."

"Feck him, he doesn't deserve you," Karen stated, then jumping up from the sofa took two wine glasses out of the cupboard. "I think we could both do with a drink."

"Are you absolutely sure that you and Shane are finished?" Jenny asked, while her friend rummaged in the drawer for a corkscrew. "After all, he'd only be a couple of hours' flight away. A long-distance relationship might not be as difficult as you think."

Karen shook her head firmly. "He made his choice without consulting me, so why should I be the one doing the running?"

"But do you think it's wise to make such a snap decision? You and Shane have been together for yonks."

"That's exactly my point. If the relationship meant anything, he wouldn't be swanning off without a second thought, would he? Anyway, I don't want to talk, or even *think* about it any more." Karen filled each glass to the brim and handed one to Jenny, careful not to spill some. "So what about the ... other issue? It's curable, isn't it? I mean ... it won't affect you permanently or anything?"

"The doc gave me some antibiotics and told me to abstain for a while, which *won't* be a problem – so hopefully, I'll be fine."

That was a relief. Karen figured that some of this stuff if left undetected might be dangerous. She was glad that her friend hadn't been too embarrassed to see about it and even better, Jenny was prepared to admit now, even to herself, that everything hadn't been rosy in that relationship.

With the way things were going, their friendship would be back to normal in no time and they could have some fun together, just like they used to.

She'd arrange it with Tessa for the three of them to go on a rip-roaring girls' night out on the town soon.

And Roan Williams and Shane Quinn could take a hike.

11

"Um, we have a ... situation." Jenny tried to stop her hands from shaking when a few days later she managed to broach the topic with Roan.

"What's wrong?" he asked. "Kevin told me that you called earlier. I had to work late tonight, sorry."

When he moved to kiss her she quickly stepped away from him and he stood back, surprised.

"As I said, there's a problem. I've been to the doctor and it seems – "

"Whoa. Don't tell me it's *that* kind of situation," he interrupted and when she flinched he softened his tone. "It's not that, is it? You're not pregnant are you babe, cos I'm not sure we're ready for –"

"I'm not."

His expression instantly relaxed.

"But I appear to have contracted ... something," Jenny was amazed at how calm she sounded when her insides were churning. "From you."

He frowned. "From me? What are you talking about?" he asked, perplexed.

"Some kind of ... infection?"

He turned away and ran a hand through his thick dark hair and when he turned back, she saw a look of utter horror on his face.

"My God. You don't think ... my God. You think that *I* passed on something suspect? I mean, how could you even think ...?"

"How else? I hope you're not suggesting ... how dare you? *I* haven't been sleeping around."

While Karen suspected that he might go down this particular road, up until now, Jenny didn't believe that he could stoop so low.

"No no, that's not what I'm saying at all," he continued, cupping her face in his hands. "I know you wouldn't. I trust you. You wouldn't cheat," he gazed at her steadily, "in the same way that I wouldn't cheat on you. Surely there are other ways you could have come across this?"

She was confused. "What are you talking about?"

"Well, what about your old boyfriend in Australia? Didn't you tell me that he had been unfaithful?"

"Well, yeah, but ..." Jenny slumped down on his couch, no longer quite so sure of herself. The doctor had told her that these things could lie undetected for some time and there was no way of knowing how long she'd had it. So there was indeed a chance that Paul could have been the culprit.

As it was, she'd been ignoring the symptoms for a

while and couldn't remember exactly when everything started.

"I hadn't thought of that," she admitted in a small voice.

Roan sat down alongside her and gathered her to him.

"Think about it. You and I are in a committed relationship. How else could it have happened?"

"Maybe you're right ... I just ... really didn't know what to think," Jenny whispered, tentatively returning his embrace. "I thought that maybe, you know ... I just wasn't sure."

As she read the concern in his eyes, Jenny realised that she had made a mistake. Why was she so quick to doubt him? And how stupid of her to automatically assume *he* was the one cheating, when there was already concrete proof that Paul had?

She looked at him, her tone filled with remorse. "I'm so sorry. You must think I'm awful accusing you like this."

"I just wondered why I hadn't heard anything from you this week. So how are things now? Did the doc get it sorted?" The look of concern on his face made her feel even more of a heel.

"No, I'll be fine but ..." She grimaced, embarrassed, "you'll need to be treated too. I'm so sorry, I really do feel awful for - "

Roan embraced her again. "Don't be silly, it's just a little misunderstanding." He kissed her on the nose. "Look, why don't you go and freshen up, and maybe we'll head for a quiet pint and chat it all through." Then he patted the pockets in his jeans. "Thing is, I seem to have left my wallet at work so I might have to –"

"Oh, I can sort it," she piped up eagerly.

"Are you sure? I'd imagine there's a few quid lying around here somewhere but –"

"Don't worry about it, it's the least I can do."

Jenny went into the bathroom and splashed cold water on her face, relieved that things were back on an even keel. She shivered with a mixture of relief and delight that he had been so understanding. She'd make it up to him. She'd make sure they had a great night out tonight and then at the weekend, she'd take him out to dinner and wouldn't let him put a hand in his pocket.

After this utterly mortifying episode, she owed him that much at the very least.

12

"How could she be so *naive*?" Karen seethed, staring out at a crowded O'Connell St from inside the cosy cafe she and Tessa were in.

She'd felt somewhat disloyal telling her friend about Jenny's situation but was so frustrated with her for believing Roan's codswallop that she had to confide in someone.

And maybe Tessa might be able to shed some light as to how the guy got away with such bullshit.

"Maybe I've been a bit hasty," Jenny had said when Karen asked her how it went. "He reckons I could've contracted it from Paul. Says there's no way it could be him."

"You and Paul broke up months ago. How would it take so long to manifest itself?" Karen ventured, unable to bite her tongue.

"To be fair, I've had the symptoms for a while – I just

kept putting off going about them." Jenny shrugged. "It could just as easily have been him?"

"Sounds a bit of a long shot to me. And you admitted yourself that you were having doubts about Roan before this."

"Maybe I misjudged him though? You should have seen his face when I told him – he was really upset about it. I felt so guilty for jumping the gun when there could well be another explanation."

Karen felt like catching Jenny and shaking her until she saw reason. Obviously, all her great intentions for dumping Roan had gone out the window.

And the sly sod knew exactly how to cover his tracks.

"I just can't understand it," she complained to Tessa now.

"What can you do? Jenny's a big girl. But now I know exactly what they mean when they say love is blind."

"*Blind* being the operative word. Seriously, could he be *that* good a liar?"

Tessa bit into her croissant. "Did you ever consider that Jen loves him and needs to believe that he's telling the truth? And for all we know, maybe he is." She shrugged. "These things *can* take a lot of time to manifest."

Karen felt annoyed at the notion that there might be any weight to Roan's pathetic explanation. But a nurse by profession, Tessa would know the ins and outs of the medical stuff.

"Well, for what it's worth, *I* don't think he's telling the truth," she grumbled. "I know for a fact that he's a lying, cheating ..."

"How so?"

"What?"

"You said that you know for a fact. How do you know that?"

"Well, I told you about that girl he was with that time in the shopping centre."

"Oh? And were they going at it there and then in the fruit and veg aisle?" Tessa inquired archly.

"No, but – "

"So how do you know that she *wasn't* just a friend? Or that Jenny may indeed have picked up this thing from her ex? STIs are often asymptomatic. Maybe give the guy a break Karen, and try to accept the possibility that you might actually be wrong for once."

She recalled Shane telling her pretty much the same thing. *Could* she be mistaken? Karen didn't know. Plus her head was going to explode if she thought about Jenny's situation any longer. Goodness knows she had her own problems. Shane was leaving the country soon.

She hadn't seen him since that night at the cinema, and he hadn't been in touch either. Karen was surprised; it wasn't like him to hold a grudge.

She also had to admit to herself that she missed him. But what was the point? He was going to Germany and she wasn't – end of story. Still, she couldn't ignore the ache she felt in the pit of her stomach whenever she thought about it.

"Have you seen Shane around lately?" she asked Tessa then, trying to keep her voice light.

Her friend paused lifting her cup to her mouth. "Aha. I wondered when we might get to that."

"What do you mean?"

"You could at least talk to him about it. He's really upset, you know."

"Has he said something to you?"

"Not to me. But Gerry reckons he's really cut up. Now he doesn't know whether he's made the right decision about moving. You should talk to him you know, you're not being fair."

"Hold on a minute. I wasn't the one that decided to up and leave for Germany out of the blue."

"Perhaps, but you should at least discuss things properly before he goes? You said yourself that you didn't give him a chance to explain."

Karen bit her lip. She desperately wanted to talk to Shane before he left, but she wasn't going to make the first move.

Tessa read her thoughts. "He's afraid to contact you. He thinks you'll tell him where to go. He didn't think that his moving abroad would put an end to your relationship. Gerry's never seen him so upset. You must be a right cracker between the sheets."

Karen had to smile at this. "I was just so angry. He dropped this bombshell and expected me to just go along with it? It was unfair of him to assume that I wouldn't be upset. After all, he'd known about this for ages, but for me, it all came completely out of the blue."

Tessa was pragmatic as always. "There's no point in being pig-headed about it though. He's leaving soon. Talk to him about it with a clear head before he goes. Then you'll both be in a better position to make any decisions about the future."

Karen shook her head, laughing. "You know, you talk an awful lot of sense for a Cork woman."

"Goes with the territory," Tessa grinned. "Why don't you pop up to his place when we're finished here? No time like the present."

"OK then. Anything to get you off my back." Karen finished eating, satisfied that the decision had been made for her.

True enough, there was nothing to be gained from mulling over this. She might as well go and have it out with Shane before he left.

Regardless of the outcome.

13

She decided to pop over to Shane's on her way home. Now that her mind was made up, there was no point in delaying things. They'd have a good chat and discuss everything properly like adults.

Who knows, maybe the move mightn't be such a bad thing after all? A break might actually be good for them – absence makes the heart grow fonder, and all that.

As Tessa had said earlier, Karen should probably show him some support. After all, it couldn't have been an easy decision to leave all his friends and family to start life in another country.

She decided against taking the bus, preferring instead to walk the short distance to where Shane lived and make the most of the fine evening.

Taking in the hustle and bustle around her, Karen marvelled at how easily she had warmed to living in this area of Dublin.

She loved the fact that she could hop on a bus and be

in the city centre within twenty minutes. Now, she couldn't imagine living anywhere else and hoped that someday she'd end up settling down somewhere nearby. The locality had everything – pubs, shops, restaurants and most importantly, good friends and great memories. Shane would definitely miss all this too.

She was looking forward to seeing him now. They had barely spent a night apart since they'd started going out, and it had been ages since the argument. Tessa was right; ignoring one another was immature and pointless; they needed to sort this out.

On the way, Karen stopped off at a nearby corner shop for a packet of Cadbury Chocolate Fingers - his favourite - as a peace offering. Or blackmail she thought, smiling to herself as she paid the shopkeeper.

Then reaching his flat, she headed down the steps to the basement entry and rapped on the door. There was no knocker and the intercom hadn't worked in years.

No reply.

She knocked loudly again, and when there was still nothing, peered in the living room window looking for signs of life. Until she heard shuffling in the hallway.

Shane opened the door in his boxer shorts, eyes half-closed as he struggled to see against the sunlight.

"Hey," Karen said shyly, a little taken aback. Now that she was here she didn't know what to say to him. He must have been asleep because he looked awful.

"Uh – what are you doing here?" His speech was fuzzy and his expression was wide-eyed.

Karen was a bit miffed. For someone who was

supposedly pining over her, he didn't look all that happy to see her.

"Can I come in? I thought we should talk."

Remaining by the doorway, Shane scratched his head and glanced around, shuffling uncertainly.

"I don't think it's a good idea. Can I meet up with you later or something?" She saw the slightly glazed look in his eyes and immediately figured out why he was acting so strangely.

"Have you been in the pub already?" she asked, surprised.

"You can't tell me what to do any more Karen – it's over between us, you said so yourself and – "

"Ah, it was just a silly argument, love. I hadn't time to take it all in. It's not a big deal – now stop being stupid and let me come inside so we can sort it all out."

"Um ... it's really not a great time," Shane mumbled uncomfortably.

"What are *you* doing here?" came a female voice from behind him. Which much to Karen's disbelief belonged to none other than Lydia Reilly. The other woman purred like a cat awarded a lifetime's supply of cream.

Bare-legged, Aidan's sister was just about dressed in a U2 T-shirt that belonged to Shane. Karen knew it belonged to him because it had been a present from her last Christmas. She was so shocked she was unable to utter a word in response.

Shane visibly paled. "Look there's nothing... I didn't know that you ... " He held his hands out in despair.

"Wow, it didn't take you long, did it?" Quickly finding

her voice, Karen turned on him, her eyes flashing and her cheeks red with fury. "Here I was feeling bad, thinking that I had let you down when all the time you've probably been screwing Miss Piggy here."

Lydia put her hands on her hips. "How dare you talk to either of us like that?"

Ignoring her, Karen stabbed Shane's chest with her forefinger as he stood there, caught red-handed.

"Good luck with Germany, pity it isn't further away. You're welcome to one other and as far as I'm concerned you can both take a running jump into the Grand Canal."

With this, Karen hurried back up the steps and down the street, her entire body shaking with shock and fury. She barely heard Shane calling after her.

How could he? How could he just take up with that .... wagon like that – after all the time they'd been together.

She tried to keep her feet moving forward, her entire body convulsed with rage as she walked. She turned onto a side street, not wanting to face the busy main thoroughfare in the state she was in. Noticing that she still had the chocolate biscuits from earlier, Karen cursed and threw the box across the road with such force that it landed in someone else's front garden.

Then she noticed Shane rush up behind her, dressed in just a shirt, his boxers and boots with no socks.

"Karen, please – I'm sorry – I didn't mean – I was out of control, nothing happened – please!"

"Don't you come near me, don't you even *think* about

coming near me." She hunched her shoulders and turned away, rushing down the road away from him.

Shane followed, shouting after her. "Please. If you would just let me explain ..."

"Explain?" She stopped and faced him, her eyes steely, "Explain what? Oh let me guess, you and Lydia were just swapping clothes – was that it?"

"Look, she was just hanging around earlier - I swear to you that nothing happened."

"Just leave me alone!" Karen cried. "I don't want to hear it and to be honest, I couldn't care less. What you do is your own business and evidently has nothing to do with me regardless. So go to Germany, Shane - or go to hell. Either suits me just fine."

14

She arrived back at the flat, still shaking with fury. There was no sound from inside, so maybe Jenny wasn't home. Karen half-hoped that she wasn't.

Here she was, dishing out advice about Jenny's love life and accusing her boyfriend of playing around. Little did she know it was her own she should have been worried about.

How could she have been so clueless?

She replayed the scene at Shane's flat over and over again in her head and Lydia gloating delightedly. The vindictive little wagon must have thought all her birthdays had come at once when she saw her at the door.

And as for him... Karen didn't realise that she could feel such anger and resentment towards someone while feeling so hurt and betrayed by them at the same time.

If she was being perfectly honest with herself, she hadn't realised her feelings for Shane had been so strong until now.

She felt as though her heart had fallen into the pit of her stomach when she saw the two of them together in the doorway. Then shook her head as she felt tears form behind her eyes again. She wasn't going to cry this time, not again. No way.

The door finally opened, and Karen walked in to see Jenny and Roan sitting in silence at opposite ends of the room. Neither of them gave her a second glance as she entered and head bent, she bade them a quiet hello and went straight to her bedroom to freshen up.

It was a difficult job, but she managed to look halfway normal when she re-entered a few minutes later.

"Jen, I'm heading out again for a bit – see you later?"

Her friend nodded distractedly and Karen was sorry she'd said anything when she barely got a grunt in reply.

Now she strode down the street, determined to make herself feel better.

Some of the girls from the office usually met up for drinks at the same spot in the city on Saturdays. Tonight, Karen was going to join them and do her utmost to forget all about Shane bloody Quinn.

"THIS IS SILLY. I don't know why you're so upset." Jenny moved over to sit beside Roan on the couch. "I wasn't implying anything. It's just ... that I'm a bit short this month, and I wondered if you could pay back some of what I lent you before, that's all," she said tentatively. "Hey, just forget I mentioned it, OK? It doesn't matter, I'll sort something out again with Karen for the rent."

Silence.

"I don't know what else you want me to say." Now she was kicking herself for saying anything.

"Well, it's nice to know that you appreciate my taking you away for a romantic break," he remarked, arms folded.

Her heart dropped. That was a bit low. Roan had announced a few days earlier that he was whisking her off to Venice for a weekend.

While Jenny had been thrilled at the prospect, and equally delighted that their relationship hadn't been affected by her recent accusations, she would have preferred that he repay some of the money she'd lent him.

And much to her surprise she felt irritated. "I do appreciate that. But the thing is," she continued, "I didn't expect that you'd pay me back like that, especially when I already owe Karen for covering my portion of the rent last month."

He looked at her, incredulous. "You're the one with the big bank job. Surely you're not stuck for a few quid."

Jenny's eyes widened at this, but before she could reply, the intercom buzzer startled them both and she jumped up to answer it.

"Jen, is she all right? Buzz me in – I need to talk to her."

"Tessa? Is who all right?"

"Just let me in, will you?"

"OK, OK." Jenny pushed the door release and replaced the handset. Everyone seemed in bad form today. Karen had also come in earlier with a face on her that would stop a clock.

Tessa appeared in the living room, gasping a little after racing upstairs.

"Is she all right? Gerry just told me ... oh, the stupid gobshite. I'll kill him. Where is she?"

"Will you calm down for a minute – what's going on?"

The other girl paused as she caught her breath. "It's Shane. Karen called to his place earlier to make up - and she caught him with Lydia. Hasn't she come home? Feck it – I hope she's OK."

Jenny looked at her wordlessly. Why hadn't Karen said anything?

"She's gone out," she managed to say. "She left about twenty minutes ago."

"What? You let her go off on her own, in that state?"

"She wasn't in a state – she never said a word." She glanced at Roan. "We were in the middle of something and I didn't get a chance to – "

He duly stood up and grabbed his leather jacket. "Don't mind me. I've had enough drama for one day. See you later."

Jenny watched wordlessly as he disappeared out the door and then she turned back to Tessa, trying to forget her own problems for the moment.

Karen had caught Shane with Aidan's dreadful sister? She knew that they were on frosty terms but this was awful.

"She said nothing to me, honestly. Just came in,

stayed a while in her room and then told me she was going out again."

"Where to, I wonder?"

"To be fair, some alone time might be the best thing for her, a chance to get some headspace," Jenny posited. "There's no point in us running around trying to find her."

"Are you sure? What if she does something rash?" Tessa wasn't convinced. "Like throttling Lydia or something? We need to calm her down."

"Nah, this is her way. Karen's never been the type to sit around thrashing things out. She'll deal with this only when she's good and ready." Jenny filled the kettle. "Now, will you sit down and take your coat off?" she urged. "Tell me exactly what happened. You've spoken to Shane?"

Tessa sat on one of the high stools at the countertop and propped her head up with her elbows. "He arrived at our place in an awful state looking for Gerry. Luckily Aidan wasn't around – he normally has dinner with us after he and Gerry finish football training and I don't know who he'd murder first, Shane or Lydia. He's very protective of his little sister."

"But why was Shane so upset? Obviously, he knew what he was doing – was it just because he got caught?"

"Lydia was probably hanging around like a bad smell and seeing Shane moping, she likely leapt on him."

Jenny was dubious. "Well, it takes two to tango."

"True and as far as he was concerned, he and Karen were finished. The problem is that *I* convinced her earlier to make up with him. She just happened to call at the wrong time – thanks." Tessa took one of the biscuits Jenny laid out and bit into it. "So I feel like it's partly my fault now. But I *certainly* didn't think he'd ..." She shook her head forlornly.

"Don't blame yourself. It's just a shame that they couldn't have sorted things out sooner."

"Amen to that. And since Karen is gone AWOL and Shane is leaving soon, that seems unlikely in the long run."

"It's such a pity," Jenny said. "I know she always pretended she wasn't that serious about him, but I thought they were a great match."

"Oh I know. But he's messed up big-time now."

"Actually, I feel a little bit bad for Shane," Jenny admitted. "Karen was the one who finished with *him*. Sod's Law that when she finally came to her senses, it was too late."

15

"Mmm," Tessa declared, polishing off a slice of banoffi. "This was a brainwave, I can't remember the last time I was on a girls' night out."

It was the following weekend and the three friends had commanded a table at one of the city's most beloved Italian restaurants.

Karen nodded. "Yeah, I know you two are trying to cheer me up and believe me,"' she grinned, clinking wine glasses, "it's working."

Going out with the girls tonight had really perked her up. It was exactly what she needed. She'd had enough of Shane Quinn. He and Lydia were welcome to one another and now there was nothing to stop Karen from having some fun of her own. "Will we head for a drink somewhere else?"

"Of course," Jenny signalled for the bill. "The town won't know what's hit it."

They moved on to a trendy cocktail bar and Karen

smiled as Jenny flirted unashamedly with the barman while she ordered another round of drinks. She also seemed to be enjoying herself - back to her bubbly self - and it was a nice change to see her out without Roan.

Although lately he'd been behaving like the perfect gentleman and he and Karen had actually held what amounted to a decent conversation. And whisking Jenny away for a romantic trip to Venice? She couldn't fault that.

Since discovering that her own relationship may have been one giant fiasco, Karen was willing to forget about her earlier distrust of the guy and for Jenny's sake, try to be a bit nicer to him.

Speaking of nice ... Right then Karen spied a cute guy smiling at her from across the room. She smiled back, and within seconds he'd made his way through the crowds.

"Hey," he said, eyeing her appreciatively.

"Hey, yourself," she grinned, while Jenny and Tessa looked on with interest.

"I was going to say something about fathers and thieves and stars," he droned, "but something tells me you're not the kind of girl who falls for lines like that."

"You'd be right. But isn't *that* a line all the same?"

He held his hands up. "OK, should I quit while I'm ahead or... ?"

Nope, she didn't want this guy to back off, not at all.

"So, are you here with friends?" Karen asked, eyeing him flirtatiously through her dark eyelashes.

"Yeah, would you three like to join us?" He indicated

a small group behind him, who had somehow managed to secure a precious table.

Karen looked at Tessa and Jenny, who both shrugged.

"Lead the way," she enthused, winking at the others as she followed him over. They were all introduced, and she discovered that the guy was called Charlie. He and his mates were in town for a birthday night out and were staying at the Conrad Hotel across town.

"We could head back to the residents' bar if you like," Charlie suggested to the others, unable to take his eyes off Karen. "It's nearly closing time and we can get a few late ones there."

After waiting forty minutes at a taxi rank, the group eventually decided to walk to the hotel. Jenny tottered along on the cobbled path, clutching an equally wobbly Tessa for support. "I'll never be able to make it in these heels," she moaned.

One of Charlie's mates knelt in front of her. "Here, I'll give you a piggyback."

"Are you sure you can handle it? I'm no Kate Moss, you know," Jenny giggled, wrapping her arms around his neck.

"I'm a big strong Wicklow farmer – the likes of me could carry twenty Kate Mosses," he said, feigning a thick country accent as he lifted her off the ground and she laughed as Brian began to carry her down Grafton St.

Charlie took Karen's hand but she flinched and pulled away.

"Ah sorry," he said. "That was a bit forward. But I thought that you..."

Karen exhaled. He was nice, he was gorgeous and he was funny.

But he wasn't Shane.

"*I'm* sorry, I thought I did too. But I've just come out of a relationship and ... " she shrugged.

He gave a woeful smile. "I knew it was too good to be true. Never mind," he added then, quickening his step to catch up with the others, "let's go and have a bit of a laugh anyway – no strings attached?"

She must be crazy. Any girl would be nuts to knock back a lovely guy like this. But it was too soon.

No matter what he had done, and no matter how much he had hurt her, Karen was realistic enough to know that it would be a long time before she got over Shane.

But in the meantime, and to help her along the way, maybe a bit of fun would be the next best thing.

16

"What's this?"

"I'm not sure. It was on the floor when I got back from work earlier. Someone must have put it under the door."

Jenny didn't like lying to her, but she couldn't tell Karen that Shane had dropped in on his way to the airport. She would go ballistic. As it was, she insisted that she never wanted to see him again. She still refused to take any of his phone calls and wouldn't talk about him under any circumstances. So Jenny knew better than to risk her friend's wrath.

"If I could just tell her that nothing happened, Jen," he'd said sorrowfully, "but she won't listen to me, she won't let me explain –"

"She's still hurting is all. Maybe nothing happened but it didn't look like that to her."

"I know ... I've been such a fool. I just wish she'd talk

to me. Will I take a chance and call back later, do you think?"

"Not the best idea," Jenny said softly. That was putting it mildly. She couldn't be certain what Karen might do or say.

"Well then ..." Shane stood up and took something out of his back pocket. "I suppose I have no choice but to leave this here." He handed Jenny a small white envelope addressed to Karen. "Maybe if she won't listen to me, I can explain things another way."

Now Karen held the envelope in her hands. "I hope it's not from that lying, cheating bastard," she said vehemently, though Jenny saw that it had piqued her interest.

"Why don't you go into the bedroom and read it in private?" she suggested, busying herself with the washing-up.

KAREN SAT on her bed and carefully tore open the envelope, her heart pounding. Was it from Shane? What should she expect? Was this good or bad?

She had spent night after night lying awake and tossing and turning, trying to get the image of him with Lydia out of her head. She had thought about little else in the ensuing days and couldn't face talking about it with anyone either, unwilling to let anyone know how much he had hurt her.

Finally, she opened the note and began to read. Then read and reread the words in their entirety a few times before going back out to the living room.

Jenny looked at her expectantly. "Well?"

Karen rolled her eyes and handed her the piece of paper. "He's just feeling sorry for himself - of course," she said airily, but her lip wobbled.

Jenny read the heartfelt note and her eyes were glistening when she looked back up. "Ah, Karen, he's really suffering."

"Just because he comes up with this sappy nonsense doesn't mean that I should run back into his arms though," she stated vehemently. "He said in the letter that I deserve better and he's right. I *do* deserve better."

Jenny shook her head as she handed the note back. "Sometimes, I just don't understand you at all. I mean, the guy has told you pretty much everything any girl would want to hear and ..." she said, hesitating a little, "you *did* dump him, remember."

Karen slumped down onto the sofa and defiantly folded her arms. "That's not the point and you know it. How would you feel if Roan went off and shagged someone else and you caught them in the act?"

"But you didn't catch them in the act. Plus according to this, they didn't sleep together, did they?" Jenny retorted. Her friend really was too stubborn for her own good sometimes. She could only guess how hard it had been for Shane to pour his heart out in that letter and it still wasn't enough. In truth, Karen was partly to blame. They had both made mistakes but clearly still had feelings for one another, so what else mattered?

The two were quiet for a while until eventually Karen stood up and stretched her arms out above her head.

"Ah sod this," she said, "I don't want to talk about it any more. He's leaving anyway, so that's the end of it. What's the story with you and Roan?" she asked, deftly changing the subject. "Are you two OK after that whole thing about the money?"

Jenny shrugged. "We're fine. I haven't seen much of him lately though – he took on a lot of extra hours so he could pay for this Venice trip."

Karen smiled, feeling consideringly more gracious toward Roan these days. "The break will do you good – you must be looking forward to it."

Jenny nodded. She *was* looking forward to spending time with him on the trip and knew that he too would need the break after all the overtime. He'd also promised to repay everything he owed once he got paid at the end of the month.

"It'll be so nice to be able to spend a bit of time together on our own. Still," she said, winking, "this little hiatus you and I are having at the mo might work to our advantage. We should give Tessa a ring and arrange another night out in town, just the three of us."

"No men? Suits me down the ground," Karen agreed, rubbing her hands together.

With that, she tore up Shane's heartfelt note and tossed it into the bin.

17

Jenny examined the contents of her wardrobe wondering what she should pack. She wasn't sure what kind of weather to expect in Venice at this time of the year.

Maybe she should pop down to the shops and pick out a few new bits and pieces. But money was tight and she'd need cash to spend on the trip too.

She certainly couldn't expect Roan to pay for everything.

But she still wasn't sure what she should bring. This capsule wardrobe that they were always talking about in magazines looked easy from the outset, yet didn't seem practical. For one thing, Jenny wasn't sure whether they would be going out to formal restaurants, or casual pizzeria-type places for dinner, and what about sightseeing? She would need to bring comfortable clothes and footwear for that and dressier stuff for the evenings.

Maybe the likes of Tessa, who was so tiny that she could fit most of her clothes in her back pocket could get away with a capsule wardrobe, but for Jenny, putting the whole lot in a freight container would be more like it.

She'd give Roan a ring and ask him about the kind of weather to expect, to say nothing of their departure time, because - typical man - he'd been scant enough on the details so far other than they were due to fly out the following morning.

His flatmate answered the landline on the first ring.

"Kevin, it's Jenny. Is Roan there?"

"How's it going? No, he's not – went home to Kildare for a while to ... um, get some stuff sorted." He sounded uncomfortable. "Do you want his home number? You'd probably get him there now."

"That would be brilliant, thanks."

Probably needed to pick up the tickets from the travel agency.

She decided to call his parent's house and find out when he'd be back – or to make it handy, maybe arrange to just meet him at the airport. She dialled the number Kevin had given her and waited while it rang a few times. Until she heard a female voice answer.

"Hello, Williams' household, Joan speaking."

"Hello there, I wonder if I could speak to Roan please?" Jenny greeted pleasantly.

"Roan? Oh, he's not in I'm afraid. Would you like to leave a message?"

Dammit, she'd missed him again.

"Yes, if you wouldn't mind. Could you tell him that Jenny called?" She waited for any sign of recognition at the mention of her name. "Jenny Hamilton."

"Yes, I'll tell him. A friend from work, is it?"

Jenny's heart sank. Mrs Williams didn't seem to know who she was. Maybe Roan hadn't told his mother that he had a girlfriend in Dublin. She remembered him saying something about how overbearing his mum could be so perhaps he preferred to keep his personal life under wraps. But he must have told her about the Venice trip at least.

She was about to say something when Mrs Williams continued. "He's in great form altogether these days," she said chattily. "Delighted about the takeover. Same as yourself, I'd imagine."

"Well, I don't work with him, actually. I –"

"Oh, sorry, pet," his mother laughed pleasantly, "I can't keep up these days. Between all his friends here and the ones in Dublin, you couldn't keep track of him. Anyway," she continued, "he left not too long ago. They're staying over tonight because of the early flight tomorrow. Venice, imagine? I don't know where he gets it. His father hasn't a romantic bone in his body."

Jenny's heart lifted. Roan was already on his way back and had arranged for them to stay in a hotel tonight before the flight. What a lovely surprise!

"Well, that's why I'm calling actually," she said smiling. "I was wondering about the flight details."

"Oh, is it you that's dropping them to the airport? I

wondered about that because I didn't think Siobhan was driving."

Siobhan? Roan hadn't mentioned that he and the ex were still on speaking terms. But then again, hadn't they grown up together in the same town and known each other for years? To say nothing of once being engaged.

Mrs Williams' voice interrupted her thoughts.

"You should have seen her earlier, I don't think I've ever seen her so excited. And the same one flies here there and everywhere with her modelling. Still, I suppose it's different when you're working. Anyway, they deserve this trip. She's abroad so much they hardly see one other . . ."

What the hell....? Jenny felt her knees weaken, and her heart quickened in panic. For a split second, she wondered if maybe she had called the wrong number.

No, maybe she had just taken it all up wrong. Or maybe *Mrs Williams* had taken things up wrong. That was it, Jenny thought quickly. Maybe Roan hadn't said anything to his mother about the break-up with Siobhan. Mrs Williams sounded as though she was quite fond of the ex, so maybe he figured she would take it badly.

Jenny clasped the receiver and tried to tune back into the woman's chatter. "Sorry – you were saying? About the trip to Venice."

"Oh, I was just saying that I worry whether they'll fit their suitcases on the plane, let alone in your car." She laughed merrily. "He was teasing Siobhan about all the stuff she was bringing." Jenny felt as though she had been hit with a sledgehammer as Mrs Williams continued, blithely unaware. "Very funny altogether. The two of them carrying on like an old married couple already."

18

"What are *you* doing here?"

"Can I come in for a few minutes?"

"I'm not sure ..."

"Please, I really need to talk to you."

Shane looked so terrible that Karen faltered. She stood back and waved him into the hallway, and as he passed she caught the familiar scent of Hugo Boss after-shave – her favourite. She tried to collect herself as she trundled upstairs to the flat behind him.

She was alone; poor Jenny had gone home for a bit, reeling upon discovering that Roan had - with no explanation - upped and offed to Venice with his supposed ex-fiancee.

"What do you want?" she asked when they reached the living room. "And why aren't you in Germany?"

She made no motion for Shane to sit down, so he stood there fidging awkwardly.

"Did Jenny give you my note?"

Karen shrugged her shoulders, her expression defiant.

"I don't know what you expected. I haven't changed my mind about anything if that's what you want to know."

"But you believe what I wrote – that nothing happened with Lydia that day?"

"I'll never know one way or the other, will I?"

Shane slowly shook his head from side to side. "I think you do know that nothing happened – you're just too stubborn to admit it. You won't give an inch, will you, Karen?"

She put her hands on her hips."Why the hell should I? Did you call here expecting me to greet you with open arms? If you thought that, then you can think again. It's not that simple."

She felt her hands shake as she spoke. It was so difficult having him so near, and yet she couldn't bring herself to forgive him. It was too hard. Although Karen knew from his face that he was indeed telling the truth. She also knew that if he *had* slept with Lydia that day, he would have admitted it. It wasn't in him to lie.

But what should she do now? She wasn't going to run back into his arms just like that. What about Germany? And speaking of which, why wasn't he ...?

"Will you marry me?" Shane asked suddenly.

She looked at him, stunned. "What did you say?"

He moved closer and taking both of her hands in his, looked deep into her eyes.

"You heard me. I love you, and I want to marry you.

You're the most important person in the world to me and I realised just how important you were when I lost you." When she said nothing, he continued. "Yeah, I went to Frankfurt and started the new job, got a place to live, met some new friends, you know – the whole shebang."

She smiled despite herself at his well-worn expression.

Buoyed by the softening of her demeanour, Shane continued. "Everything was going brilliantly. The job is terrific and the social life is too, there are so many other Irish lads over there, I had no problems settling in but –"

"But what?" she interrupted. "Let me guess," she said before she could stop herself, "you missed Lydia so much you had to come back?"

Karen saw something in his eyes then and instantly regretted her outburst. He looked as though she had just slapped him across the face.

"What's the real problem here?" Shane demanded, and she heard his voice begin to rise as something snapped within him. "Why are you acting like this? I've been nothing but honest with you from the very beginning. OK, we've had our ups and downs...no," he shook his head, "I take that back – we've had *one* down and *plenty* of ups throughout this relationship, and yet you're carrying on as though I'm some kind of serial asshole. I've told you time and time again that nothing happened. I've *never* been unfaithful. I made one misstep in not discussing my plans for Germany, but now I'm back. I've even given up the stupid job for you. And it's *still* not enough. What more do you want from me ...." He walked back and forth, running his hands through his hair. "I just can't win, can I? No matter what I say or do, I just can't win."

Karen wasn't sure what to think. She'd never seen Shane so angry. *She* was usually the one who needed calming down in any arguments – it had always been him doing the calming. His face was bright red and his fists so clenched she was afraid he might try to put one through the wall.

"I'm sorry," she conceded. "It's just a shock, seeing you here – I suppose it's just my way of hitting back at you." She shrugged her shoulders again. "Please, go on with what you were saying...about Germany and everything."

Did he just say he'd given up the job? Or was she imagining it? To say nothing of the fact that he'd just bloody *proposed?*

But Shane seemed to have lost patience. "Doesn't matter," he said, waving her away, as he stomped towards the door, "forget I said anything, forget my question, forget about the whole bloody lot of it." He opened the door, went to walk through it, then paused and looked back at her, his eyes tired and sad. "I think I have your answer now anyway."

Karen stood alone in the flat for a moment, her mind reeling as she tried to get to grips with her feelings.

Shane had just proposed. *And all she could do was stand there and insult him.*

She ran out the door and caught up with him on the landing. "Wait."

He stopped and looked back up, the expression on his face unreadable. "Yes?"

"What do you mean? I *haven't* given you an answer yet," she said indignantly. "You can't propose to someone and then just tell them to forget you asked."

They looked at each other for what seemed like an age. Then to Karen's surprise, she saw his mouth break into a grin.

"God, you're so damn stubborn," he said, shaking his head as he started back up the stairs again. "You *have* to have the last word all the time, whether you're right or wrong don't you?"

"I don't always have to have the last word," she mumbled contritely.

"So are you going to apologise?" Shane urged, waiting.

"For what?"

"For *once*."

A flicker of a smile crossed her lips, but she didn't say anything.

Shane shook his head. "Sometimes, I really don't know what to do with you."

"So what *are* you going to do?" Karen grinned, as he took her in his arms.

"I'll show you." Shane scooped her off the ground and headed back inside and onwards to her bedroom, kicking a pile of discarded clothes and shoes out of his path as he went.

Laying her carefully on the bed, he kissed and made

love to her with such intensity, that Karen thought all the time they'd spent apart had nearly been worth it.

After, they lay beneath the covers, bodies entangled.

Shane glanced across at her, smiling. Then his eyes lit up as if remembering something, and suddenly he threw back the covers, jumped out of the bed and onto his knees.

Grinning, he took her hand in his. "Karen Cassidy, for the *second* time, will you marry me?"

This time there was no hesitation in her reply.

19

"Oh – that's fantastic news!" Jenny gasped with genuine enthusiasm. "How romantic."

"Well, it wasn't exactly romantic," Karen laughed down the phone. "We had an argument beforehand and I took my time before I eventually said yes."

"Typical," Jenny said with a grin. "Poor Shane's got his work cut out for him."

"Poor Shane? Traitor – don't you mean poor me? Still, Jen, I wasn't sure whether to tell you or not. I know what you're going through now, and –"

"Are you mad? I'd murder you if you didn't. This is such lovely news, exactly what I needed to cheer me up, to be honest."

"How are you feeling?"

"A lot better now, I think."

"Good. Well, come back whenever you feel like it. We're heading to Shane's family's place at the weekend, but otherwise, I'll be here. Give me a ring when you're back, OK?"

Jenny nodded, forgetting that Karen couldn't see her. "Thanks. And tell Shane I said congratulations too. We'll have to organise a big engagement celebration soon."

Hanging up, Jenny tried to sound brighter than she felt. Although she was genuinely delighted for her friend, she couldn't help feeling envious too.

It was the same old story, really. Her love life was in tatters while Karen's couldn't be better. Her friend was on top of the world, while Jenny was home in her parent's house and feeling so low she might pop out Down Under again.

She was genuinely thrilled for Karen, though. She had handled the break-up with Shane in her own way and on her own terms. Having had a quick cry, she had taken some time to figure out her feelings and then moved on with her life. She definitely hadn't collapsed in a heap and wanted to crawl into a hole, shutting herself away from the world. Not for the first time, Jenny wished she possessed just a tiny piece of Karen's resilience.

This last week had been an absolute nightmare, and she hadn't slept more than a few hours at a time. Her dad had been curious as to why she wasn't at work, while Jenny's mum had been more sympathetic because she'd known about the Venice trip, and must have figured out that all wasn't rosy in her daughter's love life.

Jenny had lied though, when she told Karen she was feeling better. The hurt was still very much present, underlying her confusion and disappointment since discovering that Roan had gone to Venice with his ex (though presumably, they were now back together) and hadn't said a word. The same trip that he was supposed to be whisking *her* away on.

Wearily, Jenny went upstairs to her bedroom hoping to sleep for a bit but an hour later, she was still lying on the bed eyes wide open. So many thoughts kept going round and round in her head. She thought about the two of them in Venice. Were he and Siobhan together now, at this very moment? Was it better with her?

Venice was one of the most romantic places in the world. They were probably at it like rabbits, just like the way she and Roan had been at the beginning before Jenny had torpedoed everything by undermining his trust and ranting about money.

And here she was alone again, another relationship in tatters.

Story of her life.

20

"Which do you think I should wear – biker jacket or blazer?" Karen asked later that week.

She and Shane were going to meet his family, and even though she kept insisting to Jenny that she wasn't nervous, she had to admit to herself that she was.

"The biker," Jenny said firmly. "The blazer is too ... officey or something?"

"Officey? What kind of word is that?" Karen asked, studying her reflection with a critical eye. She wanted to look smart, but not too formal. The dress was elegant, but the biker jacket made the outfit look casual and easy-going, exactly the image that she wanted to project.

"I don't know what I'm so worried about, anyway," she grumbled, trying to find a stray trainer from the pile of shoes at the bottom of her wardrobe. "We're already engaged – it's not as though I have to pass a test." She finally found the one she was after and dusted it off with a tissue.

"It's a test of sorts though, isn't it? She's going to be your mother-in-law, after all," Jenny pointed out. "If she doesn't like you, she could make your life hell."

"Well, if she doesn't like me, tough," Karen said airily, studying her makeup closely in the mirror. Was she wearing too much mascara maybe?

Jenny collapsed laughing. "I'm only joking, don't start getting defensive. Of course, Mrs Quinn will like you, why wouldn't she?"

A car horn beeped twice from outside.

"Right," Karen said, jumping up and looking out the window at the street below where Shane waited in his newly purchased second-hand Astra. "Wish me luck, OK?" She checked her appearance once more in the mirror, before rushing out the door.

"Don't worry, you'll have a great time," Jenny shouted down the stairs after her.

Then she slumped back down on the couch and checked her watch.

Roan was due in half an hour.

"HEY," he greeted, handing Jenny a flower bouquet, and kissing her on the cheek.

"If you think that a bunch of supermarket flowers will soften me up, you have another thing coming." That was good, she thought, exactly like something Karen would say. Act tough and don't let him away without a proper explanation. "Did you have a nice time in Venice?" she asked, arms folded.

"It was OK," he said. "I missed you though."

Her eyes widened in surprise. "You missed *me*. Where did you get the time to miss me? I thought you would have had enough on your hands with Siobhan." Jenny felt her hands shake as she spoke. This was no good – she was going to crack soon. She had great intentions of telling him where to go, but it was so hard now that he was standing in front of her.

"Siobhan? What are you talking about?" he asked, with what sounded like genuine surprise.

"Your supposed ex – the one you brought to Venice instead of me?"

He looked perplexed. "What? I didn't go with Siobhan – who told you that? She gave me a lift to the airport, that's all."

Jenny stopped short. That's exactly what she had thought at the time. Was there a possibility that she might have been mistaken – no, that his mother was mistaken and his ex had merely given him a lift?

"What? Then who *did* you go to Venice with?"

"Nobody. I went on my own."

"But your mother said ... "

"Ah, for goodness sake, Jen, my mother doesn't know her arse from her elbow. I've told her a million times that Siobhan and I are finished but she won't accept it. She and Mrs Hennessey – Siobhan's mam – are always trying to get us back together."

"But ... but why did she say that you were like an old married couple?" Once again Jenny felt unsure of herself. Was it possible that Mrs Williams had lied? No mother would do that, would she? Yet Roan seemed so adamant. "And why on earth did you go on your own when I was supposed to be coming too?"

He slumped down on the sofa. "I was angry with you for banging on about the loan when you know I'll pay you back. And then, when I saw you out on the town with that other guy ... "

"What other guy?" she asked, flummoxed.

"On Grafton St. I was in town for a few pints with the lads and saw you pass by, laughing your head off with some fella carrying you down the street. I felt like a right mug."

"What?" For a moment she didn't get what he was talking about. Then she remembered. On the most recent girls' night; Charlie's friend Brian gave her a piggyback up the street.

Roan had witnessed that?

"But that was harmless! We were just having the craic. This guy started chatting up Karen and his friend –"

"Was hitting on you?" he finished shortly. "I know how it works, and I know what I saw. Do you have any idea how embarrassed I was? All the lads there too."

Jenny tried to gather her thoughts. Her mind was racing a mile a minute.

"So you went off to Venice without me because you wanted to get back at me? Why the hell didn't you just ask me about it straight out?"

He wouldn't look her in the eye.

"I dunno. I was angry. I arranged this trip and you

didn't seem to care – you just kept going on at me to pay back the money." He stood up and threw a roll of notes on the breakfast bar. "I told you that of course I'd pay you back, but you didn't seem content with that either. I knew you were annoyed but – "

"So when you saw me that night on Grafton St, it was the last straw ..." Jenny sat down, guilt flooding through her. He had got the completely wrong idea. And to be fair, she wouldn't have been impressed to see *him* crawling all over some strange girl either, would she?

"I'll admit I was stupid not to talk to you – but I suppose I can be a bit like Karen, I tend to simmer," he continued. "But the trip was coming up, I had the tickets and I couldn't waste them. So, I decided I might as well head off by myself, maybe have a think about things."

Think about things? Now she had *really* ruined everything. Jenny honestly hadn't meant to go overboard about the money. She was merely trying to stand her ground. But when she thought about her recent behaviour and the various accusations she'd made, she didn't blame him for being angry.

"I'm so sorry," she said. "Maybe I can understand why you thought I was being ungrateful. But when I rang your mother and she told me that about Siobhan, well ... I just didn't know what to think. Put yourself in my position – what would you have thought?"

"Put yourself in *mine,* Jen. One minute, you accuse me of sleeping around and giving you some ... disease. So to prove myself to you, I organise a romantic – *expensive* – weekend away for us. Next, you're ranting about the money you lent me and then I see you all over some stranger in the street? So I snapped. I've done everything I can to make you trust me, but you still don't. And I've done nothing wrong." He sank down on the sofa and put his head in his hands. "What more do you want from me?"

Jenny sat beside him and tentatively put her head on his shoulder.

"I'm sorry, really I am. I just didn't know what to think or who to believe. You're right, I was out of order. And I do trust you. It's just sometimes – "

He pulled away and stood up. "Look, let's just forget this, let's forget about the whole thing. This isn't working. I've always tried to be honest with you but I'm tired. If you don't - won't - trust me, then I'm wasting my time. I know Karen certainly doesn't and obviously, she's been in your ear too." He moved to the door and then turned back. "It's a pity because I truly do care about you, Jen." He looked away for a moment before opening the door. "I'll make sure you have the rest of your money by the end of the week."

"Wait," she cried. This was awful. What had she done? Jenny raced into his arms and as she went to kiss him, thought she saw something flicker in his eyes – relief, maybe? It didn't matter.

As he kissed her back, Jenny felt all doubts and uncertainty melt away. She was going to make it up to him and make every effort to ensure that this relationship worked. Maybe like Karen and Shane, things needed to come to a head like this so they could figure out what came next.

No more second-guessing, she decided happily. From now on, she'd just have to prove to Roan how much she trusted and cared about him, and all would be well.

21

Later that evening, following their return from Meath, Shane looked up from his TV when Karen came in and slammed the living room door behind her.

Catching her dark expression, he gulped. "What's up?"

"That was Jenny on the phone," she said, gritting her teeth. "You won't believe it, but she's gone and fallen for his bullshit again."

"Who has? What bullshit?"

"Roan's concocted some cock-and-bull story and Jenny believed it again. What is *wrong* with her that she swallows his claptrap?"

"Ah, he's not that bad," Shane said. "We met him down the pub the other night and he bought me a congratulatory pint. We had a right laugh – Aidan had just come off duty and he cheered him up."

A fireman by profession, some of the more challenging work incidents affected Aidan's mood and

Shane routinely brought him out to help take his mind off.

"Roan's not that bad because he bought ye a *pint*? Come off it, the guy's a snake."

"I don't know what you have against him. OK, maybe he can act the lad a bit but that's no crime, is it?"

"You don't know what I have against him ..." Karen was aghast. "Am I really the only one that can see through it?"

"See through what?"

"This big act he has going! For goodness sake, it's sticking out a mile that he's a player. I need to say something, tell it to her straight."

Shane shook his head. "I told you before that you shouldn't get involved. Jenny's personal life is her own business. How would you feel if she started questioning your relationship with me?"

"I might at least listen to what she had to say. But Jen sticks her head in the sand and believes every word that comes out of his lying little trap. It'll end in tears, I guarantee it."

"Well if it does, just make sure that *you're* not the one doing the crying. Anyway, Jenny's a big girl – she doesn't need you to look out for her."

"Maybe, but I'm glad I'm not going back there tonight. I couldn't be responsible for what I might do – to either of them."

"Speaking of which, what did you think about what Mam said - about the house?"

During their visit to the family home earlier that day,

Shane's mother had suggested that he and Karen start looking for a place to buy.

"No time like the present and prices will just keep going up," Nellie had said in the bossy tone that Karen noticed she used on all the Quinn children.

She seemed nice enough and had been gracious and friendly throughout the visit, but Karen had quickly got the impression that the older woman retained a strong influence over her offspring.

Though just because her own parents were happy to let Karen live her life without interference didn't mean that Shane's family dynamic would be the same. She had sensed that immediately upon her arrival.

"So you're the reason he gave up the job of a lifetime," Nellie greeted.

Karen had taken that as a joke at the time but as the evening wore on, she wondered if there was indeed resentment that Shane hadn't taken full advantage of the opportunity offered to him by his older brother.

Jack, home from London for the weekend came across as a very serious type, not at all friendly. He had barely uttered a word throughout the visit, but then again Karen thought wryly, he would have hardly had a chance.

Shane's family home had been absolute bedlam. Her fiance had warned her about the family dog, who tended to hump unsuspecting visitors' legs, and Paddy had indeed behaved exactly as predicted.

But he *hadn't* warned Karen about the kids. Shane's sister Marie had brought her brood to the farmhouse for the visit, and while there were only three – a five-year-old boy and two younger toddlers – it was like being caught in the middle of a chimpanzee's day out. They seemed to be everywhere all at once – the baby screaming, the older one demanding that Karen brush Barbie's hair and then her own with a sticky, sweaty comb. Then more screaming when the boy decided to frazzle poor Barbie in the microwave.

By the time she left the Quinn household, Karen was doubly determined that she would never put herself through the misery of having kids. Not much of a child-lover in any case, her experience with Shane's nieces and nephews not only put the final nail in the coffin of her maternal instinct but encased it in reinforced steel.

"You have it all ahead of you," Marie chuckled while trying to prevent her eldest from choking his sister under the coffee table. "They're just at the stage where nothing will keep them quiet."

Karen had smiled sympathetically, but it was obvious that the poor girl hadn't an ounce of control over any of her boisterous lot. Nope, she told herself – as the baby screeched loud enough to shatter eardrums – she was *never* having children.

But she couldn't be certain whether Shane felt the same way. The noise levels didn't seem to affect anyone else in the household. During dinner, while ducking a spoonful of baby food hurtling past her nose, Shane's mother suggested they get cracking on buying a place of their own.

"There's a site going over by Corbally's," she

suggested, and Karen realised to her horror that Nellie was talking about somewhere local. "You should ask Jim about it before it's snapped up."

"We're planning to settle in Dublin," Karen put in quickly. She and Shane hadn't discussed it– in fact, they hadn't made any plans other than getting engaged – but there was no way Karen would consider living in the wilds of Meath.

To her relief, he agreed. "Yeah, and the commute wouldn't be ideal for Karen either."

"I could put in a good word for her at the council," Marie piped up. "My husband works for the County Council," she explained proudly.

"Thanks, but Karen is happy where she is," Shane said quickly, evidently spotting the horror on his fiancée's expression. He took a bite from his thickly buttered scone and washed it down with a mouthful of tea.

Upon this, Karen felt momentarily relieved. It was obvious that his family must often interfere like this, and Shane had expertly headed them off.

But the visit had shaken her a little. The Quinns all seemed so involved in one another's lives, whereas her parents had always left it up to Karen to decide how she wanted to live hers. She was used to her independence and wouldn't tolerate her parents' intrusion. Her folks had been thrilled with the news of her engagement but had no intention of rushing away from their real estate business in Tenerife to celebrate.

And Karen didn't expect them to. She and Shane

would go out and visit them sometime and they could celebrate then.

No pressure.

But she sensed that things were somewhat different in the Quinn family.

"Was Jack upset with you for not taking the job in Germany?" she asked Shane now.

He shrugged. "I suppose he was a bit miffed. After all, he had pulled a lot of strings to get me the job in the first place."

Shane's dad died when he was ten, and Karen deduced from Jack's haughty demeanour and his siblings' reverential manner that the older brother was considered something of a father figure in the household.

"Anyway, about the house," Shane continued, "I'll have a chat with a lad I know from college – he works for an estate agency. I'll ask him to put a few feelers out around here – what do you think?"

"Here? Do you think we could afford to buy in this area? Prices are manic."

"Well, I know you don't want to commute. With the new job, I'll have to travel regardless, so that doesn't matter to me." Since his return, Shane had secured a job with an older, more established engineering firm and was currently on the design team for the construction of a second toll bridge on Dublin's main thoroughfare. "Be brilliant to settle around here if we can stretch to it." He shrugged easily. "We're happy here, all our friends are here – what could go wrong?"

22

"How about a video game?" Jenny suggested a potential birthday present for Shane, as she and Karen sat over a coffee in St Stephen's Green.

"Won't be any of that juvenile nonsense in our house – I can tell you," Karen replied, spooning sugar into her cup.

"What house?"

It took her a second to realise her slip and she reddened a little. "Oh, crikey. I wasn't going to tell you until we had something concrete, but ... Shane and I are thinking of buying a place together."

"Oh."

"It won't be for a while yet," Karen added quickly, seeing her friend's crestfallen look. "I'm not going to leave you in the lurch or anything. We've just thought we might as well start looking. Sorry, I didn't mean to break the news so casually."

Jenny waved her away. "Don't be silly. Of course you'll be moving in together. Makes sense."

"Are you sure you don't mind?" Karen still felt like an absolute heel. "As I said, it won't be for a while yet."

"Where are you planning to buy?"

"Somewhere close by if we can stretch to it. Maybe just an apartment or a duplex. Whatever comes up."

Karen took another mouthful of tea. She didn't yet want to tell Jen that something had already come up. A block of newly renovated apartments in Terenure Village had just come on the market, and she and Shane were going to take a look this week.

It would probably come to nothing, but she didn't want her friend to think that she had everything planned without saying anything first. After all, when Karen moved out, Jenny would need to find someone else to share their place.

Though maybe she was thinking of keeping it on by herself? The rent was expensive for one person though and it would be crazy to let the extra bedroom go to waste.

Enough, Karen scolded herself. There was no point in wondering about what Jenny might do in her absence. It was good though that she knew a move was in the offing.

Regardless she and Shane were only starting to view properties now. They mightn't end up moving for ages, and there she was running away with herself already.

. . .

A FEW DAYS LATER, she and Shane looked around the apartment in dismay.

"It's a bit... small," he remarked.

That was an understatement. The place wasn't much bigger than a shoebox. How could anyone be expected to live there?

"It's cosy but the developer has made exceptional use of space," said the estate agent, an uppity so-and-so to whom Karen had taken an instant dislike. Though hardly even a man, she thought wickedly; the guy looked as though he was barely out of secondary school. A colleague of Shane's college buddy, he'd been downright rude when they'd enquired about any wiggle room on the asking price.

"You mean a discount?" he replied, in an affected accent that had got right up Karen's nose. "These apartments will be snapped up at auction. They're in a prime location, as I'm sure you know. Price means nothing these days."

"Exceptional use of space, huh?" Shane repeated, catching her eye, and nodding towards the doorway. She followed his gaze and noticed that the interior doors were not yet installed. There was no way that even a two-seater sofa would fit there once they were hung. Karen and Jenny's little flat in Leinster Square was bigger than this *'exceptionally spacious and tastefully decorated deluxe residence'* promised by the brochure.

"If that's what we're up against, this is going to be an absolute nightmare," Karen said afterwards when they made their excuses and broke for lunch.

"I think it's probably the location," Shane said, tucking into his roast beef dinner. "Anything around these parts will command a song."

"I don't fancy living too far away though. I'd hate to have to spend hours commuting." She sighed. "Nor do I want to settle for something resembling a dog kennel though."

"Don't panic, that's not an option yet. Anyway," Shane added with a glint in his eye, "I have a bit of an ace up my sleeve."

"What do you mean?"

"Well, you know how we only qualify for a small mortgage at the moment? Jack knows a guy that can get us a bit more."

"Your brother? How so?"

"He knows a fella who works as a mortgage advisor with one of the building societies. Jack has a house up home that he's renting out, and he's going to put that up as collateral for whatever extra we need. What it means is that we can get a much bigger mortgage than what the bank has offered. The salary restrictions will still apply but because there's a guarantee, this guy can organise a bigger loan."

Karen was stunned. "Jack would do that for us?"

Shane shrugged. "He knows the score, and how hard it is to get on the ladder. The only risk he's taking is that we might default on the repayments, and he knows that won't happen. I'll have my yearly salary scale and bonuses to rely on. And of course, your job is very secure too."

Karen was contemplative. This was very generous indeed. "So you two have it all worked out already?"

Shane speared green beans onto his fork. "More or less. Now we just have to find a place. Gives us a bit of head-start though, doesn't it?" he grinned.

"I'll say. Shane this is brilliant, why didn't you say anything about it before?"

He shrugged. "I wasn't sure what we were up against price-wise. But, after that cubby hole this morning, I knew we'd have to pay more for anything even half-decent."

This was fantastic news, Karen thought, finishing the remainder of her club sandwich. With his brother's kind offer, they now had extra leeway.

"Right," Shane said then, pushing his plate away. "We'd better head on up to Harold's Cross and see what the next place is like. Who knows," he winked at Karen as he went to pay the bill, "could end up being the house of our dreams."

23

Weeks later, once the paperwork was complete, Jenny visited Karen and Shane at their starter home in the thick of charming Harold's Cross, another locality characterised by its red brick Victorian-era houses.

"It's gorgeous!" she exclaimed, glancing around the cosy living room. An expansive bay window looked out onto a small front lawn, giving the tiny room additional character despite the dreadful seventies swirling wall-paper and nosebleed-inducing carpet pattern.

She followed Karen upstairs to the bedrooms.

"These things could have been designed just for me," her friend said elatedly, opening a sliding wardrobe door to reveal a plethora of shoes and piles of clothes bundled up inside. "I don't have to keep everything tidy and folded ..." She promptly slid it shut again, "and poof! The mess just disappears by magic."

Jenny had to smile. Karen was deliriously happy with

her new home. She took a quick look around the other bedroom, which judging by the *Barney* wallpaper was previously used as a children's bedroom.

"You'll have to do some work on that one," Jenny said, nodding at the dinosaur décor, "I know you have a bit of a thing for purple but …."

She laughed as Karen pretended to push her down the stairs.

"What are you two skitting about?" Shane asked as they rejoined him in the kitchen where he was busy wiping down the insides of cupboards.

"I was just teasing your wife-to-be," Jenny said, giggling as she sat down at a small round table. The kitchen was also compact but cosy. The units were tired and old-fashioned, but Shane had already undertaken to replace those once he had the time.

"Tell Williams to get his ass down here next time. He promised he'd give me a hand with the wooden floor."

Roan – laying a wooden floor? Jenny was astonished. But pleased afresh that he and Shane seemed to get on so well. It often helped diffuse the once-again frosty atmosphere between him and Karen.

"We don't yet have a washing machine or tumble dryer so we're going to the shops on Saturday, aren't we, hon?" Karen said, winking.

Shane groaned, washing out the J-cloth he was using in the sink. "It's all very well getting a house, but I didn't realise I'd be dragged around the country looking for stuff to fill it."

Jenny watched them both enviously. They were so

happy and incredibly lucky to be able to afford a lovely house like this, and the rest of their lives to look forward to.

She'd love it if she and Roan could go down that road eventually. But, baby steps.

Much to her delight, he'd moved into her flat following Karen's absence, and so far it was working well. Jenny enjoyed coming home from work and having him there to greet her. Sometimes he even made dinner.

The only snag was his unwillingness to partake in housework. Roan wouldn't dream of picking up a sweeping brush or a cloth, to say nothing of cleaning the bathroom. Karen might have been a slob, but at least she did her share. With the longer nights drawing in, the last thing Jenny wanted when she got home from work was domestic drudgery. But if she didn't make the effort, their flat might well end up like his old place.

Then again, as he pointed out, he did work a lot harder than she did, and for longer hours. An American tech company had since purchased his employer, and the new MD expected nothing but complete dedication from staff. So she shouldn't really expect Roan to slave away at home too. He had enough on his plate and couldn't come visit here tonight because he was working late again.

And then there was the ongoing problem with Kevin and his ex-housemates. There had been some dispute over rent outstanding at his previous place. Jenny wasn't sure what it was all about but until everything was sorted, Roan couldn't contribute any rent just yet. He would eventually he assured her, but for the moment, things were a bit 'up in the air'.

"You're so lucky," she said to Karen, as she went to leave. "Shane is such a pet."

Her friend smiled. "He is. But I could have murdered you earlier when you mentioned something about setting a date. That's been a bone of contention, to be honest."

Jenny frowned. "How so?"

"Well, like yourself, Shane thinks that now we've got the house sorted, we should start making plans for the wedding, but I want to put it off for a while"

"But why get engaged if you don't want to get married?"

"I *do* want to get married, but not just yet. The mortgage repayments are higher than we'd like, so I want to try for a promotion. I'd prefer us to be more financially comfortable before considering another big outlay. Plus there are a few jobs to do with the house so I just don't think we're ready."

"I suppose you got the house sorted sooner than you expected," Jenny mused, "but does Shane know how you feel?"

"We've talked about it, and he sees no reason to wait. He reckons that things are tight for everyone starting in life. But I don't see why it has to be that way, so the wedding can wait. What harm?"

As she walked home, Jenny couldn't help but think how she would give *anything* to be in Karen's position – a proud homeowner with a devoted fiancé and a wedding to plan.

Still, she supposed she wasn't doing too badly all the same. She had a gorgeous boyfriend who was madly in love with her, and they'd just moved in together.

Surely the rest was just around the corner.

24

"Guess what?" Tessa squealed down the phone line. "Gerry proposed. We're getting married!"

Jenny gasped. "Wow. When did this all come about?"

"He just popped the question out of the blue. We went out to dinner at the weekend and he got down on one knee and everything."

"Fantastic. What's your ring like? Did Gerry choose it himself?"

"He wouldn't dare. No, we're going into town to pick it out together soon, so I suppose it's not *entirely* official just yet," she giggled. "Anyway, we're all getting together on Friday night to celebrate. I've booked a place in the city for food, and then a few drinks after. Will you come?"

"I wouldn't miss it for the world," Jenny said warmly. "Tell Gerry I said congratulations, won't you? I can't wait to see the ring."

"Me neither!" Tessa laughed, before saying goodbye.

Another one.

Everyone Jenny knew seemed to be settling down these days. Olivia from work had recently announced her engagement; her boyfriend having proposed on holiday. And one of her old friends from home was getting married soon too.

Was there something in the air?

First Karen, Olivia, and now Tessa. How was it that all her friends were settling down and heading for happily ever after, while Jenny was in a relationship that at the moment seemed to have run into a brick wall?

Things with Roan had started to go downhill not long after her promotion, she reflected. In trying to get to grips with new work responsibilities on top of general day-to-day tasks, she could barely keep her eyes open on the train home in the evenings.

Now she shook her head wearily as she caught sight of him snoozing on the sofa while all the used dinner dishes and pots and pans were still piled high on the counter. Could he not make an effort to tidy up – for once?

Things weren't great between them since he'd moved in, Jenny admitted sadly. He didn't seem to understand the work pressure she was under, nor why she 'encouraged' him to help out with the housework. He still insisted that he worked too hard all day without having to come home and get into 'domestic crap'.

She soon learned to her dismay that he'd likely never done a tap of housework. A mummy's boy, clearly Mrs Williams had let him get away with murder. He was lucky he hadn't been born in the Hamilton household. In their teens Jenny's brothers had been trained in everything from making beds to cooking stew.

Now, he muttered out loud as she cleaned up, annoyed at the noise she was making. Tough, she thought, scraping leftovers into the bin with more force than was necessary.

"Do you have to be so loud?" he growled.

"No, I don't *have* to be so loud – though maybe you'd prefer to do it instead - for a change?" she retorted, waving the washing-up liquid at him.

"Ah, don't start," he said, rolling his eyes. "I get enough hassle at work without having to put up with it when I come home too."

Something snapped in Jenny. She'd had just about enough of Roan and all the hassle he was supposed to be under. "Well, sorr-y. But you're not the only one under pressure, you know. And then I have to come back to a pigsty and clean up after you and – "

"Jesus, if it's that much hassle, give it here." He jumped up and nudged in beside her at the sink. "Talk about a bloody nag," he whispered under his breath.

"Hey, I am not a nag," Jenny retorted, "and even if I was, I don't have a choice. You make as much of a mess around here as I do, and yet you expect me to clean up after you? I'm not your slave."

"What? What are you on about? Wasn't I the one who did the shopping last week?" Water splashed out of the sink and onto the floor as he vehemently scrubbed a saucepan. "And the place is never that bad – you obviously have OCD issues."

"It's not that bad, because I make sure it doesn't get that bad!" Jenny was getting angrier by the second.

Roan threw a handful of cutlery into the water, then turned and glared at her. "I don't know what's wrong with you lately. Since you got that bloody promotion you've become really uppity."

"What? What are you on about?"

"You act like you're the bee's knees, thinking you can boss me around like you do everyone at work."

Jenny opened her mouth but no words came out. She couldn't believe what she was hearing. How dare he?

"Roan, that's very unfair. I hardly ever ask you to help unless I'm very tired. And I'm very tired tonight. Coming home to a tip and seeing you all tucked up and snoring on the couch doesn't exactly improve my mood."

"Well, I've had enough of your moods. I don't know what's got into you. You're no fun." He looked at her disdainfully. "You've let yourself go a bit too."

She whirled around to face him. "What the hell does that mean?"

"You dress like a dowdy schoolteacher these days, you hardly ever wear make-up, and you haven't bothered getting your roots redone. Honestly, it's a bit like shacking up with my mother." Then when he saw her expression, his voice softened. "Ah I'm sorry. I just lashed out because I'm tired and you were ranting on at me for being lazy. I'm not trying to be hurtful, Jen – I'm only telling you these things for your own good."

Jenny looked at her reflection in the mirror over the fireplace. Maybe he was right. She *had* been putting off a visit to the hairdresser. She was just so bloody tired all the time.

So maybe Roan had told her some home truths, however hard they might have been to hear. No wonder he had lost interest in sex. In the beginning, they had been tearing each other's clothes off at every opportunity – these days, they were lucky if they managed it once a month.

He embraced her quickly, before kissing her softly on the forehead. "Tell you what, why don't you sit down and put your feet up while I finish this and then I'll make you a cuppa?"

Jenny hesitated. "I'm sorry too. You're right; I probably have been difficult to live with."

"It's OK, babe." He patted the sofa cushions. "Go on, sit down and take it easy."

But afterwards, I'm putting on trainers and going for a good long run, Jenny resolved, wondering if any of the local hair salons might fit her in after work sometime this week.

She'd make sure she was looking her best for Tessa's engagement party. After all, her friends rarely looked anything other than glam.

Which was probably why they and not she, Jenny reflected sadly, were the ones shopping for engagement rings ...

25

"What do you think – isn't it gorgeous?" Tessa sang, proudly displaying the almond-shaped solitaire on her engagement finger. "Gerry wanted to get something smaller, but once I saw it, I knew it was the one for me."

"It's fabulous," Karen said, trying it on, and wondering how on earth Gerry could afford such a rock. Her diamond was like a crumb in comparison.

Not that it mattered she thought, looking lovingly at the back of Shane's head. He could have done a Homer Simpson on it and bought her an onion ring for all she cared. She waved at the others, who were sitting at the bar with some people she didn't know – work friends of Tessa's probably.

"Where's Jenny and Roan?" the bride to be asked, looking anxiously at the door. "Everyone else is here, and I thought they'd be arriving with you two."

"Don't ask," Karen said dryly.

"Trouble in paradise – again?"

"Paradise it ain't, not these days, anyway. We'd arranged to call for them in the taxi on the way and when we got there, Jenny told us to go on ahead – that Roan wasn't back from work yet, so they'd meet us here." She shook her head. "It was obvious that she was covering up. I'd say he was upstairs and they were in the middle of an argument."

"It's happening a lot lately isn't it?" Tessa bit her lip. "Since they moved in together, I mean."

"She's been under a lot of pressure in the new management role, and he's not giving her any support from what I can tell."

"I haven't seen them in ages. I really hope she comes out tonight though, for her own sake at least."

"We'll see," Karen said, "but I'd be very surprised if he's with her. After all, he doesn't ever make much of an effort where her friends are concerned, does he?"

"Wondering about Jen? Wonder no more," Shane said, pointing to the door, where a harassed-looking Jenny had just appeared.

"Told you he wouldn't show," Karen murmured under her breath.

"Hi, everyone," Jenny greeted shyly.

She looked miserable, Karen thought, studying Jenny as she examined Tessa's engagement ring. For an occasion like this, the old Jen would have dressed up to the nines. Instead, she wore an uninspiring all-black ensemble and very little make-up. Her hair seemed much lighter too, almost brassy.

Jenny smiled wanly at her as they took their seats. "Before you ask, I don't know where he is, he hasn't come back from work yet, and I haven't been able to contact him."

Typical. Roan had obviously ducked out at the last minute, letting her down again. Karen could throttle him.

"Jen, your hair looks different, did you get it cut? *Ow.*" Shane felt the full force of his fiancee's kick in the shins, and a low blush appeared on Jenny's face.

"I know – it looks awful," she said, touching her hair self-consciously. "I got one of those home-colouring kits and did it myself yesterday. I usually get it done at the salon but they couldn't fit me in. That's why it looks a bit ... off."

"No, no, I meant it looked nice." Shane was relieved when the waitress appeared to take his order.

Karen's heart went out to her. She had to resort to a home kit because she probably couldn't afford to have it done at the salon. Same reason she hadn't dressed up tonight, probably. Come to think of it, she hadn't seen Jenny in anything new for a long time and her friend adored fashion.

The bastard still wasn't paying his share of the rent, and Jen was making up the difference. He must owe her a fortune by now, Karen harrumphed silently.

Sir Galahad, my ass.

. . .

AFTER DINNER, Jenny wistfully regarded her coupled-up friends walking hand in hand down the street ahead of her. They were so lucky she thought, watching Shane put his arm around Karen and plant a kiss on the top of her head.

And Tessa and Gerry were just as happy with everything to look forward to.

Watching them all together just made her feel worse. She had told Roan about tonight and he'd said he would catch up, so where was he? He'd told her that they were a little behind on their current project but surely staff weren't expected to stay that late on a Friday night?

"My feet are killing me," Tessa groaned later. "We should have got a taxi to the club."

"Oh yeah? And who's the one that wanted to go dress shopping?" Karen teased.

On their way to a popular Dublin hotspot, Tessa had a drunken notion to go window shopping for her wedding dress on Grafton St. The men had quickly continued onwards to the club, arranging to meet them there.

"Can you see any sign of the lads?" Karen shouted now, craning her head to see past the dance-floor, as the three made their way through to the crowded bar.

"If they're here, the dance floor is the last place they'll be," Tessa joked.

Drinks in hand, the trio then moved through the crowds.

"Looks like it's turned into a girls' night," Tessa commented after searching for their partners to no avail.

"Oooh I love this song– come on." Setting her drink on the bar, she grabbed at Karen and Jenny, trying to drag them onto the dance floor.

"I'll just stay here with the drinks," Jenny murmured, and the others looked at her in amazement.

"But you love this song!"

"No, you two go on ahead – seriously."

Jenny numbly watched her friends strut their stuff in the overcrowded club. She didn't want to be here at all. The crowds and the noise were getting to her. In truth, the whole night was beginning to get to her. She just couldn't get into the spirit of things, and was feeling oddly removed from it all.

When the girls returned, damp with sweat from their exertions, they seemed to be giggling and whispering amongst themselves and she felt a fresh wave of irritation. She was just about to tell them she was leaving when she heard a familiar song start up.

"Your favourite!" Karen exclaimed, grinning. "We asked the DJ to play it. Come on – you *have* to come out now." It was a boppy tune that always made her smile, so despite herself, Jenny had little choice but to follow the others onto the dance floor.

Little by little she started to get into the swing of things, letting loose and beginning to enjoy herself for the first time all evening, until a familiar face at the edge of the crowd caught her eye.

And all of a sudden, Jenny stopped dancing.

26

Roan couldn't believe his luck. The Ice Maiden had finally cracked.

Everyone in the office had been surprised when their gorgeous new line manager had joined them for after-work drinks. Normally, Cara never deigned to go out with colleagues on Friday – she always made it seem as though she had something better to do.

He'd noticed her from the very beginning – any red-blooded male would – but the fact that she was cool, distant and completely uninterested in him intrigued him all the more.

Roan wasn't used to not being noticed.

Admittedly she had been a little wary when they'd started chatting in the pub. He'd started out using tried and trusted lines that made most birds weak at the knees. Not her, though.

But little by little, as the evening wore on and the

drinks kept flowing, his efforts finally began to hit the spot.

"Do you want to go somewhere quieter?" he heard Cara ask him now over the loud music. "It's too crowded in here."

He studied her face for a moment, trying to read it. It would be the easiest thing in the world to go somewhere with this girl, have mind-blowing sex and then home to Jenny, who'd be fast asleep and wouldn't suspect a thing.

Impatient at his hesitation, Cara promptly cupped his jaw and brought his mouth to hers, intending to make up his mind.

For some reason, Roan pulled back. He was just about to tell her that he was going home – without her - when he got the sense that he was being watched.

Then turned to see Jenny watching motionless and horrified from the dance floor.

27

SIX MONTHS LATER

Jenny checked the time. She and Karen had arranged to meet for lunch by Dun Laoghaire seafront. She didn't see her friend as often as she'd have liked since moving out to the coast.

She knew Karen still thought she was crazy to just pack up and leave the area. "You need friends around you more than ever."

But Jenny had been insistent. She didn't want to remain in the home she had shared with Roan, nor the same locality; there were just too many painful memories.

The spacious harbourside one-bed rental she lived in now was calming and restful, plus it was walking distance to work. In the immediate aftermath of the breakup, she'd spent evenings on her balcony looking out over the sea, watching the sailboats and ferries coming in and out of the harbour, and going over every word Roan had said, every last thing he'd done, every lie he'd told.

How could she have been so naive for so long? She cringed remembering all the times he had let her down, and the pathetic excuses she'd swallowed.

Yet, despite herself, even now Jenny wished for him to put his arms around her and tell her that he'd made a mistake – that it was all a horrible misunderstanding and that she was always the one he wanted.

Not surprisingly, he *had* tried telling her all this after that night.

Jenny had immediately recognised the girl he was with in the nightclub. They'd met briefly at his office Christmas party and Jenny had found her a standoffish at the time. Maybe they'd been carrying on behind her back all along.

She hadn't realised that something could hurt so much. That night, it was as if something had reached right inside her and grabbed her heart in a vice-like grip. She had felt dizzy and sick to her stomach as she watched them together, yet still couldn't quite believe it truly was Roan, until he noticed her.

That was the very last time she saw him, Jenny reflected, her eyes filling afresh with tears.

That night, she had rushed straight out of the club, quickly pursued by Karen. As always, her friend had been an absolute rock, making sure that Roan kept away when Jenny flatly refused to see him afterwards - much as she wanted to.

She knew that if she saw him face to face, she would

fall for his excuses and lies all over again. For her own sake, she couldn't let that happen, not any more.

Karen had made up the spare room in her new house and supervised when Roan moved his stuff out of the flat and the coast was clear for Jenny to do the same.

It had been very difficult not to talk to him, or let him explain himself, but Jenny knew that if she didn't hold her nerve then, she never would.

It had taken a lot of introspection before she came to understand how wrong and toxic the relationship had been. With distance came the time and space to look at it all more clearly.

Yet, time hadn't quite diminished her love for him. That was something Jenny couldn't run away from.

Not yet.

A LITTLE LATER, Karen groaned and pushed her plate away. She and Jenny were having lunch at a lovely seafront bistro.

"I bought a slinky number for Tessa's wedding, but if I carry on eating like this, I'll never be able to fit into it. Did you get your invite?"

Jenny sipped her mineral water and nodded. "It came last week. Fancy - looks like it'll be a very lavish affair."

"Lavish is not the word for it." Karen agreed. "I honestly think she's trying to outdo royalty with her designer wedding dress and her custom-made wedding rings - though I don't know where she's going to get the thrones from."

Jenny smiled.

"And you should see all the wedding magazines," Karen laughed. "She's a woman possessed."

"I'm looking forward to it. I haven't had a decent knees-up with you all in ages."

"It can't be good for you, being out here on your own."

"Don't start – you'd swear I was a million miles away. I'm fine as I am, really."

Karen wasn't convinced. She couldn't believe the change in Jenny since the breakup. Her friend looked so thin and drawn and the clothes were practically hanging off her these days. A completely different person to the bubbly, fun-loving girl she'd always been.

Jenny seemed to read her thoughts and smiled softly. "Don't give me that look. I'm grand, honestly."

"I know you are. I just wish you'd come and see us more often, that's all. Shane is always asking about you."

"I must call and see what else you've done with the house. Did you get the bedrooms decorated?"

Karen looked sheepish.

"Don't tell me you haven't done anything since?"

She made a face. "Ah, you know what I'm like – full of great ideas at the beginning of something, and then I just get bored."

"But it's your house – you can't have a load of unfinished rooms. What does Shane think?"

Karen snorted. "He's as bad. He got it into his head

that he'd be able to replace the tiles around the bath and borrowed one of those tile cutters from some guy he knows from work." She rolled her eyes and sniggered. "You should have heard the cursing and spluttering coming from the bathroom."

"So, did he finish it?" Jenny asked, unable to keep from smiling herself. Despite his engineer's brain, Shane wasn't known for his handyman skills.

"Not at all. I made him get a professional in to tidy up after him. Cost a fortune, but you couldn't leave it like it was, one wall dark blue and the other yellow. It looked like a GAA flag."

Jenny shook her head fondly. "The two of you are so well matched, you know."

"Yeah, shame about his family ..." Karen muttered darkly.

"What do you mean? I thought you and Mrs Quinn got on OK."

"No, Nellie's all right *sometimes* – it's the brother I can't tolerate. Remember the one who helped with the mortgage finance?"

Jenny nodded.

"Well, he's been acting the prat about that ever since. Shane is sorry he asked."

"I don't understand. I thought he *offered* to help," Jenny said, frowning.

"So did I. But seems Nellie was the one who suggested he offer us a leg-up. I think she made Jack feel guilty about having two properties and earing all this money, and here's poor old Shane starting out with nothing." She signalled to a passing waiter for a pot of tea. "He was home a while back and we went up to visit. I wanted to thank him in person for his kindness." She rolled her eyes. "Big mistake."

"What happened?"

"He kept making sly digs about Shane's job. Said straight out he'd blown it with Germany and insinuated that the job he has now isn't good enough, even suggesting we might have trouble paying the mortgage. We went to the pub and he was watching Shane like a hawk every time he bought a pint. You'd swear we were out on the razz every night of the week, and didn't give a hoot about mortgage repayments."

"That's awful. Poor Shane."

"Well if I had my way, I'd tell Jack to stuff his bloody guarantee. But we have the house now so feck him ..." She trailed off and spooned sugar into her tea.

"Have you made any plans for your wedding then?" Jenny asked, changing the topic. "Or would Jack disapprove?"

"Ah, I'll see what happens after Tessa's. Maybe that might get me in the mood."

"I take it that you won't be commissioning a famous dress designer for your big day," Jenny said mischievously.

Karen laughed. "Not my style." She glanced at the clock. "I think I might do a bit of shopping after this though. Might as well make the most of my day off."

"I need to buy something to wear for Tessa's wedding

myself," Jenny said. "I can't remember the last time I went clothes shopping."

Karen knew that Jenny was still tight for cash after all the money she had lent to Roan, which had never been repaid. Not to mention the rent that had built up on their old flat, which she also had to settle before vacating.

She sighed heavily. Sod it, she might as well say something.

"Hey, I don't know whether I should tell you or not but ..." Karen took a deep breath. "Not sure if maybe Roan's been in touch ... " She noticed Jenny flinch a little at the mention of his name. So she didn't know then. Good, at least he'd left her in peace. "Seems he's moving to the States."

"Oh ... I see," Jenny replied, her voice strained. "How ... how do you know that?"

"He bumped into Shane. You know how the two of them always seemed to get along so well?" Karen had to resist the urge to add that she couldn't figure out how her fiancé found anything in common with that ass. "He and a few others from the Dublin office are transferring to the parent company in New York."

"And *her*?" Jenny asked in a small voice, still refusing to meet Karen's gaze.

"No. He insisted to Shane that nothing was going on. Apparently she has a two-year-old son, so maybe Roan just didn't want to play daddy." Karen could have kicked herself when she noticed Jenny swallow hard. "Ah, Jen, I'm sorry," she said softly. "I didn't mean to be callous."

"It's all right, it's just ... it still hurts to talk about him." Her eyes glistened brightly.

She looked so sad, so broken. Despite her earlier protests about being fine, Karen could see that Jenny wasn't fine at all, far from it.

"I'm so sorry. I wanted to tell you because I thought you should know. Believe me, if I had my way I'd have kept it from you until he was long gone, but just in case you wanted to –"

"What?" Jenny cut in sharply, "In case I wanted to say goodbye? He said goodbye to me a long time ago. OK, it's a jolt to hear that he's leaving but it shouldn't bother me and it doesn't." A fiercely determined look appeared on her face then and she sat up straight in her chair. "At least now I'm rid of Roan Williams - once and for all."

28

Later, Karen struggled to fit through the front door with all she'd bought on a satisfying bout of retail therapy.

But stopped short when she saw the state of her living room. Granted it was never tidy at the best of times, but today it looked as though a dozen Andrex puppies had been let loose. What looked like a full roll of toilet paper – *wet* toilet paper – was strewn across a coffee table that now resembled one of Picasso's rejects.

Green and blue paint handprints had also been smeared on the wall beside the TV, and on the screen itself. Small handprints – *children's* handprints.

Karen was trying to make sense of the situation when suddenly realisation dawned.

The crazy gang.

"Hey!" A smiling Shane stuck his head around the kitchen door. "You're back early."

"What's going on?" she asked, still surveying the devastation.

"Hi Karen," she heard his sister's voice call out from the kitchen, and was almost afraid to put her head around the door for fear Marie's errant brood had targeted the kitchen too with their guerrilla warfare tactics.

But mercifully the chaos there was confined to the dining table, now covered with half-eaten chips, half-digested chips and squashed-into-the-kitchen-table chips.

Not to mention the ketchup. If she didn't know better, Karen could have sworn that Shane's five-year-old nephew was performing open-heart surgery. While his younger sister was happily dipping Barbie into a jar of Hellmann's. The little girl licked mayonnaise off the doll's head before promptly lowering it back in for another helping.

The baby was resting happily in Marie's lap while Shane sat chatting with his sister at the table, both oblivious to the surrounding bedlam.

"Karen, you're on babysitting duty tonight. Myself and Frank are going to a show and Nellie thought it might be nice for you two to get in a bit of practice." She winked.

What!!?

"Ah, can I have a word please, hon?" Karen asked, eyeing Shane.

"What?" He queried, once they were in the next room and out of earshot.

"What do you mean – *what*? Why did you agree to babysit?"

He shrugged. "I thought it would be nice to give them a break. They rarely get out on their own, so when Mam told me about the show it was the perfect opportunity."

Karen now understood what it felt like to be a goldfish. She kept opening and closing her mouth but no words would come out.

"I've tidied up the spare room so Marie and Frank can spend the night here afterwards," he said, mistaking her silence for assent. "Then they can both have a few drinks instead of having to travel back to Meath. We can take the cushions off the couch and put the kids on the floor in our room, and she brought a cot for the baby so... what? Why are you looking at me like that?"

"Shane – did you not think to check if *any* of this was OK with me? I don't fancy spending my Friday night running around after those three nightmares."

"Jeez, will you keep your voice down," Shane said, dropping his own to a whisper in case his sister might overhear, "I know they can be a bit boisterous, but –"

"A bit – *are you kidding me*? Look at the state of the living room – not to mention the kitchen."

He looked hurt. "They're family. Now that we have a place of our own, I can see them more often. I couldn't invite them to the old flat – you know yourself how crummy that was."

"But fine to let them loose here?"

"It's hardly that bad," he said, following her gaze

around the room. "The toilet roll can be picked up and I'm pretty sure that the paint is washable and –"

"Nope, that is – I mean *was*, a solid pine coffee table," Karen interrupted. Despite her offhand protestations to Jenny, she was proud of what decorating they had done. "It's not varnished. The paint will never come off – they might as well have used Ronseal – beautiful but tough. Which is what your sister would be well advised to be on that lot – *tough*."

Shane stepped back. "You're talking about my family Karen," he said, his tone changing.

She took a deep, calming breath. "You're right," she conceded wearily. "I'm just not used to having children around, that's all."

"I know. But I *like* having them around. And I'd really like to do Marie a favour tonight too."

She bit her lip. "Well I suppose, but it's just ... well ... I really don't have a clue – I won't have to breastfeed them or anything, will I?" She had seen Marie do this once and it had terrified her.

Shane's eyes twinkled with amusement. "You really don't know anything about kids at *all,* do you? They won't bite."

Karen smiled weakly. "Are you sure – the boy looks dangerous."

Shane put an arm around her shoulders. "Go on back into the kitchen and I'll make you a cuppa. And Marie can pass on a few tips," he added devilishly.

Maybe it wouldn't be too bad, Karen conceded;

surely the kids would be worn out from running around already. Maybe she wouldn't have to *do* anything.

Back in the kitchen, she smiled faintly at Marie, who offered her the baby to hold.

"Say hello to Auntie Karen," Shane's sister sang.

Karen's hands shook as she held the infant in her arms. Was she holding her the right way? She did seem to be squirming an awful lot – maybe she was hurting her. She sat down and awkwardly laid the child on her lap, then looked up to see Shane watching her. He nodded gratefully and her heart melted.

Regardless, she'd suffer through tonight, Karen decided. Purely for her fiance's sake.

29

"I was scared witless," she grumbled to Tessa the following evening, "Didn't have a notion what what to do."

"What do you mean, scared? They're only toddlers, for goodness sake."

The two were sitting on Tessa's sofa, three-quarter ways through a bottle of wine and most of the way through her bridal magazines.

"I'm an only child remember? They're like a foreign species. I dunno – it's hard to explain. I just – I just don't have a clue what to say to them – or even how to *speak* to them. That baby voice people use - with me, it doesn't come out right and I just feel stupid – like they know I'm faking it."

Tessa laughed. "Not planning to have any of your own anytime soon then, I take it?"

"Honestly? I think I'd be a terrible mother. I'm kinda

scared too – not so much of the kids, more the idea of them."

Tessa waved her away. "Don't be silly, everyone's different with their own. And from what you said before, Shane's crowd aren't exactly little angels."

"No, but," Karen exhaled deeply, "to be perfectly honest, the thought of having kids has always petrified me and I don't know if that's ever going to change." She made a face. "And the way his family are always going on dropping hints about our starting a family, I don't know what I'll do."

"What does Shane think?"

"I'm not sure. He knows that I don't exactly fall all over them whenever they visit but ..." She shrugged.

"You said his family are always dropping hints?"

"Yup. Particularly his mother."

"And do you get on well with her – enough to maybe tell her to back off a little?"

"Ah, Nellie annoys me sometimes when she visits the house, in fact, *every* time she visits. She always seems to find some fault with the place."

"How so?"

"Well, one day for instance, she picked up the sweeping brush and started poking around at the ceiling. Told me that she had spotted a few cobwebs up there."

"Cheek." Tessa arched an eyebrow.

"That's what I thought. Another time, she came out of the bathroom and announced that the towels were damp. I wouldn't mind, but earlier I had been nagging Shane to pick up after his shower. And sure enough,

Mammy Dearest had to spot them. I don't think she means anything by it – probably just trying to help."

"Maybe, but I don't think I'd put up with Gerry's mother telling me what to do under my own roof – if we ever get one, that is."

"Oh, how's the building going?"

"Not too bad. Just waiting on the plasterer to come now."

Once they were married Tessa and Gerry planned to move to the pretty West Coark village where she was from. Her dad was overseeing the construction of their new build. Gerry, who worked as a website designer, was planning to set up on his own and work from there, while Tessa hoped to secure a nursing position at a hospital close by.

Karen was going to miss her. With Jenny shutting herself away out in Dun Laoghaire and Tessa leaving for Cork, all her friends seemed to be disappearing.

"Oh, I met Jenny yesterday," she said, changing the subject.

Tessa smiled. "Ah, how is she these days?"

"Much improved, but I think it got to her a little when she heard about your man's impending departure."

"So he hasn't been in touch then."

Karen shook her head. "Maybe he's developed a conscience and decided to let her get on with her life? Or more likely he hasn't even given her a second thought. Prick."

"I met him one day in town," Tessa said. "And he seemed miserable to be fair."

"So he should be. She's been miserable for long enough." She harrumphed. "Probably just feeling sorry for himself because he was caught out in his true colours."

Tessa paused. "Don't you think that sometimes you might have been a little bit too hard on the guy?"

"You can't be serious. You were there that night; you saw what happened – what he was up to. And how devastated Jenny was too – what do you mean I might have been too hard on him? Roan is an ass, always was."

"Calm down, that's not what I meant. But for what it's worth, I do think he cared about her."

Karen set her glass down on the table and folded her arms across her chest. "You're as bad as Shane. Tell me this, would you be as forgiving towards Gerry?"

Knowing she was fighting a losing battle, Tessa gave up. "You're probably right. It's just he seemed genuinely sorry for what had happened and when I spoke to him he was keen to find out how Jenny was doing."

Karen sniffed. "Probably wondering if she had calmed down enough for him to weasel his way back into her affections."

Tessa had to laugh. "Karen, do something for me, will you? Keep reminding me for the rest of my life that I should never, *ever* make an enemy out of you."

She giggled. "Maybe. But you didn't see half of what I saw throughout that relationship. When Jenny came back from Oz, she was so bubbly, happy, and *confident*.

When I saw her yesterday ..." She shook her head. "I don't know – it was hard to believe I was talking to the same person. He wore her down, eroded her confidence, took all her money ... crushed her, even."

"Do you think she'll be OK – eventually, I mean?" Tessa asked.

Karen gave a firm nod of the head. "Jen will be fine – once Roan Williams stays well enough away."

30

"What the hell's got into you?" Jenny's manager paced up and down his office in front of her, first thing Monday morning. "A trainee wouldn't do something as stupid."

Mortified, she stared at her lap. She had never seen Barry so annoyed and it was not a pretty sight. His face was bright red, screwed up in anger and his eyes flashed dangerously.

For her part, she still couldn't believe what she had done either. Friday afternoon after her lunch with Karen, she'd been asked to step in and cover Commercial Cash when another employee had gone home sick. Jenny remembered that they had been especially busy that afternoon and that she had been rapidly doling out more cash than she was taking in.

She also remembered finding it difficult to concentrate after learning that Roan was leaving the country and didn't know how to feel about the likelihood of never seeing him again.

A director from a local firm had come up in a terrible rush, looking to withdraw a large sum from his business account. Jenny had been so harassed and harried by his impatience that she had absent-mindedly included a wad of dummy notes in the cash pile. A security precaution to be given out in the event of a hold-up, when triggered the fake bundle of notes exploded coloured dye onto any would-be thief's hands, clothes, or other stolen cash, tainting it.

And Jenny had mistakenly given this 'bomb' to a corporate client.

"How am I supposed to pacify a man who had one of his Armani suits dyed pink?" Barry raged. "And his hands are still covered. He was on his way to an important meeting and had to cancel it. Sure he couldn't face anyone in that state. He was raging."

"Barry, I don't know what to say. It was a mistake – I truly am very, very sorry."

She *was* sorry, but the image of this self-important guy covered in irremovable pink dye was comical to be fair.

But her boss was anything but amused.

"I'll speak to Mr. Kennedy," she offered. "Maybe he'll have calmed down a little by now."

Barry picked up a file and slid it across the desk to her. "InTech is the company. His contact details are all there. I suggest you write a personal letter of apology and then follow up with a call. Sweeten him up – send flowers or something – I don't know Jenny, just make sure he knows that this bank is not in the habit of putting imbeciles behind a cash desk."

THE EPISODE HAD MADE Jenny instantly famous throughout the bank network. The incident had been gleefully shared all over the district and her workmates continued to tease her unmercifully all through the week.

"Armani suits," ribbed another. "Don't they cost an absolute *bomb*?"

The banter took her mind off the fact that Roan was moving to the US and Jenny was becoming resigned to the fact that she was unlikely to hear from him ever again.

The idea didn't disturb her nearly as much as she thought. It meant that she could finally move past the heartbreak and get on with her life instead of hiding away from it. It would certainly be easier to do that without the risk of running into him again. Dublin was a small city and chances were that their paths would've crossed sometime. This was for the best. Maybe she could finally begin to let go.

Now, a young trainee called up to warn Jenny of Mr Kennedy's impending arrival and she got the sense that the apologetic letter and chocolate gift basket she'd sent in the interim, weren't nearly enough to mollify the esteemed director of InTech.

She headed out to the waiting area where a heavyset

man in his late fifties sat on the sofa, flicking through *Banking News*.

"Mr Kennedy?" she greeted. "Jenny. Pleased to meet you." She smiled and nervously offered her hand. He hesitated for a moment and then shook it, confused. She was surprised at his appearance. He didn't look like the executive type at all with his brown tweed ensemble. And where was the famous Armani?

She certainly couldn't remember the guy anyway. Then again, it had been so busy that day she could've served George Clooney and it wouldn't have registered.

"Did you get me box?" the man asked in a thick Wicklow accent. "I'm waitin' for me box."

Jenny looked at him blankly.

"Mr Kenny, you can use this room." One of her colleagues appeared with a safety deposit box, indicating a room just behind. "I'll be back to you in a few minutes, OK?"

The man looked from the other woman to Jenny, then duly took his belongings into the room and closed the door behind him.

"Oh!" Jenny put a hand to her throat and exhaled. "Katrina told me your man from InTech was looking for me. She must have misheard. Thank goodness, I was dreading it."

"No, your receptionist was correct," said a deep male voice from nearby and they both turned to look as a tall, much younger guy appeared at the top of the stairs. He stepped forward and offered his hand to Jenny.

"Mike Kennedy," he greeted.

"Oh ... pleased to meet you - again" she stammered, gulping. "My office is just back here."

Could it get any worse? Now the cranky CEO had caught her blabbering about him behind his back. For some reason when Barry mentioned he was a company director, she'd pictured a much older man.

"First of all, thank you for the gift basket," he said when they'd retreated to her office. "Nice touch."

"Um, you're welcome," she replied nervously. "Take a seat."

Kennedy duly sat down and set his briefcase on the floor. "I'm sorry that I haven't had a chance to return your calls. I've been on the road."

His trusty PA hadn't bothered telling her *that.* He smiled then and Jenny couldn't help noticing how attractive he was. *Stop it,* she warned herself, *this guy could get you fired.*

"Ms Hamilton –" he began.

"Please, call me Jenny."

"OK, Jenny. The reason I came to see you is because I wanted to put your mind at ease. I understand that it was a simple mistake and I'm sure these things happen."

"But it shouldn't have happened," she blurted, embarrassed. "I wasn't concentrating. If a junior staff member had done something like that, fair enough but –"

"Please, let's just forget about it," he interjected. "I blew my top with your manager but that was because I had to cancel my meeting, and it was just a heat-of-the-moment reaction. You must have got into terrible trouble."

Jenny managed to raise a smile. "Barry's expression wasn't a pretty sight, that's for sure."

"Neither was I afterwards," he chuckled. "That stuff went *everywhere*. Impossible to remove."

She grimaced. "I really am so sorry, Mr Kennedy. If there's anything at all I can say or do to make it up to you ..."

"Call me Mike, and honestly it's fine. There are worse things in life." He smiled at her again, his blue eyes alight with amusement.

Jenny couldn't believe how decent he was being. No wonder she had been petrified about meeting him; Barry had made him out to be an awful monster. But he was ... lovely.

"So I was in the area and firstly wanted to apologise for not returning your calls. And I also wondered if Barry might be free. I want to reassure him that I won't be moving my account, despite recent threats to the contrary." He chuckled and pushed a lock of fair hair out of one eye. "Though between you and me, I did enjoy that bit - putting the frighteners on the bank manager. You'd never know – this situation might work to my advantage after all."

Jenny stood up to see him out.

"While I'm at it, I must also check who's taking care of my replacement suit."

She looked worried. Yikes, he wouldn't expect *her* to pay for *that,* would he?

Barry must have been trying to listen in because he was right outside the door all smiles when Jenny opened it,.

"Mike!" he boomed. "Hope all well? Jen, get us a cup of coffee and maybe pop down to the bakery for a few doughnuts," he ordered dismissively.

Mike winked at Jenny as he disappeared into the manager's office. And the conspiratorial look he gave her with those twinkling blue eyes somehow managed to put a little spring in her step.

31

It was a warm late September day, and many native beech trees surrounding the little country chapel retained their golden leaves, adding an autumnal feel to the quaint pastoral setting.

"I can't believe these temps," Karen said, struggling to appear ladylike in her high heels while getting out of Shane's car. She stood up straight, positioned her hat and looked up at the sky in wonder. "You wouldn't get weather this good in June."

The church was the tiniest Jenny had ever seen and the setting was so picturesque amid the Cork countryside. A truly beautiful place to get married.

She'd travelled down from Dublin with Karen and Shane. The rugged mountainous scenery on the journey there completely enthralled Shane, who'd grown up in the relatively flatter lands of County Meath.

Throughout the trip, Jenny wasn't sure which was worse, Shane driving distractedly, or Karen driving as only she knew how. She was doing at least a hundred on the winding by-roads, beeping and honking at every tractor or slow driver in her way.

For her part, Jenny spent the majority of the journey with her eyes closed, knowing she would surely throw up if she looked out at the countryside whizzing past, and had been more than a little relieved when they finally pulled into the church car park in one piece.

Slightly late, the three hurried in to take their seats and were inside only a few minutes when the organist started up the bridal march.

Tessa's sixteen-year-old twin sisters wore rust-red bridesmaid dresses, which looked particularly striking against their dusky complexions. Then the bride herself appeared close behind, a glorious vision in ivory satin, her dad walking proudly alongside.

Tessa looked amazing in her Vera Wang wedding dress. Her hair had grown longer since Jenny had seen her last, and today she wore it curled and piled high on her head, a few tiny tendrils framing her face and a gold tiara completing the overall 'fairy princess' effect.

She inclined her head towards her dad as he whispered something in her ear, and Jenny saw her eyes glisten as they walked towards the altar. Mr Sullivan looked at his daughter with such pride and love that she felt her own eyes smart with the beginning of tears.

As she watched the two walk towards the altar, she understood for the very first time why so many people cried at weddings. The fairytale atmosphere in the tiny church was almost ethereal. Even Karen was softening a little, she realised, catching sight of her squeezing Shane's hand as the bride and groom took their vows.

The reception was being held in a hotel not far from the location. When they got there, Shane spotted Aidan and his plus one sitting at the bar.

"We couldn't find the bloody church," he said, throwing his hands up in despair. "I must have asked for directions from about ten different people but I couldn't understand a word any of them were saying. What's a boreen, by the way?" He winked at Shane.

"Nice try. It wasn't too bad though, only an hour long. I thought these things went on for ages."

"It was long enough for me," Gerry exclaimed, coming up behind them, looking especially dashing in his morning suit.

"Congratulations, mate." Aidan stood up and clapped him on the back. "Where's the missus?"

"Running around chatting to everyone – you know yourself," Gerry beamed as the barman handed him a pint of Guinness. "I've been looking forward to this – cheers, lads."

"It was a really lovely ceremony," Jenny said, sitting at a window table beside Karen. "Must really get you excited for your big day."

Karen shrugged and poured diet Coke into her vodka. "I suppose. But I thought that the horse and cart thing was a bit over the top." She giggled. "Imagine myself and Shane going down Main Street Kilkenny in a horse and cart. We'd be the talk of the town."

They were both laughing so much that they didn't notice someone come up beside their table.

"Hello there."

Surprised, Jenny looked up and felt her cheeks redden. Mike Kennedy was standing there, looking very dapper in a tuxedo. What was *he* doing at Tessa and Gerry's wedding?

"Mr Kennedy ... hi," she managed to say. Out of the corner of her eye, she could see Karen watching with interest.

"It's Mike and this is a surprise – I didn't expect that I'd know anyone here. Hello." He nodded pleasantly at Karen.

"Oh, forgive my manners. This is Mike Kennedy, a customer of the bank. Mike – my best friend Karen."

"Hello," Karen said coyly. "Pleased to meet you. How do you know Tessa and Gerry?"

Just then, a redhead wearing the shortest dress with the longest legs appeared at his side and tugged impatiently at his arm.

"I need a drink. I just met Sandra Thompson and she bored the face off me talking about baby night feeds. Save me ..." She turned and nudged through the crowd at the bar, nearly toppling Aidan off his barstool. Jenny noticed him give her an appreciative look as she ordered.

"Duty calls," Mike smiled politely. "Catch you later."

Karen waited until he was a safe distance away. "Who was *that*?" she gasped, eyes wide with interest. "What a hunk. No wonder you were blushing."

"Ah no, was I?" Jenny was mortified. "He's the one I told you about before, the one who got covered in dye."

"*That's* the guy? I got the impression he was one of those stuffed shirts, not an Adonis."

She laughed. "Well, his date is a good match." She watched Mike's attractive companion cross her long toned legs as they sat at the bar. And despite herself, felt an inexplicable hint of envy.

Soon, they all took their seats in the banqueting room. Tessa had really pulled out all the stops. A bouquet of heart-shaped helium balloons in red and gold had been placed in the centre of every round table, and two huge bride and groom air-walkers hovered behind the happy couple at the top table.

"I have to admit, I like the balloons," Karen said to Shane, taking a seat at their table. "That's something I wouldn't mind doing for ours. What do you think?"

"Mind if we join you?" said a female voice from behind. "It's just we don't know anyone else, and I saw Mike talking to you two earlier." She rolled her eyes conspiratorially. "And I don't want to get stuck with Miss Baby Bore again."

"Sure," Karen said, pulling out a chair for Mike Kennedy's date.

"Thanks. I'm Rachel, by the way. Mike's still up at the bar, chatting to some 'oul fella he met a few minutes ago." She plopped happily into the chair. "I'm kinda sorry I brought him now – he's useless. Asked him to help me find a man and what does he do? Chats to old-age pensioners." She lowered her voice and looked around her. "Any decent singles at this table?"

Karen laughed. "Not this lot I'm afraid," she said. "Well, Aidan maybe, but I wouldn't wish him on my worst enemy. So, you're not with Mike?" she added, side-eyeing Jenny pointedly.

Rachel looked at her as if she was mad. "God no, he's my brother."

With that, the aforementioned appeared at the table.

"I'm very sorry about this," he said, frowning at Rachel. "She tends to be a little … forward."

"Not at all. You guys are more than welcome to join us."

"So how do you two know the bride and groom?" Karen enquired. "Are you related?"

"Truthfully I don't know them from Adam," Mike shrugged. "Rachel trained in nursing with Tessa and she asked me to come along as her plus one."

"I haven't seen Tessa in years, but we keep in touch. I went to work in London after we qualified," Rachel explained, pushing her flame-coloured hair behind her ears as she buttered a bread roll. "What do you reckon on yer man over there?" she asked Jenny. "A bit on the old side but I could get past that."

Jenny followed her gaze and laughed out loud. "That's Tessa's dad."

"Oops!" Rachel looked duly bashful.

"What about you?" she asked Jenny. "Where's your date?"

She shifted in her seat uncomfortably. "I've just come

out of a relationship …"

"Rachel, don't be so nosy," Mike admonished. "You can't go around asking personal questions of people you've just met."

She made a face. "I honestly don't know why I ask him to go anywhere with me," she grumbled, turning to Karen. "He's so dry. Wait until I tell you …"

Mike rolled his eyes apologetically, while Rachel engaged Karen in conversation. "I'm sorry. Sometimes she acts like a ten-year-old."

Jenny waved him away and took a sip of her wine.

"It's fine honestly. She's great fun – I'm glad you two joined us. We thought you guys were together at first."

He grimaced. "Please. She's my sister, and I love her but someone like Rachel would be the *complete* opposite of my type."

Jenny felt herself idly wondering what his type might be, and quickly caught herself. Was she mad? Mike was a customer and she'd already embarrassed herself enough.

"So, did Barry organise a new suit for you?" she asked, keen to get the thorny subject out of the way. "He's a bit stingy, so I hope you were able to get a suitable replacement."

Mike frowned confused, and then realisation dawned. "Ah, you mean the famous Armani?" He chuckled. "Promise me you won't say anything, but …" He beckoned her forward, and the back of Jenny's neck tingled as she felt his warm breath against her ear. "My so-called Armani cost a hundred and fifty quid from

Next," he whispered, then laughed at her shocked expression. "Well, I have to keep up appearances for the bank manager, don't I? Don't worry, I'll tell Barry the truth – eventually," he added with a grin."I couldn't resist laying it on thick at the time. It was comical – I thought the poor man would explode."

Jenny noticed Karen watching as she and Mike laughed together over shared encounters with her boss. And when she retreated to the bathroom in between courses, she knew it would only be a matter of moments before her friend followed.

"He's gorgeous," she gushed. "And he fancies you like mad."

"He doesn't know anyone else here that's all," Jenny said, dismissing the thought as she reapplied her make-up in the mirror, though the very notion made her blush again.

"Nope. Rachel says that he couldn't stop talking about you earlier in the bar."

"That's because of what happened at work. 'There's that idiot from the bank,' he probably said."

"Whatever. But you like him too, don't you?" Karen challenged.

"He's a customer."

"And you're not a doctor. Are there any rules about dating customers outside of working hours?"

Jenny shrugged.

"Didn't think so. Ah, go and have some fun, Jen – you deserve it. It's plain enough to see that he likes you – he hasn't been able to take his eyes off you all day, more's the pity," she added glancing at her reflection in the mirror. "I quite fancy him myself." She took a brush out of her bag and ran it through her hair.

"Karen Cassidy – you're an engaged woman."

"Only joking. I wouldn't change my Shane for anything. Seriously, though," she added sombrely, "it's about time you started having fun again. You've locked yourself away for long enough– it can't be good for you. And *he's* out of the picture now. Isn't he?"

Jenny nodded, the combination of the wine and Mike Kennedy's supposed interest sending her a little euphoric. "You're right. And it's been a fun day so far." She winked mischievously at her friend's reflection. "OK, you've convinced me."

"Good woman," Karen clapped both hands together. "That's more like the Jenny I know and love."

"Anyway, we're running away with ourselves – Mike might already be involved with someone for all we know," she pondered.

Karen shook her head. "Rachel would have said something. I haven't been able to get a word in with her. She's funny, isn't she?"

"Poor old Aidan hasn't stopped staring since she sat down at our table."

"Seriously? I hadn't noticed – I'll have to introduce them. Aidan could do with a good woman in his life."

"Then we'll put them both out of their misery and maybe get them talking. Who knows?" Karen joked as they wandered back out. "This wedding could be the start of more than one grand romance."

32

Once dinner ended, the speeches began. Tessa's visibly nervous dad gave a short but loving account of how proud and happy he was for his eldest and her new husband. Soon after, a red-faced Gerry stood, greeted by whoops and jeers from around the room.

The wedding speech had been a long-standing joke amongst his mates and they all knew that he was petrified at the thought of standing up in front of everyone on the day. Sure enough, his hands trembled as he clutched the microphone.

But by the time he had finished speaking, every single woman in the room including Tessa, was in tears. Even some of the men looked suitably moved by his words. It had been heartfelt and moving and as Jenny watched him sit down and reach for his new bride's hand, she envied her friend enormously.

"I didn't think he had it in him," Shane said, eyes

watering suspiciously. He turned away from the table and feigned blowing his nose. "Every woman in the place will wish they married him after that."

Karen dabbed at her eyes with a table napkin. "The things he said about her – and the way he looked at her – the room might as well have been empty but for the two of them."

And that was it in a nutshell, Jenny realised. In all the time she and Roan had been together, he had never once looked at her like that - probably never would've.

She found herself studying Tessa at the top table. She had been smiling all day long, and anyone could see how deliriously happy she was. With all her fussing beforehand, they'd expected this to be more of a showy affair, but now Jenny understood that her friend was simply trying to make the most memorable day in her life special.

As she watched the new bride glow with undisguised happiness, she couldn't help feeling envious. It must be wonderful to be that happy, knowing that the person you loved returned that love, easily and without question. Best feeling in the world, she guessed, suddenly feeling sad, afraid that she might never experience something like it.

"Penny for your thoughts?" she heard Mike ask upon returning from the bar. She looked up and smiled, taking the glass of wine he offered.

"I was just thinking about everything Gerry was saying – how he knew from day one that Tessa was the one for him and still knows without hesitation that she's the love of his life. But how can he tell for sure?" she pondered."How can anyone tell?"

"I don't think anyone can – really." Mike sat down and moved his chair closer. "Emotions always run high on days like these. People say a lot of things and make a lot of promises that they might not be able to keep." He shrugged dismissively.

"What do you mean?"

He took a sip from his pint. "That it's impossible to know how things will pan out once reality hits."

"Sounds to me like you've got a dim view of marriage," Jenny said, a little taken aback at his cynicism. "I'm pretty sure Gerry meant every word of what he said today."

"Of course he meant it all – *today,*" he replied evenly. "All very well but it's what happens afterwards that counts and believe me, words can be very easily forgotten."

He had a distinct edge to his tone so Jenny decided to drop the subject. She took a sip from her wine glass and looked across the table at Rachel and Karen, who were chatting together easily.

"Does Rachel still work in London?"

"No, she moved back a few months ago. Now she works in the Mater hospital and she's staying with me until she gets a place of her own." He rolled his eyes. "Can't come soon enough, I can tell you. Sometimes I find it difficult to believe that we were raised by the same parents. And I truly can't figure out how my little sister ended up as a nurse. She's so flighty, how anyone would put her in charge of a hospital ward, let alone rely on her to give out medication is beyond me."

Jenny laughed. "I'll bet she's brilliant at her job." She watched Rachel expressively waving her arms as she chatted with Karen and Shane. "Seems like she'd be excellent with patients, so chatty and down to earth. I'm sure everyone adores her."

"Maybe. But I can tell you one thing – you won't ever catch me near that hospital if she's on duty. I'd rather suffer."

Jenny chuckled, and as the waitress cleared the last of the food, she slumped back into her seat. "Thank goodness – the sight of all those leftovers was making me feel ill."

"Fancy a walk?" Mike asked. "I'm stuffed after all that too."

"Good idea." She picked up her handbag and pashmina. "I could do with stretching the legs."

The air had grown colder as the evening began to draw in. Jenny wrapped the flimsy material around her arms and hugged it towards her, shivering.

"It's a little chilly all the same," he remarked. "Do you want to leave it?"

"I'll warm up as we walk," she said. Freezing or not, to her surprise, Jenny wanted to spend some time alone with him.

They walked together for a bit, chatting amiably about the day's events and she found herself steering the conversation back to their earlier discussion.

"I'm curious about what you said before – about

marriage. What do you have against it?" Jenny asked simply.

She sensed him stiffen beside her. "I'm sorry – forget I said anything ... " Then recalling his reticence to discuss it, a sudden realisation dawned. "You're married?"

Mike said nothing in reply for a moment and Jenny felt a rush of disappointment.

"I *was*," he confirmed then, "but not any more."

"Oh." She wanted to know more, but yet didn't want to pry. Was he a widow, separated ...?

"I'm divorced," he answered her unspoken question.

"Oh."

"No big deal. It was a long time ago. But the experience has made me more than a little cynical."

His wife must have left, or cheated on him, maybe. "I'm sorry, I feel really bad now. I didn't mean to pry, I hardly know you ..."

"Forget it. But," he added, with a grin. "Tit for tat. You mentioned earlier that you'd just come out of a serious relationship. What's your story?"

She sighed. "No story as such, and it wasn't that serious – not to him anyway," Jenny added darkly. "In the end I caught him cheating, but I think all along I knew it wasn't the first time. I just wouldn't admit it." To her surprise, she felt liberated by her own words, relieved that she could finally admit out loud, not just to herself, but to a stranger that her and Roan's relationship had been a sham.

"Well, I know it sounds cliché," Mike said, giving her a sideways glance, "but he's a fool – whoever he is."

She laughed, gratified. "You're right – it is clichéd. But thanks anyway."

They chatted for a while longer and Jenny discovered that she had been correct in guessing that his wife had left him.

"We'd been together for years before we married – I studied in London and we met in college," he told her. "Rebecca was one of my lecturers. I set up the company not long after our wedding and it was difficult for a while – I was rarely home and under a lot of pressure – and I suppose Becky was bored. She seemed to have her heart set on starting a family too. I thought she understood that InTech was my priority, for a while at least. We argued a lot, mostly about that ..."

"You didn't want kids until the business was fully up and running."

Mike nodded. "I thought that was reasonable but Rebecca is a few years older, and her biological clock was ticking, as it were." He looked sadly into the distance. "Plus I just wasn't ready. Having a family would put me under twice as much pressure to make the business work. She agreed to wait at least until I was sure InTech was viable. When I say agreed, I mean reluctantly," he added. "And then ... then it wasn't long before things got strained."

Jenny thought she could guess the end of the story. "She resented having to wait?"

"Something like that," he said hoarsely. "Anyway, to

cut a long story short, she ended up leaving me for someone else."

He said this in such a way that despite his earlier protests, Jenny knew he was still hurting.

Seems she and Mike Kennedy had a lot more in common than they thought.

33

Shane nudged Karen's feet as he tried in vain to vacuum the carpet beneath her while she lounged on the sofa. "Will you get a move on? They'll be here soon."

"Honestly, you're like a mother hen going around with your polish and duster." She flipped a page of the magazine she was reading, looking up at him through narrowed eyes.

"Ah, make a bit of an effort, will you? I'm trying to make this place look respectable." With feigned sternness, he handed her a cloth and a bottle of Mr Sheen. "Here – move your ass and get going on that coffee table."

"All right, Mammy." Karen reluctantly got up and checked the clock on the mantelpiece. "Shane, it's only two. They won't be here for another hour at least, and you know what Tessa and Gerry are like for timekeeping. Relax."

Just then the doorbell rang on cue.

"Feck." Shane shooed her out of his way and went to answer the door.

Karen shook her head in amusement. Sod the newlyweds, he was obviously trying to make an impression on Mike Kennedy. Shane had really taken to him on the day of the wedding. Mike too was an avid Liverpool FC supporter and her fiance was thrilled to find a like-minded soul. Not to mention a season-ticket holder at Anfield.

She heard a shriek from the doorway and went out to see a very tanned and overexcited Tessa engulf Shane in a bearhug, while Gerry looked on.

"Mr & Mrs Burke," she greeted, kissing Gerry on the cheek. "Welcome home. How was Bali?"

"Oh Karen," Tessa said elated, "you wouldn't believe it. The hotel was fabulous and the weather! Unreal."

"Well, you got plenty of sunshine anyway. I thought honeymooners weren't supposed to be out long enough to tan like that."

"Don't worry – there was plenty of that too," Tessa chuckled, heading for the kitchen. "We have to make the most of it at the moment, don't we, Gerry?" she added, with a wink. Her husband blushed a deep shade of red and hunkered down at the kitchen table. "Tell you later," she mouthed when Karen looked at her questioningly.

"So – any news? What did we miss while we were away?"

"Well, you already know about Jenny and the delicious Mr Kennedy."

"Yes – but you didn't tell me any of the nitty-gritty. I only met him for a second at the wedding. Rachel's brother. What's he like?"

Shane groaned at Gerry. "Come on," he took a couple of beers from the fridge. "We'll go in and nab the comfortable seats and let these two natter in peace."

"Sounds good to me." Gerry duly followed him out of the kitchen, while Karen opened a bottle of chardonnay and took out a pair of wine glasses. "From what I can tell he's an absolute dote. Seems mad about her, too."

"Is that a good or a bad thing?" Tessa said, with a frown. "I know it's been a while, but is Jen ready?"

"I thought the same myself at first. But your wedding was exactly what she needed."

"So what's Mike's story? He's a little older, isn't he?"

"Yep, divorced and the wife left him, apparently. I'd like to see the guy she's with now if she ditched a hunk like that."

Tessa giggled. "Maybe he's not great in the sack."

"Well, compared to that lump Williams, I'd say he's a demon," Karen remarked bitterly. "With the way he carried on, you'd swear he was God's gift. To everyone but Jenny it seems."

Tessa shook her head. "I felt so bad for her that night at the club. How did she stick with him for so long?"

"Must admit, I couldn't picture her with anyone for a long time after Roan but having met Mike, I can see why she likes him. He's a pet – the complete opposite."

Tessa chuckled. "You really hated Roan, didn't you?

Wouldn't give him an inch. And you were right as it turns out."

"Hate to say it Sullivan, but I told you so."

"It's *Mrs* Burke now, thank you." Her friend wiggled her left hand.

"That sounds so weird. Hard to get used to."

"Not as weird as Karen Quinn is going to sound – whenever that comes about." Then Tessa stopped when she saw Karen's expression turn serious. "Hey, is everything OK?" she asked, touching her arm softly.

"Oh, I don't know," Karen looked into her glass. "All this stuff with Shane's family seems to be going from bad to worse."

"You mean the kids? Are they still driving you mad?"

"It's not just that, though believe me that's bad enough," she said, rolling her eyes. "Marie was here with the brood last weekend, and kept saying how great it was to be young enough to enjoy your kids when they're young, and how Shane and I would want to 'get a move on'."

"I can't imagine you being afraid to tell her where to go," Tessa remarked. "That'd be a first since I've known you."

"Yes, but they're Shane's family, aren't they? I can't very well tell them to feck off. And it's not just that," she sighed again, "Jack's around a lot too these days."

"The brother from England? You're not keen."

"I think he's a pompous prat to put it mildly," Karen growled. "Whenever he's in town he expects to stay here whether it suits us or not."

"And you're not over the moon about that arrangement."

"That's the problem. It's never *arranged*. He just turns up whenever the mood takes him. Never calls beforehand and just takes it for granted that we'll be happy to put him up."

"What does Shane make of it?"

Karen looked towards the doorway, keeping her voice low. "He won't say anything to him, because Jack's been 'so good to us'. He seems to think we owe him free room and board because he helped out with arranging our mortgage." Her face was red with indignation. "I like my privacy and good to us or not - I don't agree with Shane's family appearing on our doorstep at the drop of a hat. His mother did the same thing last weekend. Decided she fancied a cup of tea after some shopping and just popped in like she owned the place. It's still our house and our mortgage – we're the ones making the monthly repayments. It's like being in the bloody Mafia or something."

"Sshh," Tessa whispered. "You don't want Shane to hear."

"Do you know, I couldn't care less if he did." Karen refilled her wineglass, took a large mouthful and gulped it down. "You know he's too bloody placid for his own good."

"Well have you told him that you're not comfortable with all this?"

"There's no point," she said flatly. "As far as Shane's

concerned, Jack is Big Brother Wonderful. What I think doesn't matter."

"Well, you'll have to try and sort this stuff out somehow. If you're unhappy now, what will it be like when you two are married? I know they say that you marry the man and not his family, but in your case that doesn't appear to be true."

"I know," Karen said, standing up. "But you know what we're like – any problems we have are only ever sorted after a huge blow-up." She grimaced.

"Seriously, get it sorted. It won't do you any good to bottle it up – and will surely get a lot worse if you let it fester."

"OK, Mrs Burke, I promise. Come on then, let's go in and join the boys. The others should be here soon."

"SO WAS IT FANTASTIC?"

"Oh yes." Tessa gave a broad wink at Gerry. "Absolutely fantastic."

"Oh, I don't mean *that*." Jenny said, pink-cheeked. "I meant Bali itself – what was it like?"

"Amazing – wasn't it, love? I have to admit when we got off in Bangkok after a ten-hour flight, and then another four onwards, I couldn't care less what the place was like. I just wanted to sleep for a week. And then ..."

"Then we got to the hotel," Gerry finished.

"Just paradise," Tessa said. "Bounty Ads, Robinson Crusoe – you name it. The hotel was on its own beach – there was hardly anyone else around."

"Sounds like paradise, all right," Shane mused turning to Karen. "Where'll we go for ours?"

Jenny let out a squeal. "Have you two *finally* set a date?"

"I think she's having second thoughts about marrying me altogether," Shane joked, his smile not quite reaching his eyes.

"Pity. I wouldn't mind another day out. I so enjoyed your wedding."

"I'd say *you* did, all right," Tessa teased, hoping to change the subject for Karen's sake.

"It was OK," Jenny glanced sideways at Mike, "apart from this weirdo I met. Keeps following me everywhere, and won't leave me alone – ouch." He pinched her thigh.

Karen went out to the kitchen for more drinks and Tessa followed.

"Can you believe those two?" she asked, her eyes wide.

"I told you, didn't I? Completely besotted with one another."

"But it's lovely," Tessa said. "Means that she's finally over Roan. Mike's an absolute pet too. I have to admit, I didn't really believe it when you said she was back to herself."

"Didn't you notice how she hasn't stopped grinning since she walked in the door?" Karen was struggling with the bottle opener.

"Who hasn't?" Jenny asked from the doorway.

"Speak of the devil." Karen handed her a freshly

opened bottle. "Get another glass from the cupboard. Tessa's dying to know all the gossip."

"There's no gossip," Jenny blushed. "We're just – friends, that's all."

"You lying madam," Tessa gasped. "I've seen the looks the two of you are giving one another. Don't give me that 'just friends' rubbish."

"Honestly – that's all it is. He's good fun, and I enjoy spending time with him, but I'm not interested in Mike that way."

"Not interested ... are you half-cracked, girl. What's not to like, for goodness' sake?"

"It's not like that. It's just a friendship thing."

"Are you sure he feels the same way?" Karen asked. "Because it seems to me as though he's interested in a *lot* more than friendship."

"Nope. We get on great, but that's it. He's still in love with Rebecca – that's his wife – well, ex now. I think that could be why we get on so well, there's no expectation, no pressure, nothing like that."

"And how do you feel about Roan now?"

"To be honest, I've hardly even thought about him – don't look at me like that, Karen – I mean it," she said with a grin. "Thinking back over it now, he was completely wrong for me and I'm finally beginning to realise that."

Karen raised her wine glass. "Girls, I think a toast is in order."

"To what?"

"To us," she declared, "The new Mrs Burke, obviously." The three girls clinked glasses."Then Jenny and her new Mr Wonderful."

Jenny smiled as they clinked again, then paused, a little surprised that she and Tessa's glasses were still in mid-air, while Karen had already started on hers. "What about you?"

"Yep," Karen replied, decidedly glum as she set her glass down firmly on the countertop, "what about me."

34

Jenny studied the list of names on the report on top of her desk. Great, a stack of overdrawn letters to be dictated on top of everything else she had to do today. Her extension buzzed but she finished what she was doing before picking up.

"About time." She knew that Mike was smiling when he spoke. "I thought you were going to keep me on hold forever."

She grinned too. "Just ringing for a chat, or does the high-and-mighty director of InTech have a cash-flow problem?"

"Very funny. But that may well be the case after today. Can't talk long, but I need to ask you a favour."

"Fire away." As she listened, Jenny began to doodle on a pad of Post-it notes.

"I'm going to view some houses this evening and wondered if you'd be interested in acting as a second pair of eyes."

Since moving back for the UK after the divorce, Mike was living in what he called his 'bachelor pad' – a rented house in Wicklow. He was keen to move closer to the city and the office, and with Dublin house prices rising at an alarming rate, plus the ongoing success of InTech, the time felt right for him to buy a place of his own.

"Definitely – I'd only love the chance to see how the other half lives," Jenny teased. "I'm finished here around five – what time will I meet you?"

"Why don't I pick you up? We can go for a bite somewhere after."

A little after five, Jenny exited the branch and smiled as she caught sight of his car across the road.

It never failed to amuse her that Mike drove one of those tiny Smart motors when he could easily afford a Merc or Jaguar.

But that was him in a nutshell. Unpretentious and practical, he'd pointed out that he only needed 'enough room for himself and his laptop'. Jenny idly wondered whether he would apply the same criteria to buying a house. She opened the car door, the scent of his aftershave assaulting her nostrils.

"Phew. Do you have a date tonight or something?" she teased, settling herself in the passenger seat. "What's with the barrel of Brut?"

"You don't like it?" He feigned a hurt look. "Your woman in Arnotts told me that I'd have 'em falling at my feet. And it's not Brut – I can't remember the name, Packie something."

"*Keeling* over maybe," she chuckled, "and I think you

mean Paco Rabanne."

"Hmmm, never trust a woman pointing a tester bottle at you," he said, pulling out into the traffic.

"Where are these houses, then?"

"The estate agent is showing us two in Blackrock – one on Newtownpark Avenue and another close to the seafront."

"The one on Newtownpark would be easier for the office commute," Jenny pointed out.

"True – but I kind of fell in love with the view from the other one."

"You haven't seen inside though - it could be an awful kip. Online brochures can be deceptive."

"Which is why I'm bringing you along," he stated simply. "I need you to keep me on the strait and narrow. If I get too excited about either, you can mitigate by acting disaffected. Otherwise, the agent might well have me sign there and then and I couldn't trust myself not to. I'm useless when it comes to stuff like that. Rebecca ended up negotiating the sale of our London place – I'd have taken the first offer we got."

"I don't believe a word of it. A businessman who could buy and sell for Ireland, and you can't trust yourself with a pushy estate agent?"

"No word of a lie," he insisted, turning onto the Rock Road. "I'm terrible under pressure. That's why I have Frank in Sales and Marketing. I can design software to beat the band but when it comes to promoting and selling anything, I'm no good. Frank won't let me in the room when he's trying to negotiate."

"You take it too personally – because you're so close to it all, I suppose."

"Exactly. Bet you never had me pegged as the emotional type, huh?"

"Actually I always knew you were a bit precious, getting so upset over your beloved suit."

"Huh. Now I have a good mind to turf you out on the road and get some other leggy blonde to accompany me."

"I've never been called a leggy blonde before," Jenny flicked her hair exaggeratedly.

"It was supposed to be an insult."

They eventually pulled up in front of a two-storey, red-brick 1950s bungalow with a big 'For Sale' sign posted outside. The seaside location was indeed appealing but on first impression, the house didn't look especially so. The garden was overgrown and weeds ran along the edge of a broken path. The estate agent who greeted them was immediately at pains to explain that it had 'lots of potential'.

Potential for a wrecking ball maybe, Jenny thought dubiously, spying patches of mildew along the dirty grey skirting, and walls painted the colour of diarrhoea. She couldn't see why anyone would want the hassle of renovating to such an extent. Mike was looking for somewhere to live, not a lifelong hobby.

It seemed that he too was unimpressed, and after visiting the other equally disappointing option with the same agent; was no further forward in his quest.

Afterwards, they went for dinner nearby.

"So what do you think?" Mike asked, ordering the biggest steak on the menu he could find

"Don't think I could manage a sixteen-ounce. I think I'll just have the pork instead," Jenny said.

"I meant the properties – what did you think of the houses?"

She shrugged. "I wasn't impressed with either, to be honest." She smiled at a waiter who had brought a glass of wine for her and a Coke for Mike. "They both needed a lot of work – considering the asking price."

Then again with his money and a successful company behind him, he probably wouldn't have too many worries on that score.

"I know what you mean," he said grimacing, "the living room in the second one looked like something out of a bad sixties porno." He chuckled when she raised an eyebrow. "I don't want anything that needs a lot of work because I don't have the time or more importantly the inclination, for tearing down fireplaces and replastering walls." He traced a finger along the Coke bottle, catching droplets of condensation as they fell.

"Isn't there anything you've seen so far that you like?"

"Nope. They're all either much too big or much too small."

"Nothing that's 'just right'?" she teased."I thought *I* was the only Goldilocks around here."

"Hey. Watch your cheek or you'll be paying for your own porridge."

Jenny chuckled, realising that she was thoroughly enjoying herself. It was difficult *not* to enjoy being with

Mike. Whenever they got together there was always something to talk about or more often than not, something to laugh about.

"So any plans for the weekend?" he asked nonchalantly, but before she got a chance to reply, his phone buzzed. Conscious of disapproving stares from the other diners, he answered on the second ring. "Hello? Oh, hi Becky," he greeted, a smile breaking across his face.

Becky? Jenny had known that he and his ex were still on good terms, but not that good. She played with her food, trying not to listen as he laughed heartily at something Rebecca was saying.

"I can imagine. Typical ..." Mike prattled on for a few minutes more, before promising that he would 'sort it out' and speak to her tomorrow. Then he put the phone back on the table. "Sorry about that. Anyway, what were we talking about?"

"You were asking about my weekend."

"Yes, I've a few more properties to view on Saturday, so if you're not doing anything, fancy coming along again?"

"Only if you promise to come shopping after. I need to get something for Karen – her birthday's coming up. Actually," she said, the thought of another outing with Mike pleasing her more than she cared to admit, "you could come in very handy, now that I think of it."

"Handy," he said flatly, his chin resting on his hand. "I've been described many different ways in my lifetime – intelligent, funny, sexy, gorgeous – but handy? That's a new one."

35

Karen hurried down the street in the pouring rain, battling against the wind with her umbrella as the bus drove away from her stop.

She put the key in the front door, dived inside and slammed it behind her, relieved to be home at last. She removed her sopping wet jacket and wiped the dirty rain spatters off the back of her tights. A nice warm bath with some lavender oil and plenty of bubbles was exactly what she needed she decided, the thought of it warming her up already.

But first, she needed something to eat.

"Please, please, let there be something decent in the freezer," she muttered out loud to no one in particular. Luckily, there was a frozen lasagne at the very back of the icebox. Perfect. That would only take ten minutes in the microwave. She was starving too and in no mood for cooking this late on a Friday evening.

Shane was out with workmates for a leaving party, so

she was looking forward to having the place to herself. She switched on the microwave and padded upstairs in wet stocking feet to switch on the hot water. Grabbing a towel, she changed into a T-shirt and tracksuit bottoms, sorely tempted to put on her comfy bathrobe, but that could wait until after her bath.

Then went back downstairs to check on her lasagne. It was a little overdone and rubbery at the edges, but what the hell. Karen shrugged, plonking it unceremoniously out of its plastic tray and onto a plate, tomato sauce and pasta running everywhere.

She moved into the sitting room and cringed a little at the sight that greeted her. It looked a state, even by her standards. Yesterday's newspapers were strewn all over the sofa and the coffee table was covered with overflowing ashtrays, empty glasses and crisp packets. A plate of dried-up noodles lay on the floor alongside Shane's armchair, along with a pair of trainers, a fleece top, and a copy of this month's *Cosmo*.

She'd clean it up later – or nah, it could wait 'til tomorrow. Tonight, all she felt like doing after her bath was flaking out on the sofa in front of the telly by herself in a big fluffy bathrobe, bottle of wine, and a ginormous bag of crisps.

She finished her ready meal and leaving the plate on the coffee table along with the rest of the previous night's debris, went upstairs to run her bath.

Minutes later, Karen felt the weariness simply melt away as she closed her eyes and sank into the warm, frothy bubbles. She was still smiling happily to herself when she heard the phone ring. Let it, she thought, there was no *way* she was giving up this for anyone. Not after staying behind for two extra hours in the office on a Friday evening trying to clean up the mess her assistant had made, *and* getting drenched trying to battle home in the pouring wind and rain.

No way.

She sank further and further into the water until her ears were covered and she could no longer hear the ringing.

Some twenty minutes later, feeling revived and wrinkled, Karen dried off and stepped into her precious comfy bathrobe; fluffy, full-length chenille embroidered with yellow stars and blue moons. It had been a Christmas present from Shane one year, and she absolutely adored it. She wondered if he'd be late home tonight. Didn't matter, she decided, wrapping a towel around her head and rubbing moisturiser on her face. They could stay in bed for as long as they wanted at the weekends.

Karen loved Saturday mornings almost as much as quiet Friday nights. She and Shane would wake up whenever they fancied, and enjoy some sleepy, lazy sex, before getting up and lounging around for the rest of the day, reading the newspapers and watching the football results on the telly. One of the major plusses of having your own place really - no housemates or anyone else's schedule or needs to consider. Just her and Shane lazing about and doing what they liked when they liked.

She padded back across the landing towards her

bedroom to grab a pair of slippers before going downstairs. As she did, she thought she heard rustling or movement downstairs. It wasn't even ten o'clock yet – her fiancé must have decided to come home early after all.

Coming back out of the bedroom, the pile of wet towels and underwear on the bathroom floor briefly caught her eye. Nope, that would be a job for tomorrow too, she decided firmly. The towels were all due a wash anyway, so it wouldn't matter at this stage whether they got damp on the floor or damp in the laundry basket - which at any rate was downstairs in the kitchen by the washing machine.

Putting on her slippers and sliding a hair comb into the robe pocket, she went downstairs, idly hoping Shane had picked up a pizza or something on the way home from the pub. She was still a bit peckish.

Then Karen did a double take.

There was – not Shane – but *Nellie* Quinn pottering around the living room, picking up newspapers and emptying ashtrays.

"Nellie?" she gasped incredulously. "Is Shane with you?"

"Oh, hello Karen," his mother said airily, scraping the remains of yesterday's noodles into a refuse sack. "I didn't think there was anyone here. I phoned ahead to let you know I was on my way over. I was in town for a bit of shopping and with it being such a stormy night, I thought I'd stay over."

She thought she'd stay over ....

Then Karen thought of something. "But how did you get in?" she asked, her voice rising in confusion as she had visions of Nellie unceremoniously climbing in the back window or something.

"Sure, don't I have a key?" the older woman reached into her pocket and held it up as if Karen had never seen a key before. "I got Shane to cut one in case any of us ever needed it when you're not home – like tonight, for instance. It came in very handy altogether. Otherwise I would've been stuck out in that rain."

Unperturbed, Nellie happily returned to tidying up. "You really shouldn't leave noodles dry out overnight, you know," she scolded. "It's impossible to shift them. I'll have to soak those plates overnight."

"Nellie," Karen said, through gritted teeth, "I'll be tidying the place myself tomorrow. There's no need for you to be putting yourself to any bother."

"But love, why do it tomorrow when you can do it today?" the older woman said sweetly, but with a distinct edge to her tone.

"Don't take this the wrong way," Karen replied, trying to keep her voice level, "but if I wanted the place tidy, it would be tidy or if I prefer to leave it messy then I'll leave it messy."

Nellie flinched as if she'd been slapped.

"Well..." she said huffily. "If I'd known how strongly you felt about someone trying to help, Karen, I wouldn't have bothered." She perched on the edge of the sofa as if afraid to sit down for fear of getting the remains of yesterday's dinner on her clothes. "There's a pile of washing-up in the sink and I thought I'd save you having to do it - since you seem to have an aversion to housework. Even so," she continued as Karen's blood pressure rose even further, "it's not for me to decide how you want to keep your house. However, Shane happens to live here too and I'm not at all happy about my son living in filth."

Her jaw dropped. "How dare you call me filthy? I work long hours and can't be mopping up every little crumb when I get home. Shane is well able to do it either. Regardless, it's my house."

"If it wasn't for me, dear, you wouldn't have a house," Nellie countered sharply.

Karen struggled to keep her anger in check. She couldn't *believe* what she was hearing. She tried to calm down before she said something to the older woman that she'd really regret.

She could almost hear her dad's voice in her head telling her to count to ten like he always did as a little girl when he sensed her temper rising. She felt her heartbeat quicken with rage. This wasn't the first time that Nellie had tried to undermine her either.

During another one of her visits, Karen had found her sweeping the kitchen floor, claiming that 'with that colour linoleum it needs to be swept every day, not just once a week'. And on another occasion, she had taken down the curtains from the spare room, protesting that she'd have them 'washed and ironed in no time'. Karen had been livid but hadn't mentioned either incident to Shane.

This time though, swords were drawn. She'd murder

him for giving the Quinns a key. There was no way she was going to have his family crawling all over the place whenever they felt like it. She wouldn't have her own family do that. She'd never be able to relax in this house again if she thought that any of Shane's motley crew could arrive in on top of them at any minute.

It was out of order and Karen would be damned if she was going to put up with it. She'd have it out with him when he got home. In the meantime, she supposed she'd have to mollify Nellie; otherwise, they'd soon be at one another's throats.

She took a deep breath and tried her utmost to sound amiable. "I know you're only trying to help. And to be fair, the house isn't usually so untidy. But I've had a very hard week, I only just got home from work and to be frank, the last thing I wanted was visitors tonight – you know what I mean," she added quickly, when Nellie looked huffy. "All I wanted to do was chill out for the evening instead of going on a cleaning frenzy. I was just surprised to find you here, that's all." Her voice softened. "Forget about the plates and the washing-up – I'll get rid of the newspapers and we'll have a cuppa, alright?"

So much for her relaxing glass ... Karen duly picked up discarded newspapers and put them into the refuse sack. Then she went into the kitchen to put on the kettle, noting that the cupboards were wide open and Nellie had put what looked like every dish, plate and piece of cutlery they owned soaking in piping hot water in the sink.

A fresh burst of annoyance erupted. Obviously

thought she'd give their 'filthy' kitchen a good spring clean while she had the place to herself, Karen fumed as she filled the kettle with water. The kitchen was *not* filthy. Nor was she. Untidy maybe, but not dirty. If that wasn't good enough for Mrs Quinn or her darling son – tough. They'd just have to go take a running jump.

She felt a surge of misdirected annoyance towards Shane and tears smarted behind her eyes as she reached for the box of teabags she kept (still in the box, not some fancy jar) in the cupboard. She'd thought that owning their own home and planning a future together would be fantastic, but so far it was turning into a complete disaster.

His overbearing family's involvement; what with any one of them arriving on the doorstep at any time, constant digs about having children or setting a date for the wedding - all of it was bit by bit driving a wedge between them.

Karen knew for certain that she did *not* want to marry Shane if it meant being routinely saddled with his family too.

She went back into the living room with a cup of tea for Nellie and a bottle of wine for herself, thinking that if the 'oul bag said anything about her drinking, she'd throttle her altogether.

However, they appeared to have reached an impasse, because her future mother-in-law was sitting quite happily in front of the television watching the *Late Late Show*.

Karen handed her a cup of tea and plastered a smile

on her face. So much for her grand plans for a cosy evening. Hopefully, Shane wouldn't be out too late.

"Any nice biscuits with it, pet?" Nellie asked, smiling beatifically. "It's good manners to offer a visitor something extra too."

Karen harrumphed. She'd get Nellie her precious biscuits and then she was going straight to bed.

She'd confront Shane in the morning. This time she'd have it all out with him, no holding back. Definitely.

Without A Doubt.

36

The next morning Karen awoke with a start and opened her eyes. What was Shane doing banging around in the kitchen so early on a Saturday?

She looked groggily at the alarm clock. Almost eight AM. Then she felt movement beside her in the bed. Obviously not Shane making all the noise then. She hadn't heard him come in the night before.

Then she shot up in the bed, remembering. Nellie...

"Shane, wake up," she said, elbowing him none-too-gently on the shoulder.

"Whah? What time is it?" he asked blearily.

"It's eight in the morning, that's what time it is," Karen hissed. She couldn't believe that not content with ruining her evening, now Nellie was trying to intrude on her precious Saturday mornings too.

"Aw, great – smells like Mam's making a fry-up," Shane declared sitting up in the bed and sniffing the air.

"Well, what in God's name is your mother doing

making a fry-up in our house at this hour?" she gasped, incredulous.

"Calm down – it's no big deal. Mam always gets up early." He threw back the duvet and got out of bed. "Brilliant." He pulled on a pair of jeans and a T-shirt. "I haven't had one of her fry-ups in ages, and I'm starving." Rubbing his hands with glee, off he went downstairs, completely oblivious to her indignation.

Karen sank back down and pulled the covers over her head. Let Shane have breakfast with his mammy. There was no *way* she was getting up at this unearthly hour.

She closed her eyes and tried to return to sleep, until a few minutes later heard a shout from downstairs "Karen – stop lolling around like a lazy lump. Your breakfast is ready."

She sat bolt upright on the bed. The cheek of Nellie ordering her around like she was a ten-year-old – in her own house! Well, she could go sing – Karen would 'loll around' for as long as she wanted. Then she heard footsteps on the stairs and Shane stuck his head around the bedroom door.

"Karen," he said delightedly, "you should see the place downstairs – it's spotless. Mam must have been up since cockcrow, hovering and polishing. Now neither of us has to do a tap this weekend– isn't it brilliant?"

She resisted the urge to throw a pillow at his grinning face. Why didn't this level of intrusion bother him – or why couldn't he see that it was bothering *her*? Or was it perfectly reasonable to Shane that his mother could just swan in and do as she pleased?

"I'm not getting up 'til she's gone," she huffed, letting her head fall back hard on the pillow.

"What?" He was puzzled. "But you're awake now – and she's cooked us breakfast."

"I don't care. I don't think it's right that your mother is wandering around this place like it's her own," she pointed out. "*And* I certainly don't think it's kosher that you gave her a key without consulting me first."

"What? But how else was she supposed to get in if none of us were home?" he asked, mystified.

She sat up and turned back to face him, her eyes flashing. "Why *should* she get in if none of us are here, Shane? This is *our* house – not a stopover for your family's city jaunts."

"I don't know what you're getting so worked up about," he said, lowering his voice and glancing at the door, afraid that Nellie might hear.

Karen was livid. She couldn't believe that he was trying to turn the tables and make it seem as though *she* was the one being unreasonable.

"Just feck off, Shane," was all she could think of in response. "Feck off downstairs to your mammy."

"Fine. I will," he retorted, turning back towards the door. "But whatever your problem is, you'd better get over it. I don't know what's going on with you these days."

Couldn't even bring himself to slam the door behind

him, she thought sourly. Too afraid that he might upset Mammy Dearest.

Realising that she needed to use the loo, Karen got out of bed, opened the door and tip-toed across to the bathroom. Downstairs, she could hear Nellie merrily telling Shane how she had to go out to buy food since there was nothing in the fridge.

"Barely a scrap of milk," she trilled. "I can't understand how you can live like this, pet."

Karen slammed the bathroom door behind her, noticing that her discarded wet towels and clothes had been picked up, the washbasin looked freshly scrubbed and the tap handles on the bath were gleaming.

Bloody Nellie had been *everywhere*.

What did she do, wait until Karen went to sleep so she could go over every room in the house with a J-cloth and a bottle of Cif?

But what should she do? She couldn't go downstairs and confront her again in front of Shane. That would only force him to take sides and Karen couldn't be sure at this point where his allegiance might lay. Not that it would be fair to put him in such a position she supposed, heading back to the bedroom. After all, he was very close to his mother.

What was she supposed to do though? She couldn't let Nellie take over their lives like this. Glumly, Karen pulled on a pair of jeans and a fleece. There was no point in hiding – this was *her* house after all.

"Morning, Karen," Nellie chirped brightly, when she

joined the cosy tableau at her kitchen table. "Or should I say, 'good afternoon'?"

Shane looked at her and winked as his mother took a plate of food she had been keeping warm under the grill, and set it on the table in front of her.

This is bloody ridiculous, Karen thought, trying to defuse her annoyance. Ordered around like a teenager in her own home and there was absolutely nothing she could do about it. She looked in dismay across the table at Shane, praying that he would notice that something was off, but no, mammy's boy was happily munching on his third piece of buttered toast.

This was definitely not the happy ever after she'd envisioned.

37

Jenny examined her reflection in her bedroom mirror, satisfied that today, she looked good. She'd been to the hairdresser the day before for a trim and to touch up her highlights, and now her hair gleamed healthily.

She wore a black T-shirt with a metallic oriental print over a pair of bootcut denims that she'd picked up on sale in Brown Thomas. A pair of black chunky heeled boots completed the outfit. Those were new too.

In fact, Jenny thought, spraying perfume on her wrists; she had rediscovered her passion for a lot more than fashion. Although she hadn't relished the thought initially, she now found that she truly valued her independence. She had her own apartment, a good job and great friends. She hadn't felt this good in ages and was looking forward to heading out with Mike today.

As if on cue, the intercom buzzed and she went to

answer it. "You're early. I'm not ready yet – you'll have to come up and wait."

When she let him in, Mike stood back and wolf-whistled. "Look at you, all rock-chick raunchy – do you have a date or something?"

Jenny made a face, secretly delighted with the compliment. He didn't look too bad himself. Today was her first time seeing him out of work attire, and the tan combats and navy rugby top he wore made him look a lot more laidback and she had to admit, sexy.

"These look deceptively small from the outside." He looked around the living room with interest, and she realised that this was the first time he had been inside her apartment.

"Yep, but at a cost," she replied, wondering if she should offer to give him a tour, then instantly decided against it. Once he spied the pile of clothes scattered on the bed, he would think she'd been making a concerted effort to impress. Which wasn't the case, Jenny assured herself, applying a slick of Vaseline to her lips.

She followed Mike downstairs and out into the bright morning sunshine. It was still chilly, but spring was on the way. Daffodils and tulips burst out of the flowerbeds at the building entrance, reminding Jenny of her dad's flowerbeds at home and of the fact that she hadn't visited since Christmas.

"What a fabulous day," she commented, following Mike's gaze out to the pier. The water beneath the yachts and boats moored in the harbour sparkled with reflected sunlight.

"It is, isn't it?" he nodded, a thoughtful expression on his face. "Actually, way too nice to spend it traipsing around dreary houses."

"What do you mean?" she asked, disappointed at the prospect of their outing being cancelled. "Do you want to call off the house hunt?"

"Most definitely," he said. "I can do that any time – let's do something interesting instead, like take the Dart out to Howth or a ramble along Killiney Hill – what do you think?"

"Well, great – but haven't you already made arrangements with the agent?"

Jenny was in two minds; the first eager at the thought of doing something 'interesting' with Mike, and the second unsure as to whether she should show it.

He was already on his phone before she had time to think any more about it.

"Sorry, something's come up. I'll need to reschedule ... yes ...OK great, talk to you soon." He put the phone back in his pocket and grinned. "Right – that's that sorted. And I just had a brainwave while I was on the line... have you ever been to Brittas Bay?"

Jenny hadn't so they got into his little yellow SmartCar and headed towards the Wicklow coast, all thought of house-hunting forgotten. On the way, they stopped off for brunch at a cosy café in Ashford, whereupon Mike admitted that he rarely cooked for himself at home.

"It takes too much time and effort for one," he said, "even if I tend to eat enough for two or three."

"I'd noticed," she remarked dryly, watching him stuff two sausages and a piece of white pudding into his mouth all at once.

"Rebecca used to go mad," he said, gulping tea to wash it down.

Watching him smile at the memory, she felt a tinge of jealousy. He was always talking about Rebecca, commenting on things his ex might do or what she might like. Still, Jenny supposed, you couldn't so easily forget someone you were married to.

In contrast, she rarely spoke about Roan, other than that time at Tessa's wedding. Mike knew that she'd been let down, and it seemed that was all he needed to know. He had never pressed her for more information and she appreciated that.

Mike paid the bill and they continued the drive, reaching their destination within twenty minutes or so.

Jenny gasped on arrival when she spied a series of spectacular dunes framing a wild and remarkly empty beach of powder-white sand.

"This is fantastic," she gasped, the cool breeze whipping through her blonde curls. "Like something out of a holiday brochure." Being more familiar with the dark and stony beaches of the south, she couldn't believe that the east coast could be so different.

"Pity the temperatures don't fit the comparison," Mike chuckled, then casually held out his hand. "Come on, let's go for a ramble."

A little giddy, Jenny took it and together they walked along the mainly-deserted shoreline. He took his shoes off, unable to resist testing the water with his bare toes. She wasn't quite so adventurous though and regretted wearing her chunky-heeled boots as she watched him turn up his combats to the knees and wade further into the water, urging her to join him.

"No way I'm getting my feet wet. It's bloody freezing," she exclaimed, grimacing as the water hit her fingers.

While it was chilly on the beach, the sky was completely clear and she could feel the warmth of the midday sun on her back. "I can't believe I've never been here before," she said looking around in fresh wonder as Mike rejoined her,.

"Glad you like it," he smiled and Jenny was conscious of the fact that he'd taken her hand again. "But there are some other gorgeous beaches further down this direction too. Will we keep going? Make a day of it, maybe?"

She nodded happily, deciding this was one of the nicest Saturdays she'd spent in a while.

38

Later that evening, having spent the day visiting numerous beaches and beauty spots along the coast, Mike suggested dinner in Wexford.

"There's a lovely beachside hotel I stay at when I'm down on business," he said, "or we could look for a restaurant in town if you'd prefer."

Jenny told him that she didn't care where they went, as long as they ate soon. She didn't know if it was the excitement of the day, or the sea air in her lungs that was making her feel so hungry.

They opted for the hotel he knew and were soon comfortably seated, enjoying their food.

"You'd better eat some of this too," she said, pushing a plate of garlic bread towards his plate of fried brie. "Otherwise, you'll refuse to have me in the car with you on the way home."

"Agreed," he said, picking up a slice and popping it in

his mouth, clearly delighted at the prospect of extra food.

"Pig," she teased, amused at his unbridled appetite. "Do you always eat this quickly?"

"Yep," he said, swiping another piece as if to illustrate. "There were five in my family and it was every man for himself when it came to mealtimes. If you didn't eat quickly, you didn't eat, simple as that."

She chuckled. "You make it sound like something out of a Dickens novel."

"God no, I'm not trying to say that we were penniless, just that we were savages. Even now, when we all get together at Christmas or whatever, it's still the same and Rachel is as bad." He sat back in his chair. "You should come along sometime – see exactly what I'm talking about."

"Ah, no thanks," Jenny joked. "From what I've seen so far, one Kennedy is more than enough." She indicated the empty plates in front of them. He'd even polished off the salad.

She took another sip of wine and licked her lips. "It's a pity you have to drive back, otherwise you could have a glass too." Checking her watch, she looked up in surprise. "Crikey, I hadn't realised the time. It's nearly nine o'clock! No wonder I was so hungry."

"It'll be late by the time we get back. Sorry."

It must have been the wine because the words were out of her mouth before she could stop them. "Why don't we stay? I mean, we could both relax and have a few drinks and then you wouldn't have to worry about driving or ..." She could feel her cheeks reddening as she spoke.

Please don't let him take this the wrong way,

"Great idea," he agreed easily. "When we're finished here, I'll ask for a couple of rooms at reception."

Jenny spread mint sauce over her lamb, relieved that he didn't seem to read anything into it. As if to demonstrate his newfound freedom, Mike poured a generous measure of wine into his glass and ordered another bottle. The waiter was about to uncork it when his phone signalled an incoming text.

"Ah – somebody loves me," he said, searching for the phone in the pocket of his jacket and then Jenny looked up to see him chuckle at the message.

"What's so funny?" she asked, a little miffed about their cosy dinner being interrupted.

"It's from Becky. Sent me the most stupid meme – here, take a look."

Oh. Jenny reluctantly plastered on a weak smile and handed the phone back to him.

"Well?" he asked guffawing. "Did you get it?"

Jenny didn't. She didn't get the joke and she certainly didn't get the unnervingly close relationship he still had with his ex. She pushed her food around the plate, her appetite as well as her good mood having worn off all of a sudden.

"I didn't realise you two got on so well, considering ..." she ventured.

"Considering?"

"The reasons for your break-up, I mean," she stammered. "Since she left you for someone else and –" Seeing his expression darken, she faltered.

"Things are never as straightforward as you might think." He drank from his glass. "We both went through hell at the end. Believe me, I was no saint either. In throwing myself so heavily into my work, I abandoned her too, in a way."

"Hey," she interjected, annoyed with herself for saying anything, "I'm so sorry – I didn't mean to pry."

"It's probably my fault for making it sound like I was the one hard done by. But you don't know how much it means to me that Rebecca and I are adult enough to stay friends, after everything we went through together. There's no animosity, she's always been and still is one of my closest friends. I even get on with Graham – her new guy. I know what you're thinking," he smiled when Jenny struggled to keep the shock from registering on her face, "but there's no point in being bitter. I'm glad that she's found happiness with someone else, really I am. I still love her but not in that way, not any more."

His eyes looked suspiciously bright then, and Jenny resolved to change the subject. How could she have been so flippant? Sounded like Mike and his ex had been to hell and back, yet still managed to maintain their friendship. It was a very mature and deeply admirable attitude.

She shook her head. "Really, I didn't mean to – "

His eyes twinkled with good humour. "Just forget about it. So," he continued, pushing his empty plate away, "will we go for dessert or what?"

"No way," Jenny put a hand on her stomach, pleased

that the uncomfortable moment had passed. "If I eat anything else, I'll explode even more out of these jeans."

"Hah! If anything, you could do with a bit of extra meat on your bones."

She laughed, her early good humour returning."Don't try to justify your gluttony by forcing food on me."

"OK, I won't have anything else either - maybe just another drink," he said, getting up. "Why don't you head on into the lounge and I'll pick up our room cards?"

As Jenny watched him stride confidently through the double doors to reception, she admonished herself once again. Was she jealous of Rebecca and Mike's relationship? It wasn't as though she and Mike were anything more than friends, so what was the problem?

"Right," he said, rejoining her in the lounge a few minutes later. "We're on the third floor, across the hall from one another. I'll tell you though," he looked at his watch and yawned, "I'm fairly beat and after all that food, I don't think it'll be a late one."

"I know what you mean," she agreed. "I feel like I've eaten enough to keep me going for a week."

He sat down beside her on the comfy banquette against the wall as they watched the various comings and goings at the hotel bar. Jenny was practically horizontal, the combination of the food, wine and the day's adventures making her drowsy. Mike was so close; she'd only have to lift her head to lay it on his chest.

He smiled lazily across at her. "Are you thinking what I'm thinking?"

She nodded with heavy-lidded eyes. "If it involves a bed, most definitely yes."

"Are you propositioning me?"

Mortified, Jenny looked up and saw his eyes twinkle with humour. But as their gazes met, his expression changed and he must have seen it in her face, because she couldn't help what she did next.

Putting a hand around his neck, she pulled Mike towards her and planted a gentle kiss on his mouth. He pulled back a bit, looking at her questioningly, but she reached for him again, answering his unspoken question.

This time the kiss wasn't so one-sided and as it deepened, longing swept through her like a thunderbolt - until Jenny remembered where they were.

"Mike," she gasped, opening her eyes and looking around in embarrassment.

"You're right," he said breathlessly, sitting up straight, "I'm sorry – it was all my fault, I shouldn't have – "

"No," she said with a grin, tightening her arms around him. "I meant, maybe not here."

They were upstairs and inside his room within minutes.

There was no point in trying to kid herself. There was, and probably had been from the beginning, Jenny admitted, a lot more between the two of them than friendship.

With Mike, it was all about touching, teasing, and laughing, not about racing to the finish line, which was mostly how it had been with Roan.

Afterwards, she nestled easily into the crook of his arm and fell fast asleep, waking only when she felt Mike kiss the tip of her nose at dawn.

They dozed happily until around eleven whereupon he declared that he was once again ravenous.

"Typical," Jenny teased, sitting up in the bed. "You and your bloody stomach."

He laughed and kicked her under the sheets. "Come on, woman. You don't think a man can go like that all night without the need for sustenance?"

"You make a good point."

He dragged her back down beside him and kissed her deeply. "And," he added, "you'd better get used to it."

Jenny looked at his face, not sure what to say. It certainly seemed like this could be the beginning of something good between them, but she wasn't quite sure how he felt about getting involved with someone else after Rebecca.

"I'm really happy," he stated matter-of-factly, searching for his boxers at the end of the bed. "You probably know that I've fancied you for ages."

Jenny burst out laughing. He sounded like a schoolkid and she realised then that this childlike honesty and unyielding good nature were the things she liked most about him.

This time would be different. He was nothing like Roan - there would be no game-playing, second-guessing or lies.

Mike just didn't have it in him.

39

"You look fantastic!" Karen enthused, as Jenny skipped across the pedestrian crossing at Stephen's Green. "You've put on some weight too, haven't you?"

"You honestly think that's a compliment?" Jenny retorted, but the glint in her eye suggested she wasn't in the least bit offended.

"It is in this case. You fell away over the last few months, so it's nice to see you with a bit of colour in your cheeks again."

"So what's up?" Jenny asked, studying her friend with some concern. There was no mistaking the strained look on Karen's face.

"I'll tell you later," she said glumly, not wanting to go into the details just yet. "Let's go somewhere nice for bite – I had an early lunch today and I'm pretty famished."

They decided on a little pizza pasta spot just off Grafton Street.

"So, tell me your news first," Karen urged, once they were comfortably settled at a table for two, a bottle of the house white cooling on the table between them. "You haven't stopped smiling since earlier. Let me guess, you and Mike?"

She leaned in rapt as Jenny excitedly relayed the previous weekend's events. She was thrilled for her friend, but in truth it also highlighted how deflating and hopeless her own situation was becoming.

How was it that when she had been at her happiest, Jenny had been going through the wringer with Roan, and now that her friend had found happiness, Karen was the one in trouble? It seemed cruel.

Shane hadn't got home from work until after ten most evenings lately, and barely uttered a word when he came in. He went straight to the kitchen to make himself a cup of tea and a sandwich, and onwards to bed in the cluttered spare room.

Karen had hoped that they might discuss the Nellie situation without it turning into a screaming match, but so far there hadn't been an opportunity.

They had had some stupid fights throughout their relationships, but this was without a doubt the worst. Shane could never keep an argument going for long and was usually the one to capitulate. This time though he seemed to be sticking to his guns. This time, *she* might have to break the ice.

"I'm so pleased for you," she told Jenny now. "You know I've always thought that Mike was a good one.

When I met him at the wedding, I *knew* he had a thing for you."

"That's what he said too!" Jenny chuckled as if the thought had never crossed her mind. "I'm trying not to get too excited though in case it all goes pear-shaped. But he sent me two dozen roses at work yesterday." She giggled excitedly, then put down her fork. "Hey, I'm sorry. Here I am rabbiting on about Mike and how wonderful everything is. I've never even asked you about Shane. Did you get everything sorted out?" Karen had already told her about Nellie's unexpected drop in.

"We haven't spoken in days. He's mad at me because I dared to question why he gave his mother a key to our house, and all the cleaning up and the family criticising me and – oh, I'm just so sick of them all." Suddenly close to tears, Karen gripped her napkin so hard that her knuckles were white.

"Shush, shush, relax," Jenny soothed.

"The thing is, sometimes I'm not sure whether it's just me. I know I can get a bit wound up sometimes, but ..."

"Of course, it's not just you. Shane *was* wrong to give his mother a key without asking you first. Anyone could walk in on you at any time."

"Exactly," Karen agreed, "but he seems to think it's all perfectly reasonable. What I think doesn't seem to matter at all."

"Doesn't sound like Shane to be so inconsiderate of your feelings. Have you two been arguing a lot lately?"

Karen hung her head. "There's more. He keeps

pushing me to set a date. Like I told you, I have no intention of getting married so that the Quinns can start annoying me about having kids. Nellie is determined to get a grandchild out of me." She laughed bitterly. "Can you believe it? In this day and age? So I've told Shane that we'll get married when we're good and ready, but certainly not to suit the bloody Quinn's timeline."

"Karen, can I ask you a question?"

"Sure, what?"

"You keep talking about what they want, and what you're determined you don't want. Have you asked Shane how he feels? You keep saying, 'Nellie Quinn says this and she thinks that'. Has Shane ever explicitly said that he expects you to start mothering a brood once you two get married?"

"No, but – "

"You can't think straight, so you're conflating the issues. I can't imagine that he'd expect that. For one thing, you could hardly afford the drop in salary with a new mortgage." Jenny looked her straight in the eye. "And I'll be willing to bet that you've never even discussed this."

"But I have," Karen answered indignantly, "I've told him there's no way I'm giving up my job and everything I've worked for to stay at home changing dirty nappies and watching Oprah."

"Would you listen to yourself?" Jenny groaned, exasperated. "All about how you won't do this, and you won't give up that. Did you ever think for a second that Shane might just want to *marry* you? The way I see it, he can't understand your resentment because he doesn't realise the pressure you're putting yourself under. Yes," she added vehemently, seeing Karen's expression tighten, "you're your own worst enemy. If you just sit down and calmly explain to him exactly how you're feeling, I bet that he'll be bewildered as to what's been going on in your head."

"I don't think so, Jen. He knows full well how I feel – "

"Karen," she interrupted calmly, "promise me."

"What?"

"Promise that you'll go home now and talk to Shane - properly. Forget about Nellie and the Quinns; just find out once and for all what *he* wants."

40

Shane was half asleep on the sofa when Karen got back to the house. "We need to talk."

"I know," he replied flatly, his eyes still glued to the television screen.

She fidgeted uncertainly, not sure how to begin, then perched on the end of the sofa.

"Look, I've been stressing about a lot of stuff these days and I know I've been taking a lot out on you."

"You can say that again." Still, he didn't look at her.

"I'm sorry. It's not your fault and you shouldn't have to deal with it. The thing is, when you keep talking about setting a date for the wedding ... well, I -"

"Doesn't matter," Shane said, picking up a newspaper from the coffee table and flicking idly through it. "I think we're finished, Karen."

She felt as though she had been kicked hard in the stomach. "What do you mean?"

"What I *mean,*" he said mimicking her tone, "is that we're finished, over, kaput – whatever way you want to put it. This wedding obviously isn't happening."

"Shane– " She reached a tentative hand across to touch his knee.

"Forget it." He stood up, his face filled with emotion. "When we got engaged and then got this place, I was the happiest man alive. But you've changed. You're not happy with anything. Lately, I've been working my ass off on overtime whenever I can get it. I was planning to surprise you, bring you off on holiday somewhere – anything that might cheer you up. But I'm wasting my time, aren't I? You have no intention of marrying me. Did you think I wouldn't notice that every time I or anyone else, brings up the wedding, you react as though you've been burnt?"

"I know, I'm sorry. But if you'd just let me explain –"

"As far as I'm concerned, there can only be one explanation. We made a mistake getting engaged. You don't love me any more. Not to mention the fact that you seem to have some weird vendetta against my family," he spat.

"Well, what else do you expect?" Karen couldn't hold back any longer. "Nothing I do is good enough for your mother. I don't know what she has against me, but –"

"Can you not hear yourself?" he said, putting a hand to his head in exasperation. "What does my bloody mother have to do with any of this?"

She took a deep breath, sat back down and clasped her hands together. "I know you're angry with me and in a way, I can understand why. But you don't know what's been going on in my head. I've been worried and –"

"Too right I don't know what's going on in your head. So come on then – why don't you just get it all out in the open and tell me exactly what is going on, because I know I can't carry on like this any more – all this fighting and silence and sleeping in separate rooms is driving me crazy."

"Will you sit down – please?" She motioned towards the space beside her. "You mightn't like what I'm going to say but please, don't interrupt. If I don't get this out now, I never will."

"OK, shoot."

She saw that he was still angry, but seemed to have calmed a little. "Right. When we got engaged and after we went to your mum's house – I think it might have been a couple of weeks later – I had a conversation with Marie. I didn't think much of it at the time, but the same topic seemed to come up time and time again afterwards."

Shane looked at her, puzzled, but didn't say anything.

"She was telling me how much they were all looking forward to another grandchild, how your mother had said she'd thought neither of her boys would ever settle down. We were holding off on the wedding until we got the house sorted, so I just laughed it off a little and told her that - first things first - a place to live was our priority." She shrugged. "After that, it seemed like no time at all until Jack announced that he'd help us secure a mortgage. It just seemed to me as though your family were trying to smooth things along so that we would hurry up and get married and then crack on with the grandchild."

"But it wasn't like that at all," Shane gasped, unable to keep his promise not to interrupt. "Jack did us a huge favour ..."

"Please, just let me speak."

"Fine, go on," he said wearily.

"Anyway, soon after we got settled in here, we seemed to see a lot more of your mother and extended family. She or Marie and the kids always seemed to be popping in and out for whatever reason. And to me, it felt like, 'Well, you've got your house sorted – now get a move on with the rest'. Don't look at me like that, Shane, I'm just telling you how I feel."

She saw him slowly shake his head from side to side, but he didn't speak.

"Then you kept talking about 'setting a date and moving things along' and I was thinking; I'm not about to give up my job just to keep the Quinns stocked with grandchildren, to say nothing of the fact that I think we're way too young to be tied down like that. To me, getting married became suddenly equated to conceding a life that I love."

"Sorry but I have to interrupt now," Shane said sternly. "I know Marie can be a bit painful about the kids – but what made you think that I would expect you to drop everything and have babies once we were married? I'm working hard enough as it is, love. We couldn't possibly manage to keep the roof over our heads if only one of us was working. To say nothing of the fact that I'm nowhere near ready to be a parent either." He moved closer to her and put an arm around Karen. "I wish you would have told me this before. I had no idea you were feeling that way. I assumed that you'd changed your mind about marrying me, and just didn't have the guts to tell me yet."

"Well, I suppose I had changed my mind about it – in a roundabout way," she said, relief flooding through her, as she felt his arms around her.

"Karen, having a family is *not* something that's foremost in my mind, I can assure you. I just want to us to get hitched and enjoy life together. If or when we do decide to have kids, and assuming we can, it'll be *our* decision, nobody else's."

"Are you sure?" she asked, hardly daring to believe him.

"Definitely," he said, planting a kiss on the top of her forehead. "Don't mind them – they're old-fashioned and have never known anything other than marriage and kids rolled into one. As you know Marie has never worked, apart from on the farm, and neither has Mam, or Barbara. You should never have let them get to you like that. Look, I'll have a word – make sure my sisters lay off on the baby talk, OK?"

Karen nodded, relieved beyond belief.

Jenny was right. She shouldn't have let this go on for so long and let it drive a wedge between them without first finding out how Shane actually felt.

He gathered her in his arms and embraced her

tightly. "I love you and nothing or no one is going to change that. Do you believe me?"

She nodded into his shoulder. "Yes."

"OK," Shane grinned. "So, I'm asking again – for the *third* and final time, Karen Cassidy will you marry me?"

41

"Congratulations!" Jenny smiled at Mike as they clinked glasses. She had cooked him dinner at her place to celebrate his brand-new purchase.

She had gone with him to view another property and agreed that the four-bed bungalow in Blackrock fit the bill. The house had been recently renovated with an attic conversion; the owners had kept the original 1950s facade, but to Mike's delight, had favoured a stylish and modern interior.

The house itself was situated not far from the pretty little seaside village. Mike had instantly fallen in love with it; so much so that he had engaged in a bidding war and paid well over the asking price. He was hoping to have everything finalised within a few weeks.

"I can't wait to move in," he said dreamily, sitting back on the couch and putting a hand behind his head, "I was sure that the other couple were going to bid higher. Thank God they didn't; I would have needed a second job to afford it."

Jenny laughed. "Hey – cut the poor me crap. Remember where you hold your bank accounts."

"Feck, I'd forgotten you know my net worth. Maybe I should move to a different bank."

"Don't you dare! I'm already getting weird vibes from Barry. I have a feeling he thinks my seeing you is some kind of conflict of interest."

"And is it?"

"Nah." She refilled her glass with Moet. "As far as I know, there's nothing in my contract that says I can't date rich and powerful clients. Anyway," she added with a wicked grin, "never stopped me before." She ducked just in time to miss the cushion he threw at her.

"Are you doing anything this weekend?"

Jenny shook her head. "Why – were you thinking of whisking me away somewhere romantic?"

"Not exactly," he said, the expression on his face becoming serious, "it's just ..." He hesitated. "Well, Rebecca's in town and I've told her about us and she'd really like to meet you."

"Oh." For all her curiosity, the last thing Jenny wanted was to meet his ex-wife face-to-face. What on earth would they have to say to one another? And why was Rebecca so keen to meet her? To check her out maybe?

Since that time in Wexford, she and Mike had hardly spent a night apart. At first, Jenny had been a little taken aback by his openness and unbridled enthusiasm compared to second-guessing Roan's moods.

This felt more like a proper grown-up relationship. It was wonderful not to have to worry about whether he was interested, or if he was going to get bored and drop her at any moment. With Mike, everything, including his feelings, was totally transparent.

And now, he wanted her to meet his ex-wife. How very civilised.

"So what do you think?" he asked, bringing her back to the present. "Graham is Welsh and they're over for the rugby. Rebecca thought it would be a perfect opportunity for us all to meet up."

"At a rugby match? Wouldn't it be a little noisy?"

Mike laughed. "No, we'd meet them somewhere after."

"OK, great." Jenny thought she'd better agree before he picked up on her hesitancy.

"Brilliant. Becky's very easygoing. I reckon the two of you will get on like a house on fire.."

42

Tessa squealed down the phone at Karen. "So you've got it all booked?"

"Everything except the dress," she replied proudly. She was starting to look forward to the wedding now that everything had been arranged.

"June 15th – put it in your diary. And it's not at the church by the way, but the registry office."

"Oh," Tessa seemed taken aback. "But what about the flowers and white dress and bridesmaids and everything? Won't you miss having all that?"

Karen laughed. "We can still have all that; we're not getting married in The Temple of Doom."

"Really?" Tessa considered this. "It's just I've never been to a registry office wedding. I haven't a clue what to expect."

"Don't worry, you can still dress up to the nines in some slinky figure-hugging thing if that's what you're worried about."

Tessa gave a little giggle. "At that stage, I won't get an ordinary dress to fit me, let alone a slinky one."

"Ah you're not telling me what I think you're telling me, are you?"

"Yup. I'm nearly five months gone."

"Five months? But you must have known that time you and Gerry were here after the honeymoon – why didn't you tell us?"

She could sense her friend shrug on the other end of the line. "You were on an anti-kids rant at the time about all the babytalk you were getting from the Quinns. You might have exploded if I landed that on you, so I told Gerry to keep his mouth shut too."

"Ah stop, you shouldn't have had to do that on my account, though I did spot that you weren't inclined to drink much that day. Of *course* I'm thrilled for you, and Shane will be too. Pass on our congrats to Gerry, won't you?"

"Will do and likewise. I can't wait for the big day!"

They said their goodbyes and Karen had just hung up when the phone rang again.

"Karen? Nellie Quinn, here," said a prim voice at the other end.

She cursed silently. "Nellie – how are you?" Karen greeted pleasantly, trying her utmost to remain civil. "Shane's not back from work yet ..."

"It's you I wanted to speak to actually. Shane told me at the weekend that you've set a date, and I might add that it's about time. But he says the ceremony will be taking place in some kind of – of civic office in Kilkenny. Is that right?"

"Quite right." She had expected that Shane's wholly traditional mother would disapprove of a registry-office wedding, but by her tone, you'd swear that the venue was a lap-dancing club or brothel, even.

"Karen, far be it from me to interfere, but why can't you have a normal church wedding, like everyone else? I don't know if you were reared as a child of the Lord, but Shane certainly was and – "

"Really," she interjected flatly, "and when was the last time Shane was inside a church?"

"But you could ask that of any Irish couple these days," his mother retorted. "Doesn't stop them getting married in the Lord's house. Where else can you get such beautiful surroundings and backdrop? The photographs will be terrible."

"Nellie, with all due respect, Shane and I aren't getting married so that we can look pretty in our wedding photographs." Karen's voice was steely. "I'm not a hypocrite." She and Shane might indeed have been raised Catholic, but they weren't practising churchgoers.

"Well, I simply won't have it." Nellie cried, her earlier calm deserting her. "I do *not* like being stopped on the street by people wondering why my youngest can't get married under God's roof. Presumably, they think he's done something shameful like marrying a divorcee. Will you please tell Shane to phone me immediately when he gets home?"

"Fine," Karen answered and promptly hung up on her mother-in-law-to-be.

Great. Another stumbling block. She rolled her eyes. *Something shameful ...*

She just hoped that the 'oul bag would leave them alone to get on with their plans now, without belittling and complaining about every last detail. She and Shane had just come through a difficult patch, and now was certainly not the time for his mother to be throwing a spanner in the works.

Especially when Karen already knew that Nellie Quinn could be terribly persuasive in trying to get her own way.

43

Jenny spent pretty much all morning in front of the mirror, trying to decide upon an outfit. She had *no* idea what to wear.

She wanted to look stylish but at the same time not too vampish. She didn't want to wear anything too trendy because it would surely highlight that she was a good ten years younger than Mike's ex and she didn't want to come across as immature. Honestly, she had never felt this self-conscious in her life – had never agonised over an outfit choice to this extent.

Normally, she knew instinctively what to wear – tailored trouser suits to the office, funky casuals for a night out in the pub, elegant party wear for special occasions. Then there was the problem of what to do with her hair. She had let it grow much longer lately and it now reached well below shoulder length.

If she wore her hair down, Rebecca's first impression of her might be the stereotypical bimbo hoping to nab herself a rich divorcee. If she wore it up, she might look too severe or too try-hard depending on her choice of outfit.

Which brought Jenny right back to square one.

But that evening, when Mike picked her up in the taxi, she was feeling a lot more confident.

Having sought Tessa's advice, she wore a sleeveless cashmere turtleneck and black leather biker jacket over flared jeans and metallic block-heel platforms. Her friend had been adamant that she should step out in nothing less than a three-inch heel.

"It'll give you confidence," she had insisted over the phone. "There's nothing better than the clicking of high heels on the ground to make you feel great about what you're wearing. Can't go wrong with black – and there's no harm in showing a bit of flesh, either."

Mike had seemed happy enough with her anyway, she thought, recalling his appreciative wolf-whistle when she got into the taxi.

Problem was, that wasn't even half the battle.

When the taxi pulled up outside the hotel and Mike walked in front of her through the sliding doors, Jenny took a deep breath.

Inside she looked to her left towards the lounge and saw a smiling, slightly plump woman wave at them – Rebecca? But no, Mike continued straight past her towards a flame-haired bombshell sitting at the bar.

"Hey, you look fabulous," he stepped forward and hugged his ex, kissing her lightly on both cheeks.

"And you must be Jenny," Rebecca greeted in a husky

voice, her wide green eyes smiling in synch with her mouth. "It's lovely to meet you finally."

"Where's Graham?" Mike asked, looking around.

"Never far," said a lilting Welsh voice from behind them. He walked up and slapped Mike hard on the back. "How are things, man?"

"Fine, fine. You're looking very well – all those hours on the golf course are doing you the world of good."

"Hah, any excuse to get away from Becky, as you know yourself."

"Hey, thanks a lot," the aforementioned retorted wide-eyed. "You're giving Jenny a terrible impression of me already."

"Only joking." Graham put an arm around Rebecca's waist and smiled at Jenny. "Hello, my lovely," he greeted. "Nice to meet you."

She shook his hand, warming to him instantly. It was probably the accent, she thought. Jenny couldn't quite forget though that this was the guy who ran away with Mike's wife.

Although he certainly seemed to have forgotten it. The two men were already chatting away as if they were the best of friends.

Mike ordered more drinks and the four moved to a quiet table in the cosy hotel lounge. As the others chatted amongst themselves, Jenny noticed that although Rebecca wasn't conventionally beautiful, she was effortlessly sophisticated and attractive. In other words, she could see why Mike had fallen for her.

She decided she'd better make some effort to join in the conversation.

"So, you two live in Wales?" she asked.

Rebecca chortled. "God, no – we live in London. I couldn't survive all that way out in the country."

Graham rolled his eyes. "She makes the place sound like the back of beyond. Poor Becky couldn't function if she didn't have Chelsea High Street within walking distance – isn't that right, my love?"

"Well, for dining at least," Rebecca replied, winking. "Unfortunately, I'm a terrible cook."

"I can certainly vouch for that," Mike piped up and they all laughed.

Still a little taken aback at how easy and comfortable they all seemed together, Jenny relaxed. She truly hadn't expected them to be so nice. Rebecca and Graham were so full of chatter that it was difficult to get a word in.

Since Graham was also involved in the software industry, it wasn't long before he and Mike were deep in conversation about business.

Rebecca rolled her eyes and leaned towards Jenny conspiratorially.

"And they're off. Does all that tech talk bore you senseless too? Anyway, onto more important stuff," she said and Jenny's stomach tightened nervously, certain that Mike's ex was about to give her a grilling. Until Rebecca gleefully rubbed her hands together. "You won't *believe* how much I picked up on Grafton Street earlier – I'd forgotten how great the shopping is here."

. . .

LATER THAT NIGHT, lying in the darkness beside Mike, Jenny went over the evening's events in her head, pleased that the outing had gone so well.

Mike was right – they were wonderful. Rebecca, obviously sensing Jenny's nervousness, had gone out of her way to help her feel at ease.

"I know you probably think it's odd that Mike and I still have such a good relationship," she had said when he and Graham were out of earshot, "but we've known one another for a long time and went through a lot together." She smiled and put a hand on Jenny's arm. "It was hard at times, but we sorted everything out in the end."

She'd just nodded, unsure how to respond.

"I think what I'm trying to say, and please don't take this the wrong way ..." She looked at Jenny. "I can only imagine how awkward it must have been for you tonight. I'd be the same myself, meeting the dreaded ex-wife." She looked affectionately over at Mike and Graham, both engrossed in the rugby highlights on the TV. "Things went wrong for us early in the marriage. By the end, we were more like brother and sister than husband and wife and I'm pretty certain Mike would agree with that. Then I met Graham and – "

"It's OK," Jenny interjected. "Please don't feel that you have to tell me any of this, Rebecca. It's none of my business, after all."

"I think it is," she stated firmly. "I know how Mike feels about you and I'm concerned that my friendship with him might make you uncomfortable. I just want you to know that I'm not a threat, and never will be. I still love him as a friend and I know he feels the same way. We both have our own lives now – you know that Graham and I have two little girls?" Her face lit up when she mentioned her children and Jenny realised then how important having a family must have been to her – so much that it ultimately destroyed her marriage.

"Yes. Mike mentioned that."

"We're hoping to get married next year – if we can find the time, that is. Rosie and Robyn are still only toddlers but sometimes ...." She rolled her eyes.

"Anyway, I was thrilled when Mike told me that you two had finally got it together." She nudged Jenny softly. "It's wonderful to see him so happy. I hope you don't mind, but he told me all about you ages ago?"

Touched by this, Jenny smiled affectionately at him.

"So you'll have to come over for a visit sometime. I could take you down to Fulham – there's some incredible shopping there and ..."

Now, Jenny smiled to herself in the darkness. Rebecca was quite a woman. She didn't know how she would react in the same circumstances. She rarely stayed friends with her exes; she'd left Paul behind in Australia and Roan was another ocean way too.

It was hard to believe that this time last year she had been a complete wreck, trying to keep that disastrous relationship going. It seemed like a million miles away now, she felt like a completely different person, and she wasn't sure how she'd react if she were to encounter Roan again now.

Regardless, Jenny thought, rolling over and snuggling closer to Mike. She was in Dublin and Roan was in New York.

She wouldn't have to worry about bumping into him anytime soon.

44

Karen glared at her reflection with absolute horror. She scowled at Jenny who was outside the bridal shop fitting room, crumpled over with laughter.

"I'm trapped!" she moaned, trying to lift the heavy skirt over her head, but to no avail.

Jenny had persuaded her to try on what could only be described as the flounciest, fluffiest 'meringue' they had ever seen. Karen wasn't convinced but had done so just to pacify her.

She *hated* this palaver of trawling through the shops looking for the 'perfect dress'. She had hoped to just wander into a bridal shop and pick something up off the rack.

A store attendant had nearly choked with shock when Karen had told her the date of the wedding. "June? You mean June, twelve months?" the woman gasped, eyes wide.

"No. I mean June – six weeks."

"But ... but," the sales assistant spluttered, "our gowns need to be ordered at least a year in advance. You'll need to first make your choice – and this takes time to ensure it truly is the *perfect* dress for you," she added reverently as if the decision was on par with choosing the husband. "Fittings for you and your bridal party at various intervals in the run up to the big day, the dress will need to be ordered and additional adjustments to be made and ..."

"It's only a bloody dress. You'd swear it was a work of art," Karen complained, muttering expletives to Jenny as they trawled the city looking for a more easygoing option.

It was only through sheer desperation that she'd been persuaded to deviate from her quest for a simple satin sheath. Hence the meringue.

"You're right, it's woeful," Jenny chuckled, eyes watering and hand over her mouth. With her chest, the style made Karen look like an overgrown marshmallow. "You look like a, a ..."

"She looks like a *princess*. Oh, that has to be the one! It looks amazing on you. Wait, I'll go get a veil. Now stay right where you are - don't move." The sales assistant scuttled off eagerly.

"Jen!" Karen hissed. "Get me out of this yoke – *quick*!"

Jenny was laughing so much she could barely get the zip undone. Karen wrenched the dress over her head, quickly put her clothes back on and hurried out of the cubicle, nearly knocking over another bride-to-be outside the changing room preening at herself in the mirror.

An older lady, presumably her mother, reverently placed a tiara on her head, and both were moved to tears by the glorious vision in satin and lace.

"I'd be crying too if I had to wear *that* to my wedding," Karen muttered under her breath, as she and Jenny sped past them and out of the shop, laughing uproariously.

A little later, exhausted from battling the crowds and still without a dress, to say nothing of the 'perfect' one, the two nabbed a precious free table in a packed city cafe.

"It's hopeless. I haven't seen anything that could work as a prospect and we haven't even started on bridesmaid dresses. What if I don't find something in time?"

"Of course you will." Jenny put her mug down and looked at Karen thoughtfully. "Though we've been looking in the same places and there's not much variation. We don't we try somewhere different – like Belfast maybe?"

"Up North?"

"Why not? The sterling exchange rate's good at the moment and the shopping's supposed to be excellent, as good as London even, Rebecca said. "

"*Rebecca*? The famous ex?" Karen asked, startled.

"I didn't get a chance to tell you yet," Jenny beamed. "We all met up recently. She's great."

Karen shook her head in admiration. "You know, I

have to say I'm very proud of you Jen – you've come so far since this time last year."

Her friend shrugged, her face flushed with pride. "I suppose we both have, haven't we?"

She was right. They were both in a good place now, planning their futures and it felt wonderful. Karen was walking on air and looking forward to marrying the love of her life, and Jenny was as happy as she'd ever seen her. They'd grown up together and had gone through a few ups and downs over the years, but remained firm friends throughout it all. The one thing they'd always been able to count on was their friendship.

Karen squeezed Jenny's hand and smiled.

Life for them both was finally looking up.

45

Karen couldn't wait to leave the office. Today had seemed like the longest work day *ever*.

Still, only three weeks to go 'til the wedding and then she and Shane were flying to Thailand for a blissful two week honeymoon.

At this point, they both needed the break. He'd really been putting in the hours at work lately to the point that they barely saw one another. The wedding would be small, but Shane was insistent that they pay for everything themselves – reception, flowers, honeymoon etc, without having to resort to more borrowing. Hence the additional overtime.

She checked her watch again, hoping that by some miracle the hands might've reached five o'clock. No such luck.

She was also looking forward to the upcoming bridal shopping trip to Belfast with Jenny this weekend. If she didn't get a dress soon, she might have to think about wearing a suit to the registry office. Karen didn't think Shane would care either way - he loved her as she was and that was all that mattered.

Though with the hours he was putting in, there hadn't been much loving lately. She wondered if getting married would have a negative effect on their sex life. She should ask Tessa, although maybe she wasn't the best person just now. With only a month or so til the baby's arrival, her friend was getting bigger by the minute and the last time Karen had spoken with her, had been inconsolable about that.

"What if I can't lose all this weight after?" she moaned. "I'll never go outside the front door again."

Karen smiled, trying to imagine what Tessa would be like as a mum and wondered if she would ever be able to think seriously about parenthood herself. It didn't appeal in the slightest, and listening to Tessa recount tales of 'all day and all night' sickness didn't endear her to the possibility any further.

She decided to quickly check in with Shane before leaving the office. He would still be at his desk, slogging away on the new toll bridge project that was taking up most of his time.

"Sorry, Karen – he left about half an hour ago," the receptionist asked when she phoned the main switch, having got message minder on his personal phone. "Will I take a message or ...?"

She frowned. "Not to worry thanks, I'll catch him at

home." She was almost certain Shane had told her earlier that he was working late tonight.

Oh well, she mused, grabbing her jacket and knocking off for the day. Must have been a change of plan.

46

Aidan instinctively jumped up, quickly casting aside the poker game he and his fellow on-duty fire officers were engaged in, once the alert sounded.

"RTA, M50 southbound," his colleague called out as they all hurried to get changed. "Persons trapped, persons reported, two vehicles – get a move on, lads."

Aidan grimaced as he got into his gear. Road Traffic Accidents were the worst. He lifted his fire helmet from where it hung on the wall and followed the others out to the fire vehicles.

"Take Second, will you?" directed the Station Officer.

Seemed like this crash was a serious one, too.

Aidan nodded and dutifully rushed towards the truck, passing the Jaws of Life on the side of the unit. He hated the sight of that equipment and the eardrum-piercing screeching while prying open metal to safely remove crash victims. The part of this job that he dreaded the most.

Two fire vehicles soon hurtled out of the station, sirens screaming past the rush-hour traffic, and the station officer radioed further instructions from the unit up ahead as they raced towards the crash scene.

"Colin and Tony – fend off. Aidan and Donal – airbags."

Two would be responsible for sectioning off the crash scene, ensuring that the rescue team and the paramedics had enough space. Since he and his colleague had been given airbag duty, Aidan knew that at least one vehicle involved in the crash had tipped over and thus airbags would be used to lift it back up so that the rescue team could access passengers.

Paramedics and police were already at the crash site. When they reached the location, he and his partner jumped out and immediately grabbed the airbags, deploying as directed.

But as Aidan hurried toward the mangled vehicle on the tarmac, his breath caught in his throat.

"Jesus Christ ..." he whispered hoarsely, "I know that car."

47

Tessa decided to check on her patient Mrs Clearly once more, before going off duty.

"How are you feeling now?" she asked the elderly lady who had been complaining of a ferocious headache.

"Not too bad," the woman said hoarsely, "I think those tablets you gave me finally did the trick." She patted her hand. "I'll miss you when you're gone. When are you moving down to Cork?"

"Next week," Tessa confirmed. She was looking forward to it. New house, new job and new baby. And the beginning of a brand new life for herself and Gerry.

She said goodbye to the Ward Sister and switched on her phone as she left the hospital and headed towards her bus stop nearby.

As she waited idly for the next service, Tessa listened to the five-thirty news bulletin. There had been a very bad car crash on the M50 motorway, which of course meant that rush hour would be even more chaotic than usual.

She shivered again, but not from the cold. Gerry travelled that route on his way home. Tessa took her phone out and quickly dialled her husband's number.

Better give him the heads up.

JENNY NOTICED Barry switch off the light in his office and checked her watch. Just after five-forty. Time to finish up and head home.

Home.

She recalled a recent conversation with Mike whereupon she'd been moaning about the landlord increasing her rent, and whether she should renew her lease.

Life all round was good. Things were going well for her at work; there was an Officer post coming up in the district, and if Jenny was promoted again, she would hardly notice the rent increase. In fact, she could even start thinking about buying something altogether. But while she loved living in the area there was no way she could afford to buy a place in these salubrious coastal suburbs like Mike had done.

When discussing all this, Jenny got the inkling – though he hadn't said anything out loud – that he was about to suggest she move in with him. The thought of it didn't frighten her, but she was loathe to give up her independence just yet.

Was she ready for this? Ready to commit herself wholeheartedly again?

Maybe she and Mike should talk seriously about where they felt the relationship was going. She'd give him a call and check if it was OK to pop over to his tonight. She hadn't seen him since last week on account of a stomach bug she'd picked up somewhere.

She dialled his mobile and heard it ring out for a bit, until her call was diverted to InTech reception.

"Hi Ciara, it's Jenny. I was looking for Mike," she greeted.

"He's off-site today," the receptionist said snootily. Jenny couldn't stand her but Mike was full of praise for her guard dog talents.

"OK, where *is* he based then?"

"At a client's office in one of the business parks off the M50."

48

Karen sat in front of the TV, languidly flicking from *Coronation Street* to *EastEnders*. She didn't follow either show and based on tonight's narrative offerings, couldn't see any particular reason to start.

She felt a low rumble in her stomach and wondered what on earth was keeping Shane. He'd since left a message, telling her that he'd pick up Chinese takeaway on the way home.

She wished he'd hurry the hell up because she didn't think she'd be able to hold out for much longer. The thought of chicken, green peppers and black bean sauce was making her mouth water. She hoped he'd got her return voicemail asking for spring rolls and prawn crackers.

Ah sod it, a slice of bread would keep her going until he got back she decided, ambling into the kitchen. Except they didn't have any bread, Karen remembered.

She was rummaging around the back of her rarely defrosted freezer when she heard the doorbell.

Great, she thought darkly. Only the bloody Quinns would arrive at her doorstep unannounced on a week-night. But at least these days they had the decency to ring the bell before barging in. That, or it was someone looking for directions again. Living at the corner of a busy street brought its problems, and Karen couldn't count the number of times they had been disturbed by some lost soul trying to find his way to the city.

She padded out to the door in her stocking feet to find an ashen-faced Aidan in her doorway.

"Hey stranger," she greeted. "If you're looking for Shane, he's not home yet –"

"Karen ..." He came into the hallway and took both of her hands in his. She noticed that his eyes were blood-shot and his typically mischeivous grin absent. "Pet ... there's been an accident."

"Where – at the crossroads?" she asked, looking past the doorway to the street.

"Please, just sit down for a sec OK?" Aidan continued gently, and she felt a rod of panic shoot through her as she realised that another man was standing at the door too – also in uniform.

A garda car was parked a little way down from the house, its blue overhead lights flashing and illuminating the expectant faces of a small crowd gathered on the path.

A shiver of unease slithered down Karen's spine. Her

stomach constricted with fear and her heart hammered loudly against her chest.

"An accident, you said? Not sure what *I* can do – are you hurt? I don't have any bandages in the house if that's what you need but – "

"Karen – "

"I mean, I'm not a nurse or anything, I don't even know first aid. Tessa's the one you want, but she's not here. Of course not, she's probably still at work so whatever it is, I suppose you'd better call an ambulance."

"Karen, please ... sit down." A stray tear rolled down Aidan's face as he reached for her.

What the hell... Why was Aidan crying? And more to the point, why hadn't she noticed until now that he was he still in uniform?

She stepped back as if electrocuted.

"Aidan – come off it, please. If this is your idea of a joke, it's not funny, it's not bloody funny, OK? Why are you scaring me like this?" Suddenly, dizzy, Karen lost her balance and slumped heavily against the doorframe.

She knew what he was here to tell her, of course – had subconsciously known before he opened his mouth. Aidan's expression had told her enough – he didn't need to say it out loud.

And she hoped he wouldn't, because she didn't think she could bear to hear the words.

"He didn't suffer, pet," Aidan whispered, his voice constricted. He reached for her again, and this time Karen numbly allowed him to guide her inside and back to the living room. He sat down on the sofa next to her, cradling her gently in his arms. "He was on his way back from a site inspection and a car going north had a tyre blowout. It skidded across the reservation, straight into Shane. He was gone instantly, pet – there was no pain."

Karen said nothing.

"I'm so, so sorry," Aidan continued, resting his head on hers, his tears falling onto her hair as she rocked back and forth in his arms, dully staring into space.

"No," she said, sitting up suddenly, her face a mask of defiance. "No you're wrong, you have to be wrong – he couldn't be – it mustn't have been .... can't have been my Shane."

"Pet – "

"No seriously, think about it," Karen argued, her voice rising as she shook her head. "He was picking up a takeaway – he's probably down at the Jasmine Palace as we speak. It wasn't him – I'm telling you."

"Love – "

"Don't you think you should have got your bloody facts right before waltzing in here and upsetting me with speculation? The least you could've done was found out for sure ...."

Aidan shook his head, tears brimming, as he looked back at the officer in the doorway for assistance.

The policeman duly went to Karen and put a hand on her shoulder. "I'm so very sorry, Ms Cassidy. I know how difficult this is, but your fiancé has already been identified."

"What do you mean?" she implored in a small voice.

"What does he mean 'identified' ... Aidan – what does that even *mean*?"

Wiping away tears, he tried to compose himself.

"My unit was the one called to the scene, pet. I've seen him and the Astra. It is Shane and ... he's gone, Karen. I'm so, so sorry, but it's true. He's gone."

49

He's gone ... he's gone ... he's gone.

Aidan's words still echoed through Karen's brain in an agonising mantra.

She could barely remember what happened next – vaguely recalled picking up the phone and calmly informing Nellie that her youngest son had died in a head-on collision, at the same time she and much of the country's population were idly tucking into their supper.

Couldn't remember the racking sobs on the other end, nor hysterical accusations of Karen forcing Shane to work all those extra hours that he mustn't have been concentrating.

Couldn't remember Jenny and Mike getting here, plus all these other people she didn't recognise. Couldn't understand why they wouldn't just go away and leave her alone.

Alone.

Gone. Shane was gone. Her Shane.

Why him? Why not her? *She* was the one who really deserved to die in that crash – not him. He wouldn't harm a fly. All that time they had spent arguing over the wedding, all the time they had spent arguing over stupid inconsequential things, all the time she had spent resenting his family – Karen would have given anything in the world to have that time back. She would give anything just for someone to wave a magic wand and take it all back, take the nightmare away.

Why? *Why* would someone let this happen?

Was God punishing her because she hadn't been to Mass? Was He punishing her because she had been so determined not to get married in His church? Or was it simply because she was a selfish bitch who didn't want to share Shane with anyone else? She had made no secret of her bitterness towards his family. Was this her punishment for trying to keep him all to herself?

Karen couldn't find any answers. All she knew was that she would never again feel his arms around her, never wake up beside him in bed or feel his kisses on her lips. They would never again laugh together, never share another moment.

They would never be able to do all the things they'd planned after the wedding like visiting Las Vegas or New York like Shane always wanted, or Rome and Paris, like she did.

There would be no wedding, no new life together, no nothing.

Nothing.

Shane was gone.

. . .

WITH GROWING CONCERN, Jenny watched the devastated figure slumped in the armchair in front of the TV.

Karen had barely uttered a word since the authorities left the house, nor engaged with the steady arrival of sympathisers as the evening went on.

A stricken Aidan was sitting in the kitchen with Gerry, still in shock. They were all in shock, but Jenny was becoming frightened by how withdrawn Karen was right then. She just hoped that the Quinn family would stay away for the moment, and maybe give her some time by herself to grieve.

Jenny had to take the phone away from her earlier, hearing Nellie's sobbing and ranting on the other end. She knew it was a grieving mother's shocked reaction talking, but the last thing her friend needed was recrimination.

Karen had said nothing since; she'd just taken to the armchair – Shane's armchair – and wrapped one of his discarded sweaters around her. Offers of coffee, tea and invitations to talk had all been rejected with a slow shake of the head.

Jenny had never felt so helpless in her entire life. How could she possibly even imagine what her friend must be feeling? The magnitude of it all was so completely overwhelming that Karen's way of coping was to shut down and pretend that it wasn't happening, that it wasn't real.

Now Karen stood up from her chair. "I'm going to bed," she mumbled, heading towards the stairs.

"Do you want me to ... ?" Jenny's words trailed off as Mike put a hand on her arm.

"Leave her, Jen. She needs time on her own."

She felt her eyes quicken with fresh tears. "I don't know what to say to her, I don't know what to do. How can I help?"

"You can't," he said simply. "Just leave her be, let her grieve in peace."

"I still can't believe it. I mean, they were getting married next month. How could this happen? It's not fair."

"It's never fair," Mike said, sighing as he took her hand in his. "All you can do now is be there for her as a friend, same as always."

"My heart is breaking for her though – and for Aidan. Imagine being called to an accident like that. Shane was his best friend ..."

Aidan had insisted on accompanying his senior fire officer and the garda to the house to break the news of Shane's demise. While his own heart was breaking, he was adamant he didn't want anyone else to do it. While protocol demanded that a senior officer or member of the gardai should inform family members, rules were bent given the circumstances.

"I know it was tough on him, but at least Karen had someone she knew with her," Mike pointed out. "Wouldn't it have been far worse if they'd just turned up and asked her to identify him?"

Jenny was distraught at the very notion. "This is such a nightmare. How can she possibly ever get over this?"

"It won't be easy, and she'll need people around her. What about her parents? You said before that they lived abroad."

"Tenerife, yes. I wonder has anyone told them yet?"

As far as Jenny was aware, the only other people Karen had spoken to were the Quinns.

Aidan had in turn contacted the others once he'd broken the news. Jenny resolved to inform Karen's folks first thing as they would no doubt need to make arrangements to come home for the funeral.

Later, Mike sat with a distraught Aidan as he tried to cope with coming upon the tragic crash that had wiped out his best friend.

While Jenny tried in vain to support Karen through the hardest night she would surely ever experience.

50

The following morning, Jenny cobbled together some breakfast. Karen hadn't reappeared since retiring the night before, and Jenny hoped that she'd been able to get some sleep.

She managed to catch a few hours herself on the sofa once Aidan and the others had gone home. Mike had since left for the office, despite his protests to stay, but she insisted he carry on.

It still didn't seem real to Jenny, not at least until Tessa and Gerry arrived. A banner headline on that morning's newspaper announced that Shane and the other driver were respectively the eighty-sixth and eighty-seventh road accident victims that year. Emblazoned beneath was a colour shot of Shane's beloved Astra, the car's chassis bent and twisted beyond recognition.

"How is she?" Tessa asked through tears as she enveloped Jenny in a hug.

"I'm so worried about her. She hasn't come out of her bedroom or spoken a word since it happened."

"She's still in shock, God love her."

"I know, but I wish she'd do something – cry, scream, kick the walls, just *something*."

"She probably has – in her mind even," Gerry said softly from behind his wife. "Everyone copes differently."

"I know, I just wish I could do something," Jenny said filling the kettle. "I don't know how many times I've been up, but she still doesn't want to talk."

She heard the landline ring and went out to answer it, leaving Tessa and Gerry sitting quietly at the kitchen table. The caller was Jack Quinn letting them know about the funeral arrangements, which would take place in Meath.

Jenny smarted at his brusque tone, or the fact that the family hadn't consulted or included Karen in any of it. But from what she'd heard about the Quinns so far, it didn't surprise her.

And maybe Karen didn't want to be included.

She went upstairs to impart the information to her friend and knocked softly on the bedroom door, but there was no answer.

Trying the handle, she entered to find the room in darkness, and Karen lying on the bed with her eyes wide open staring at the ceiling.

"I'm not going," was all she said.

"Honey – "

"I'm not going," Karen repeated, an edge to her tone. "I heard you downstairs talking about ..." she winced, "about the funeral, and I'm not going. Don't try to change my mind because you'll be wasting your time."

With that she turned onto her side, facing away.

Jenny sat down on edge of the bed and put a tentative hand on her shoulder. "I have no idea how you're feeling. I can't even begin to imagine and it's entirely up to you what you want to do. But don't you think that Shane would want you there?"

"No," she answered simply.

"I know this is so hard but–"

"No, you don't know!" Karen shrieked, jerking back suddenly, her eyes wild with grief. "Do you know what I did yesterday morning when he was leaving for work? He came in here to kiss me goodbye. I groaned and turned away, annoyed at him for waking me up. Imagine? It was the last time he would ever kiss me and I turned away because I was too damned lazy to care. *The very last time.*"

"But you couldn't possibly have known ... " Jenny knew it was pointless trying to soothe her – Karen was in full flight.

"And then yesterday I left a message on his phone, nagging him to hurry up with the takeaway. 'Don't forget the spring rolls.' Can you believe that? *Don't forget the fucking spring rolls*! That was the last thing I said to Shane. The very last thing! I didn't tell him I loved him or that I missed him or that he was the most important thing in the world to me. I just said something so fucking ... trivial!" She thrashed on the bed, thumping her fists on the covers. "If only I could go back and say one last thing..."

"But you couldn't have known – "

"And when he was mangled in that crash, maybe still alive and crying out for help even, I was sitting here annoyed with him for being late and impatient for my bloody dinner. What sort of a person does that make me, Jenny? Why am I the one still here and he's gone? How is that fair?"

"That's not the way it works, pet."

Karen was crying openly now, tears racing down her cheeks. "To think that I spent all that time trying to delay our wedding, resenting his family and making him miserable. Well, I got what I wanted, didn't I? Now there'll be no wedding, they'll never be a wedding, because I was too damned selfish."

"Karen, you never made him miserable – you're being too hard on yourself. It could just as easily have been you or me in that car. Don't eat yourself up with guilt over this – you've enough to deal with now. If you start blaming yourself for what happened, then you might as well have died with him."

"I wish I had." She sank back heavily on the pillows and again turned away, wiping her eyes with the quilt cover. "I have nothing now, nothing. Shane was my life, my entire future. Where do I go from here? What do I do?"

Jenny touched her hand. "Honey, maybe the one thing you can do is say goodbye. I'm sure – no, I'm *certain* that Shane wouldn't want you lying here miserable on your own. You need people around you to help you through this. You said yourself you didn't get the chance to say goodbye."

As she listened to her words of supposed wisdom, Jenny couldn't be sure whether she believed them herself. She couldn't even begin to imagine how she would feel if someone she loved was taken from her like this. Maybe Karen was right to shut herself away from all the empty platitudes and tired comforting clichés. Who knew whether going along and facing into all that stuff *was* the right thing to do?

"Hey," she added softly then, "if you really don't want to go, then I'll stay here with you. Don't argue," she said, seeing her stir, "I'm not leaving you on your own. I'll stay for as long as you need me and if you want to talk, then talk, but rest assured no one will force you to do anything you don't want to, OK?"

Karen nodded, her eyes brimming with fresh tears.

"I just can't stomach going up there and facing all these people, most of whom I don't know anyway. And I don't want to have to face the Quinns either. They hate me enough as it is – don't tell me otherwise, I heard every word Nellie said last night."

"Don't forget that she's in shock too. He was her son."

"Still, maybe she was right about a few things. I did give him a hard time, you know that."

"Karen, you and Shane were two of a kind. You argued more than any other couple I've ever known, but it was obvious to all and sundry that you adored one another. I'm sorry but don't turn yourself into a martyr either. You didn't force Shane to work late or to do anything he didn't want to. Anyway, he was coming home early last night, wasn't he?"

Karen winced and Jenny felt terrible for the painful reminder.

"If the crash had happened on the road to Meath do you think Nellie Quinn would have blamed herself?" she ventured. "Please don't take to heart what she said yesterday, Karen. She's upset and grieving, the same as you. She probably has her own regrets. Everyone does."

51

It was forecast to be the warmest May Day in Ireland for years, with midday temperatures predicted to rise to above twenty degrees in the Midlands. At least according to the radio weather broadcast, but as the taxi driver reiterated to his passenger, Met Office predictions in this country could never be trusted.

"Shower of eejits they are."

The sun hadn't begun to burn through the early morning haze that had obstructed Roan's initial view of his homeland from above the clouds. The pilot had made an excellent landing because to him Dublin Airport was pretty much invisible from the air.

Now, an old road sign told him that Rathrigh was another twenty miles away. It was odd, but strangely comforting that the old black-and-white road signs indicating distance in miles were still prevalent throughout these parts.

Not that he'd travelled on too many roads in the

States, or freeways as they were called. In truth, he had barely ventured out of the city in the time he'd been there.

As thrilling as it had been when he'd caught his first glimpse of the famed Manhattan skyline on the initial journey from JFK, Roan soon discovered that living among other Irish ex-pats in Yonkers wasn't all that different from being in Dublin.

When he got the text from Aidan about the accident, the news had shaken him. It wasn't as if he and Shane were particularly close - Roan had never been close to anyone really. But to his surprise, Shane and Aidan had kept in touch after he left. Never a week went by when he didn't get a chatty text or corny social media post from one or the other.

None of his other so-called friends or ex-housemates had bothered. Roan had assumed they'd all be madly envious of his big-city job, expecting to be bombarded with requests to come and visit him in NYC. He'd been looking forward to showing off a little.

But no visits had ever materialised. In fairness, he wasn't the best himself for keeping in touch but appreciated the effort from the two lads. At least somebody back home gave a shit about what he was up to.

And now poor old Shane was gone.

Reeling with shock, Roan had called to enquire about the funeral. The very least he could do was go home for a bit and pay his respects. He felt sorry for Karen too. Granted the two of them had never clicked, but it must've been very hard to lose him so suddenly.

"Any idea where we go from here, buck?" the driver asked, interrupting Roan's train of thought. They had stopped at a T-junction and there didn't appear to be a road sign to Shane's hometown, or indeed to anywhere. Like himself, the city taximan wasn't familiar with the back roads and by-roads of County Meath.

"I'm not sure," Roan shifted in his seat to get a better look out the window. The sun had risen much higher in the sky now. Aidan had told him that the funeral Mass was at eleven.

At this stage, it looked like he was going to be late.

TESSA TOOK Gerry's hand and squeezed it tightly as the smell of incense filled the church; a signal that it was time to carry the coffin out to the graveyard.

They waited for Shane's family to exit the pews and then the small group of friends followed the priest, altar boys and other mourners down the aisle and out the door into bright sunlight.

It was a glorious day and the sun shining happily in a cloudless sky just didn't fit. If anything it seemed to mock the tragic circumstances that brought them all here today.

Walking slowly through the graveyard, Tessa caught Mike's eye and gave him a little smile. He had come to the funeral without Jenny and seemed a bit lost in the middle of it all. Tessa thought she could understand why Karen couldn't bring herself to attend, but she wasn't sure if her friend was doing the right thing.

Laying a loved one to rest was an important part of the grieving process; this she understood from her own experience consoling patient relatives at the hospital. By trying to shut it all out, Karen was simply delaying the inevitable.

Her friend's decision had been especially unpopular with the Quinn family. Upon hearing that she wouldn't be attending the service Shane's older sister was scandalised. Temporarily putting aside her grief, she had launched an all-out attack.

"I don't know why I'm even surprised," Barbara spat down the line when Jenny informed them. "Typical of that one – selfish to the end. God forgive me, but the only good thing that's come out of all this is that she'll never be part of this family."

She was an odious person, Tessa thought. At the undertaker's the night before, Barbara had been close to disrespectful with her carry-on – chatting and gossiping with locals as if at a country fair. Then turning on the tears and wailing like a banshee as soon as the priest arrived. Tessa didn't doubt that she had loved her brother, but the funeral seemed more of an excuse for a social outing at which Barbara was the centre of attention, rather than the tragic and poignant occasion that it was.

It was a terrible thing to be thinking, especially in present circumstances, but she felt that Karen was well rid of the Quinns.

The funeral procession stopped then, and the crowd began to gather in small groups by the grave opening.

Nellie Quinn was supported on one side by her daughters and on the other, a tall, wiry thirty-something who Tessa figured must be the older brother. Wreaths were laid alongside the coffin and the priest had just begun a decade of the rosary when she noticed murmuring and some additional movement behind the crowd.

Then a tragically frail Karen – her face ashen, and tears streaming down her cheeks - slowly pushed her way through the small gathering, Jenny a couple of steps behind. Tessa felt a lump in her throat as she witnessed her friend's naked anguish.

Reaching the graveside, Karen bent down and briefly caressed the brass plate atop the coffin bearing Shane's name.

Then crouching alongside it, she lowered her head and quietly began to wail. A raw and achingly mournful cry that broke Tessa's heart afresh.

52

After the burial, the funeral party retired to the village pub, where drinks and refreshments were served.

"I'm glad that you managed to persuade her," Aidan said to Jenny. "We were all so sure that she wouldn't come."

"I didn't have to," Jenny replied. "Nothing would have dragged her here at first, but when she got up this morning, something had changed. She told me that she had spent all night thinking about it and that she had one last thing to say to Shane." She glanced toward Karen, who was sitting in the corner of the lounge in gentle conversation with Gerry. "Something to say goodbye properly."

"Mike's gone back?" Tessa said, sipping her mineral water. "I noticed him leave earlier."

She nodded. "He feels so guilty about having to rush

off to London. But there's no point in his hanging around here – it's all over now."

"He's been terrific with Aidan, you know. I don't know how he does it, but he has this knack of saying the right thing to people, especially at times like this."

It was true, Jenny thought. Mike had been a rock all week, to the lads in particular: spending hours with Aidan, Gerry and the others as they reminisced until the early hours, so he would be shattered by the time he got to London for his business meeting.

Since deciding to attend today, Karen had brightened somewhat, but Jenny could already see from her friend's face that the strain was starting to get to her.

She'd get her back home as soon as an opportunity presented itself, but in the meantime, it was good to have her up out of bed, and amongst friends. Especially since she couldn't rely on Shane's family or indeed her own.

Jenny was still smarting from an earlier conversation with Karen's mum.

"I'm sorry sweetheart, but it's just *impossible* for us to get back at the moment. We have a huge American booking this week and well, we already had to keep that week in June free for the wedding. We couldn't possibly rearrange everything so quickly. Karen will understand, she knows how it is. Tell her we love her very much and we'll send some flowers."

Flowers? Jenny knew that Karen's parents were busy, but what kind of parents would desert their only child at a time like this?

"I'm getting another Coke, does anyone want

anything?" she asked, draining her glass. Then looked up, startled a little as Jack Quinn waylaid her on the way to the bar.

"Jenny, isn't it?" he said, "I'd just like to apologise for my sister on the phone the other night. She was upset – we all were."

She stiffened, unable to do anything else but nod. Though at least Jack had the decency to apologise, realising that his sister was out of order in blasting Karen for her decision.

"Barbara can be a little," he searched for the right word, 'difficult' sometimes. But it's nothing personal."

"It's fine, honestly," Jenny assured him. Out of the corner of her eye, she saw Nellie Quinn approach Karen at her table and figured she'd better intervene, just in case.

Jack moved away and as he passed by, Jenny's breath caught in her throat. Her head started spinning while the rest of the world stood still.

Roan was leaning casually alongside the bar counter to her left, chatting with someone she didn't know. Her stomach constricted and her heart started pounding at the rate of what seemed like a thousand beats per minute.

What was he doing here? No, it couldn't be him – it was just someone who looked like him. She was exhausted and her mind was just playing tricks on her.

Jenny looked away, shook her head and then looked back again. No, it *was* him.

Oh stop it, she told herself. So what if he was here? It

was no big deal, was it? Though just so unexpected to see him in the flesh, she supposed.

"You've spotted himself, I take it?" whispered Tessa, just out of earshot from the others.

Jenny nodded, trying her best to appear nonchalant. "I didn't know he was home, did you?"

"No, but I twigged him earlier at the back of the church on our way out." She leaned forward and whispered. "Are you OK?"

"Me? Oh, I'm fine, absolutely fine. A bit unexpected obviously, but ..."

Jenny stopped short as Roan approached the table and nodded briefly at the others. Aidan, who was sitting with his back to the bar turned in surprise when Roan tapped him on the shoulder. He stood up and the two amiably clapped one another on the back.

Jenny tried to avert her eyes but couldn't. Over Aidan's shoulder, he was staring right at her with those deep dark eyes she had once known so well.

Then he casually pulled up a stool and perched on it in the space between them, while she shuffled uncomfortably in her seat.

"How have you been, Jen?" he asked pleasantly, taking a sip from his pint.

She bristled at the offhand greeting.

How have I been? You broke my heart, upended my life and left me with a pile of debt but I'm grand. Thanks for asking.

"Very well, and you?" was all she said, her tone calm,

even though her heart was going a mile a minute. *Two can play at that game.*

"Great, great. No complaints."

Tessa swooped in then and swiftly monopolised the conversation while Jenny tried to appear disinterested when Roan explained that he had flown in just for the funeral and was heading back to New York tomorrow. It was quite literally a flying visit.

She digested the information with a mixture of relief and disappointment. She had tried so long to pretend she didn't care, had *told* herself she didn't care, but seeing him here now and so unexpectedly, brought all the old feelings back. Jenny knew she shouldn't be thinking like this, not when she had finally got her life back on track.

And then there was Mike, who she knew would do anything for her, who trusted her implicitly and would never even dream of treating her like Roan had.

Anyway, she thought as he moved back to the bar and she noticed Karen approach, today was not the day for thinking about this stuff.

"Jen, I hope you don't mind, but the Quinns have asked me back to the house." She grimaced a little. "They have some things of Shane's that Nellie wants me to have."

"Do you want me to come with you?"

Karen sank down on the seat alongside her. "No, you head on home. I don't want to go, but I probably won't get the chance again. After all, I have no ties with them now, do I?" Eyes glistening, she looked away for a moment. "I'm sure Jack or one of the others will drop me home later. You head back, you haven't been home for days, and probably had even less sleep than me."

Jenny patted her friend's hand. "Are you absolutely sure?" she asked, not too happy about leaving her alone with the Quinns. She hoped Barbara would behave herself because at this stage, poor Karen had been through enough. Then again, maybe this would be the opportunity they all needed to let bygones be bygones.

"I am. I think everyone will be heading away soon anyway, though Aidan looks like he's enjoying his few pints," she said, looking to where he was sitting with Gerry, a half-finished Guinness in his hand and a fresh one on the table in front of him.

"I think we all could do with some downtime after this," Tessa said. "You know, I used to hate the way everyone in this country rushed straight into the pub after a funeral. I always thought it was disrespectful. But after everything that's happened this week, I can see why people need to feel close to normal again." She saw Karen wince and could have kicked herself. "Ah love, I'm sorry. I just didn't think."

"It's fine," Karen smiled wanly, getting up from the stool. "Actually, today has been better than I expected. I know it sounds weird but I'm sort of glad I decided to come. Thanks, you two. I appreciate you being there for me."

She hugged them both and went to join the Quinns, who were waiting for her by the door.

"I'm going to go too then," Jenny yawned. "Karen was right, I've hardly had any sleep and I'm whacked."

"Are you sure that you'll be OK to drive?" Tessa asked.

"I'll be fine, honestly. Say goodbye to Gerry and the others for me?"

Jenny looked around her, but in the meantime much of the crowd had dispersed and many of the other mourners - Roan included - had left.

For some reason she'd assumed that when she finally came face-to-face with him again, it would be different - more emotionally heightened. But in the end, it had been ... anticlimactic.

He had barely even acknowledged her.

53

Feeling strangely empty, Jenny left the pub and headed out to the small car park at the rear of the building.

Getting into her car, she switched on the ignition; her vision blurring a little as she slowly made her way out, and had just reached the roadside exit when she noticed a figure run up beside the car at the passenger side.

"What do you want?" She rolled down the window, still unable to look him in the eye.

Roan began to say something, then stopped, putting both hands in his trouser pockets. "I saw you leave and I just wanted to –"

At that moment, Aidan came out a side door of the pub and wandered in their direction.

"For goodness sake, get in," Jenny snapped impatiently. She wasn't quite sure why, but she didn't want anyone to see them together.

Roan obliged and she put the car into gear, speeding

out of the lot and down the street, her thoughts going much faster than the speedometer.

Neither of them said anything until they were a little outside the village.

"Where are you staying?" Jenny asked, keen to break the silence and despite herself, completely unnerved by his proximity. "Not many hotels around these parts."

"At the Skylon, near the airport."

She exhaled. "I can drop you back on the way if you'd like."

"That would be brilliant, thanks."

Spurred by a combo of nerves and confusion, Jenny drove much faster than she would normally allow herself, especially on such narrow and winding back-roads. She was so aware of him, so conscious of the familiar scent of him. He looked good too.

When they reached the main road, Roan finally said something.

"How have you been?" he asked again, this time with a little more feeling.

"Fine," Jenny said, trying to keep her voice even. "I didn't expect to see you here today. I knew that you and Shane had kept in touch, but I didn't think you were that close."

"Shane was a nice guy," said Roan with a slight American twang, "for some reason, we just kept up messaging one another - Aidan too. It was pretty lonely out there at the beginning. I didn't know many others in the New York office and the company put me up in a hotel until I could sort out a place of my own."

"Didn't Cara go out there too?" Jenny asked bitterly before she could stop herself. "I'm sure she would have kept you company."

Damn - why had she said that? Now he would know she still cared.

"This is why I caught up with you back there. I know you're still angry with me, and you've every right to be. Look, pull in and we'll go somewhere where we can talk properly – not like this. You're getting yourself all worked up. Please – you'll get us both killed," he added, trying to make light of the situation, before realising that given the day that was in it the quip was in very bad taste. "I mean ... you know what I meant, sorry. Let's just take a breather."

Satisfied at the realisation that after all this time she was the one making *him* feel uncomfortable; Jenny eased off on the accelerator. He was right. They needed to talk. Maybe then she could get some answers, but a part of her wasn't quite sure whether or not she wanted to hear them.

A few miles further down, she pulled in and parked the car at a picnic area in a lay-by just off the main road. Although it was late in the day, a few daytrippers were still present at the small wooden picnic benches, undoubtedly taking advantage of the unexpected fine weather and the gorgeous views out towards Dublin Bay.

She and Roan sat side by side at the nearest vacant table.

"Now that you're here, I'm not sure what to say," he

said quietly. "I've rehearsed this conversation a thousand times in my head but now I don't know where to start."

For once, he looked a little unsure of himself. But Jenny wasn't going to be taken in by his little-boy-lost act. Not this time.

"How about, 'Jenny, I'm sorry for lying to you, I'm sorry for cheating on you, taking advantage of you and treating you like shit?' That would be a good start."

"You're right, you know. I won't argue with that." He turned to face her, but she concentrated her gaze away from his and out towards the water. "I *am* sorry, I'm sorry for everything. You deserved better."

"Yes," she said simply. "I did. You told me you loved me; we were living together, for goodness sake. And yet you still cheated and lied to me all the way through. Why? If you didn't love me, why not just finish it? Why the charade? Was it just because you needed a place to stay? Since the others had kicked you out."

He shook his head. "When I said I loved you, I thought I meant it – at the time I did, but I suppose back then I had no real idea what I was saying."

"Oh."

So he didn't love her after all, never had.

Jenny could feel the tears starting behind her eyes and she willed herself not to cry. They were all coming back now, all the old feelings of hurt, betrayal, and utter humiliation.

Back then, she had fooled herself into thinking that they had more. While she had put her very heart and soul into making it work, Roan had done everything to tear the relationship, and her self-esteem, asunder.

"I'm so sorry," he said finally. "Really I am. I know you did your best and I didn't know at the time how lucky I was to have someone like you. It was only when I moved away that I realised how few people truly cared about me. I had nobody to rely on. I thought that everyone, all my so-called mates back here, would be impressed by my big-shot Manhattan lifestyle. I thought they'd all be clambering for invitations to visit and I was looking forward to showing off. But after a few weeks, I realised that nobody gave a shit. I ring my mother and once in a blue moon, if she wants something she might call me back. But she's still annoyed at me for moving away. I could be dead in the Bronx somewhere, for all they care."

"And that's why you came back for the funeral? Because Shane cared?"

He nodded. "I had to pay my respects. He was under a lot of pressure before he and Karen set a date for the wedding. I think he felt that she was getting cold feet."

Jenny was shocked to hear this. She was certain too that Karen would have had no idea that Roan and Shane had been communicating like this.

"Were you really that miserable?" she asked, wondering why he had stayed in New York if things had been that bad.

"At the beginning, yes, but after a while I got a place of my own – well, a house-share in Yonkers with a crowd of Dublin lads." He shook his head in wonder. "At the shop near my place, you can buy Galtee sausages for your breakfast and Jacobs Cream Crackers for your lunch. They even stock all the Regional Irish newspapers. I buy the *Leinster Post* in there every week." He laughed, relaxing a little. "I suppose all of this helped me settle." He paused and glanced at her. "Then I met someone."

Jenny said nothing. She'd had a feeling that this was coming.

"Her name's Kelly," Roan went on. "She's American but tells everyone she's Irish-American even though she's never even been outside the state. She works as a radio dispatcher for the NYPD." He smiled at her expression. "I know what you're wondering but that's not how we met. I haven't been in any trouble over there – quite the opposite, the job is going well and I'm in line for promotion."

Jenny listened in silence as he told her all this. It was incredible, she thought how separate their lives were now. He lived in another world, completely different from the one they had shared. And he sounded happy too. He had moved on.

"I met someone too," she said, aware that she was using her words as both a shield and a weapon. She wanted him to be affected by this, maybe even a little jealous.

"I'm glad. You deserve it, Jen," he said, and then he smiled that incredible smile, the one that revealed those tiny dimples on each side of his mouth.

It had been a long time since Jenny had seen that.

He gave a short laugh. "You won't believe me but I talked to Shane about you shortly before I left and asked him to keep an eye on you." He shrugged. "Arrogant of me, I know – because I should have realised you'd bounce back without help from anyone. I wanted to tell you I was leaving too, but by then it had been what – five, six months since we'd seen one another? Shane advised me against it, said that you'd moved on and it would be better if I just left you alone."

"He was right."

"I wanted to pick up the phone to you so many times, Jen. I was lousy – I know that now. But believe me when I tell you that my behaviour back then was no reflection on you."

"Tell me about Siobhan," she asked dully, even though she didn't actually want to hear the truth.

He sighed. "I suppose if we're being honest, I might as well tell you. That night in the pub, Lydia wasn't lying."

Jenny's heart plummeted.

"We were still together right up until after the Venice trip. We'd been going out forever but after that, I think she saw through me, realised that I'd been doing the dirt on her in Dublin, that I'd been doing the dirt all along."

In her heart of hearts, Jenny had known the truth too.

"I'm sorry. Siobhan was supposed to have been away on a work shoot that weekend. So I asked you. Then she heard about the competition and cancelled the shoot to go with me ..."

"Competition? *You won the Venice trip in a bloody competition*?"

Suddenly enraged, she jumped off the wooden bench, not caring one whit about what the other picnickers thought of her. The revelation that Siobhand had finished with him was the straw that broke the camel's back.

By his own admission he was a conniving, cheating rat, but *this*. How could anyone be so deceitful?

Roan was engaged to someone else and had been throughout most of their relationship. Jenny had given him everything, and she was never even his first choice.

"Jenny – "

"Forget it," she snapped, rummaging in her handbag for the car keys."I've heard enough, I'm out of here and don't think you're coming with me. You can crawl your way back to Dublin, it's the least you deserve, you creep."

He followed her back to the car where she stood, struggling to find the right key.

"I'm sorry, I truly am," he said softly, coming up beside her.

"Do you know what I went through, trying to figure it all out, wondering what I was doing wrong? Thinking that it was me, that it had to be me, that I wasn't attractive enough, that I was fat, that I was crap in bed, that I wasn't enough. I wasn't *enough*. Did you have any idea?"

"Jen I ..."

"And all that, after wondering if you were cheating on me, after trying my utmost to keep you happy, you turn around and tell me now that I wasn't even the one who was being cheated on? *I* was the other woman. After Venice, Siobhan dumped you so you had to settle for second best?"

"It wasn't like that. I cared about you a lot – I still do."

He reached for her but Jenny recoiled at his touch, while inside her heart broke all over again.

"You just had no idea, did you?" she sobbed, "No idea how much I loved you."

54

Much later, she dropped him back to his hotel. They were mostly silent for the rest of the journey and the atmosphere hung heavily between them.

Jenny had never felt so exhausted in her life, the heavy, emotive conversation draining her. Not to mention the fact that she hadn't had a decent night's sleep in days.

She pulled up outside the hotel entrance, kept the engine running and put the car back into first gear while he got out.

"It's late," Roan said, glancing at his watch, which Jenny noticed was an expensive Tag Heuer. He hadn't been lying about doing well in New York. "Do you want to maybe get something to eat? I know I'm hungry and I'm sure you must be too."

He was ... nervous, she realised.

Jenny looked up into those familiar brown eyes, and

now saw something in them, an intensity she wasn't sure she wanted to see.

Was it merely nostalgia, this electricity between them now? After today, the rules had changed. Everything was out in the open. They'd both changed, matured even.

Yet Jenny realised there was something unfinished hanging in the air. She could feel it and she was certain he could too. Her heart began to pound and she felt beads of moisture form on her forehead.

"I'm – I'm tired," she replied quickly, afraid to meet his gaze.

There was a heavy pause. "Sure - um, thanks for the lift."

Out of the corner of her eye, she could see him watching her, almost willing her to look up. But if Jenny looked into those eyes again she didn't know what might happen.

"You're welcome." She grasped the steering wheel as tightly as she could.

"So, I guess I'll see you around?"

She nodded, still afraid to look at him, afraid to say anything more as heavy tension simmered. She moved the car into first gear for the second time, as if to convince herself that she really was leaving soon – needed to leave soon.

Roan hesitated for what seemed like forever, then softly closed the passenger door.

Jenny sped off without checking her rearview mirror, afraid that if she looked back and saw his face, she would surely falter.

Thumpety-thump, thumpety-thump – her heart raced. *Don't look back, don't look back,* she kept repeating to herself.

But when she stopped the car at the hotel exit onto the main road, she couldn't help it. It was as though an invisible force had taken control of her responses.

Jenny looked back and saw Roan still standing there, watching her outside the hotel – an unreadable expression on his face.

Waiting.

As if being controlled by an invisible force, she suddenly put the car into reverse and sped backwards into the car park, her sense of orientation all over the place.

She narrowly missed bumping into a Mondeo reversing around a corner when she saw Roan move towards her. She abandoned the car in a staff space but didn't care; she was far beyond caring.

Jenny wrenched open the door, got out and flung herself into Roan's arms, holding on to him as if her life depended on it.

He cupped her upturned face in his hands and stared into her eyes, the desire in his gaze so clearly mirrored by her own. Unwilling to break the spell, she didn't utter a word.

And when their mouths finally met, Jenny knew that she was once again, lost.

PRESENT DAY

55

Back in her kitchen, Karen's jaw fell to the floor and she almost dropped her teacup in tandem.

"*Seriously?*"

Having reached the end of her sorry tale, Jenny looked at her in nervous anticipation.

"I just ... I never expected to see him again. I was caught off guard.

Karen was still dumbstruck. "But why didn't you tell me at the time?"

Jenny shook her head. "You had just buried Shane and I was ashamed. It was such an emotional day and to be honest, I felt terrible about the timing." She dropped her hands in her lap. "I was afraid you'd think that all I cared about was myself. But it wasn't like that."

"It doesn't matter *what* day it was. I'm just annoyed that you fell for the guy's bullcrap all over again. To think of how he just left you in the lurch – "

"Another reason why I didn't say anything. I didn't

want to have to thrash it all out again. And goes without saying that I was terrified that Mike might find out. But honestly, this time with Roan - it was different – *he* was different. Maybe because we both figured we'd never see one another again."

"So you decided to have a quick roll in the hay for old time's sake?" Karen shot back sardonically. "Sorry, it's just a bit of a shock hearing all this now."

"But you're right, in a way," Jenny agreed. "It *was* for old times' sake and a purge of sorts, for me at least. Roan went back to New York and after that I think I knew once and for all that Mike was the one I wanted; the one I *truly* loved. Until then I was uncertain; still caught in the past I suppose. But once I'd confronted Roan I could finally let him go." She bit her lip. "I know it's maybe difficult to understand, but it was only until I got him out of my system that I could say for certain that I wanted to spend the rest of my life with Mike."

"Which is why you two got engaged so soon after," Karen ventured.

"Partly, yes. I think Mike realised that something had changed in me too. He knew that Roan had been at the funeral, although he didn't know the whole story, obviously. Still, I think he sensed that I was ready to move on and he proposed."

Thinking it through, Karen was silent for a long moment and she reached for another muffin.

"That's not quite the sum of it though, is it?" she stated matter-of-factly, meeting Jenny's gaze head-on. "There's more to all this; otherwise, you wouldn't be so distraught." Her friend's haunted expression told her all she needed to know. Jenny nodded, her face betraying her as she battled hard to prevent tears. "Aw, Jen. Seriously?"

For her part, Karen was still in disbelief that Jenny had fallen under Roan William's spell again - just when she was finally getting her life back on track.

She'd had no idea that the two had even spoken that day. As it was, she hadn't seen Roan at the funeral, and wouldn't have known he was there at all had Tessa not told her afterwards. But according to her, he hadn't stayed long. Suggesting Tessa didn't know about Jenny's little liaison either.

Needless to say, Karen was mired in her own worries back then, so Jenny was right – there was never a good time.

A few weeks after the funeral, when she was still trying to get her life back on track, she got a call from a solicitor in Meath asking her to come in for 'a discussion' about Shane's estate. Karen had intended to pay a quick visit to the Quinns on her way, but there had been nobody at the farmhouse when she called.

She soon found out why.

Upon her arrival at the local solicitor's practice, Jack and Nellie were sitting together in the waiting room. Nellie made small talk while they waited – stiff, awkward and meaningless chat – Jack sitting stony-faced and barely acknowledging Karen's presence. She should have suspected then, probably should have known that something was amiss.

But Karen couldn't have imagined in her wildest dreams what she would hear that afternoon. She could still recall the solicitor's soft tones as he explained that, because Shane had left no will and they weren't married, their house in Harold's Cross now legally belonged to his next of kin – his mother. She listened in disbelief as the solicitor told her that the deeds of the property were registered solely in Shane's name and thus would now be transferred to Nellie's. As Jack remained an active guarantor for the mortgage, he also had a legal interest.

It had been surreal, Nellie patting her hand and telling her that they wouldn't expect her to move out straightaway, that she should go home and consider what to do next. Home? Hadn't they just told Karen she no longer had one?

She had never once considered the legal implications of Shane's demise, hadn't considered anything other than overcoming the gaping void in her life since she lost him. While she had briefly wondered how she might continue paying the mortgage on her own, she'd assumed that life assurance would cover his share of the repayments.

She remembered Aidan advising her to get in touch with a solicitor to thrash out any related stuff, but Karen had been too wrapped up in trying to get through the days without Shane.

But that afternoon in Meath, reality had come tumbling down on top of her, much the same way that a pile of Shane's clothes had come tumbling out of the wardrobe once Karen had felt strong enough to go through his things. His scent was still painfully evident on the sweaters and T-shirts, triggering another intense wave of grief.

She had been angry then and she was equally angry sitting in that office, wanting to scream at his family. Wishing that Shane didn't have to die, wishing that he was still here and that she didn't have to suffer all over again.

But it seemed the suffering had only just begun. Jack had told her in no uncertain terms that they had every intention of selling the house. He would give Karen a couple of months to 'sort herself out' and any contributions she made towards the mortgage in the interim would be repaid.

But he hadn't bargained on her resolve. It had been the proverbial kick up the backside that Karen needed and had given her a new lease on life. Since then, she had temporarily parked her grief and set about making an absolute mission of keeping the house. There was no way she was going to pack her bags and just up and leave her home, the home she had shared with Shane.

Suddenly she had something to fight for.

She refused to move out on the original vacate date the Quinns had set, and threw every subsequent legal letter into the bin while she tried to launch a defence.

After a few false starts, her dad had put her in touch with a property lawyer in Dublin who was open to taking a case on her behalf, and as she'd learnt just that morning, she and Jack Quinn were going to battle it out in court.

So no, Karen conceded, bringing her thoughts back to the present, there had been little opportunity for Jenny to confide her secret liaison with Roan Williams had she been so inclined.

"And now he and Mike are working together?" she said to Jenny. "You'll have to say something."

"I know," Jenny was crestfallen. "But I was so sure I would never see Roan again. I thought it was all at a safe distance. I couldn't risk telling Mike back then. He wouldn't have understood."

"And do you think he'll understand now?"

Jenny buried her face in her hands. "I have no choice but to find out, do I?"

56

Much later, Jenny drove home in a daze, barely noticing the activity around her. It had turned out to be much drearier than this morning's bright skies had suggested, which she thought was fitting to her mood.

She looked out over Dublin Bay, remembering when Mike had proposed. It wasn't long after Shane's funeral and they had gone for a walk along Sandymount Strand; Mike teasing her about that time in Brittas Bay when she wouldn't get her feet wet, that very first day they kissed.

Jenny had promptly taken off her shoes and socks and rushed into the water, as if to prove him wrong and show him that, this time, she had no problem at all getting her feet wet.

He had followed, and the two spent ages jumping around and splashing in the water until they were soaked. Afterwards, they both collapsed laughing and exhausted onto the sand. Then Mike sat up, looked seriously at Jenny's upturned face and out of the blue asked her to marry him.

It was unexpected, yet it felt so right and she said yes without a moment's hesitation. Roan had ceased to exist in her thoughts once they'd said their final goodbye after Shane's funeral. Mike was the one she wanted now, pure and simple.

When they phoned Rebecca to announce the news, she and Graham were over the moon. As were everyone else, Jenny's parents, Mike's mum and all their friends, including Tessa and Gerry, who at the time had their own reason to celebrate after Tessa gave birth to a baby boy.

Jenny had hesitated before telling Karen about their engagement, mindful that the news would resurrect deeply painful memories. But she had been equally delighted for them, cognisant that Shane's death had affected their relationship, though not for the reason she suspected.

"I knew that I would marry again, eventually," Mike confessed, once they'd chosen the ring. "But I had every intention of taking things slowly. After Shane's accident, everything changed. I put myself in Karen's shoes and wondered how I would feel if I lost you. And I decided that I wasn't going to waste time, Jen; if I wanted you to be part of my life, if I wanted to be with you for the *rest* of my life, now was as good a time as any to start. Because none of us ever know how long that might be. The rest of our lives, I mean."

Jenny knew he was right. And shortly after their

engagement, she moved into the house in Blackrock and began making it a home.

Everything was falling into place, and she didn't think anything could spoil her happiness. She had well and truly moved on.

Indicating right, she turned into the driveway and got out of the car, pausing for a moment before putting her key in the door.

What was it they said about the best-laid plans?

57

Later, Mike slammed the door behind him and called out a greeting into the kitchen where Jenny sat nervously awaiting his return. "We're home!"

She looked up as he came through the doorway and despite her heavy heart, couldn't help but smile.

"There's Mummy...." he sang and the little girl's face lit up in a beaming smile as Jenny stretched out her arms.

"Hello honey." She took the baby from Mike and embraced her, kissing the top of her head. "Did you have a good time at Auntie Rachel's, Holly?"

"She was great," he soothed. "Rach said she slept through lunch and spent the afternoon glued to *Paw Patrol*. I'm not quite sure if I'm happy about our girl watching so much telly, but I didn't say anything to my darling sister." Mike removed Holly's nappy bag from one shoulder and his laptop case from the other, before bending down to kiss Jenny hello. "So did you get everything squared away today?"

For a brief moment, she started, confused. Then she remembered – the exam, she was supposed to have spent today studying. Rachel had taken Holly the night before and babysat today to give Jenny time to do so.

"I did as much as I could," she answered, which was something that resembled the truth. Since this morning, she hadn't been able to concentrate on anything other than what Mike had told her over breakfast.

"You must be zonked," he said. "Why don't you go and take it easy for a while and I'll organise something for dinner." He removed Holly's coat and sat her in her high chair, before taking her favourite teddybear out of the bag and handing it to her. The little girl began playing happily with the toy, banging it up and down on the plastic table in front of her.

"No, it's fine, I was just about to start," Jenny said. She got up from the table and took some carrots from the vegetable trolley beside the sink. "You go on up and have your shower."

"Are you sure?" Mike said gratefully, taking orange juice out of the fridge and drinking it directly from the carton. "It was a tough day, to be honest. And battling traffic from the other side of town wasn't much fun either. I don't know how people endure having to sit in that every single day."

Rachel lived on the north side of the city, close to the hospital in which she worked. Mike had left the office early, but with the inevitable motor congestion, the journey had taken a couple of hours.

She nodded distractedly. "I can imagine."

"I called earlier to see how you were getting on, but you must have been so immersed in the books that you didn't answer."

Jenny thought quickly. She couldn't tell him she had spent the day at Karen's. "I had the phone switched to silent. Sorry." She hated herself for lying to him and even more for deceiving him, but Mike noticed nothing amiss.

He tickled Holly in her chair and the baby chuckled, enjoying the attention.

"Oh," he added then, remembering, "I booked a table at that new Thai place tomorrow night. I asked Rach and she said she'd be delighted to come over and spend time with her favourite niece again. Remember I told you this morning that I was planning to bring the new guy out?"

Jenny nodded, wondering why he didn't ask her what was wrong, certain that he could hear the blood gushing through her veins.

"I think he's bringing his girlfriend – or is it his wife even?" Mike pondered. "I'm not sure. I haven't had a chance to get to know him since he started and I'm keen for all of us to start off on the right foot. After all, he'll be the one running the show when I'm on leave for the honeymoon." She tried to relax as he came up and put his arms around her, nuzzling her neck. "You should wear that dress you got for the christening. Your man would be impressed as hell if he saw you in that."

Mistaking Jenny's silence as fatigue after a tough day

with the books, he gave her a quick kiss on the cheek and then hummed a little tune on his way upstairs.

Jenny was stricken. She couldn't do this, couldn't pretend any longer.

She had to tell him – tonight.

58

"Firstly, you need to know that I never planned this ... I never intended to lie or attempted to deceive you. It was ... well it was just the way things happened."

Later that evening, after they had put Holly to bed, Jenny decided that it was time to come clean since an upcoming encounter with Roan was imminent. Swallowing hard, she took both of Mike's hands in hers and led him over to their bed, sitting on the edge of it.

"Deceive me?" Mike chuckled nervously, "What are you talking about? Hey, you're shaking, what's wrong?"

"What I'm about to say may well mean the end of our relationship, but it's something you need to know." Jenny clasped both of her hands tightly around his, steeling herself to tell him the truth and wishing that she hadn't lied in the first place. "The new guy you've taken on at the company – Roan. He was - is - my ex, the one I was getting over when I met you." She waited anxiously for his response.

"OK," Mike stated, evidently a little bemused still. "But that was ages ago. You're hardly still carrying a torch?"

She swallowed hard. "There's more. Remember I told you we met again last year when he turned up at Shane's funeral? We hadn't seen one another since ... well, since the breakup."

"I remember," he said, waiting.

"It was difficult seeing him again and to be honest, it sent me into a tailspin," Jenny continued, watching him closely, trying to gauge his reaction. "There was so much left unsaid and a lot unresolved since the last time we met." Again Mike remained silent, so she pushed on. "That day, I left when Karen went away with the Quinns because I was exhausted. It had been an emotional week and it felt like I hadn't slept in days. Plus I was stung by the fact that Roan didn't seem as affected about seeing me again, as I was about seeing him."

Mike nodded slowly. "A bit of a letdown, considering."

"Exactly," Jenny agreed, relieved that at least he could identify with her state of mind. "I don't quite know what I expected, but given how things ended I suppose I thought that he might at least try to speak to me - apologise even, rather than simply stonewall. I was angry with him and even angrier with myself for expecting him to be any different, or even sorry." She paused. 'What I didn't tell you is that after I left the pub, Roan followed me." She went on to tell Mike about his apologies and explanations and how emotional she had been.

He nodded. "To be fair, I had more or less figured that out. That you'd seen the guy and laid the ghost to rest, as it were. I hadn't realised how upset you were and you hadn't told me that you had given him a lift back either. But what does it matter now?" he shrugged. "I'm not someone who'd hold a grudge or be jealous if that's what you're thinking. OK, I'll admit it might be a little awkward from a social point of view, but we can get over that surely?" When she wouldn't meet his gaze, Mike seemed to understand that there was more. "What? Please don't tell me that you're still in love with him, Jenny. Is that what all this is about?"

Still, she said nothing, unable to come up with the right words.

His face went white. "Jesus. We're getting married soon – we have Holly and we're *happy,* aren't we? Aren't we?"

She watched Mike's expression switch from initial concern, to confusion, bewilderment and finally, hurt. She ached to touch him but was afraid to in case she would lose her nerve.

"Why didn't you tell me?" he continued hoarsely. "I had no idea that you still loved this guy." He shook his head. "If he truly was the one you wanted, if you were still holding a candle, then why on earth did you agree to marry me? Let alone start a family? Say something for goodness sake."

Her voice shook as she spoke and she tried to battle her tears as they spilled a lot faster than her words.Yet resigned herself to the fact that there would be many more tears after this.

"It isn't that. I wasn't ... I'm not in love with him. It's you I love, more than anything else, and you have to believe that. It's just ... I should never ...oh Mike, I've been so stupid." Jenny put her head in her hands and sobbed, afraid to continue, terrified to reveal the rest, knowing that the truth would destroy them both. "And now everything's ruined."

"What? What's ruined? Jenny, tell me."

She couldn't look at his face, knowing that his eyes would merely reflect her own distress.

"I'm so, so sorry," she said softly. "By the time I found out, by the time I even suspected anything, it was much too late. And I truly never thought I'd see him again. But now that he's back, you have to know the truth – you deserve to."

Mike entwined her fingers in his. "Jen we'll work through it. We've been through a lot together already. Maybe it's just cold feet – "

"Stop, you don't understand..." Her voice raised an octave as she became frustrated. She was desperate to get it all out now, as if saying the words out loud would absolve some of the guilt. "I was going to mention my suspicions, and you don't know how many times I tried, but ...." She paused and took one last deep breath, but still her voice quivered as she said the words. "I'm so sorry, but there's something else, one last thing you didn't know," Jenny met Mike's gaze for the very first time since the beginning of the conversation. "About Holly ..."

59

The baby perched contentedly in her high chair while her mother made her favourite breakfast of Rice Krispies with hot milk.

Thankfully Jenny thought, watching Holly gurgle merrily to herself, her daughter seemed oblivious to the solemn atmosphere. Or that the man she'd called Daddy for the duration of her short little life, had last night packed his bags and marched out of the house and out of their lives.

"If it wasn't for the love I have for our ... or should I say *your* daughter," Mike had spat, his face wincing in pain as he corrected himself, "it would be you packing. You can stay here until you find somewhere decent for Holly to live. It's the very least you can do after lying to us both since the day she was born."

"Mike, please," Jenny pleaded, panic consuming her as she realised that he wasn't going to give her a chance to explain further, "you can't just leave."

"Why not? It seems to me that I can do what I damn well please. God knows you did," he shot back, eyes flashing.

She hung her head. "We have to talk about it, and you need to know that it was nothing to do with you and me, nothing to do with my love for you – it just was something I needed to get out of my system."

He glared at her, outraged. "Well, good for you, Jenny. I'm so glad. Maybe next time you have something to get out of your system, we'll end up with a son."

The comment stung and she felt ashamed afresh. She had been so consumed with guilt and determined to unburden the truth, that she hadn't properly considered the aftermath.

"Please try and understand – "

"*Understand!*" Mike yelled and then remembered that Holly was sleeping in the next room over. "Understand?" he repeated, his voice dropping to a whisper, "what I don't understand is after all this time, you suddenly decided to tell me the truth?"

"I had to," she said simply. "The guilt has been eating me up since I first realised it myself. I love you too much to lie to you any longer."

Mike winced as he heard this. He looked old and weary as he sat back down on the bed, this time keeping his back to her, unable to look at her.

"How could you? How could you have kept up such a pretence? Faking being as happy as I was when she was born? How could you when you knew all along that we were living a lie?"

"It wasn't like that. I didn't know – the thought didn't even cross my mind at the beginning. I assumed she was yours, but by the time I though otherwise, it was too late. We were both there when the doctor told me I was pregnant, remember?" she said, trying to make him understand, to let him know that she had never planned to deceive him, but that things had snowballed. While he had been ecstatic at the GP's that time, Jenny's reaction to the news had been a little less assured.

How could she be pregnant? Upon discovering this mere weeks after she and Mike announced their engagement, the doctor began to trot out statistics about the Pill's effectiveness. And a beaming Mike reminded Jenny that she'd had that vomiting bug shortly before Shane's accident. The doc confirmed that this may well have interfered with the contraception's efficacy.

It was only then that it dawned on Jenny that Mike may not be the father.

"I promise, I swear the notion had never crossed my mind before then. Remember you mentioned how quiet I was after the doctor visit, and I told you that I was just letting the news sink in? That was true. I *was* letting it all sink in, trying to come to terms with the possibilities. But what could I do? I had never seen you so excited. There was no way I could have broached the subject then."

"You could have said something," he said gruffly.

"I didn't have a chance. And before long, everyone knew. Your mother, my parents – everyone. You'd told them all before I had a chance to think straight." Her parents had been thrilled; Mike's mother had been a little surprised at the speed of everything; their engagement and a baby on the way, but equally elated. "The pregnancy was shock enough."

Mike had been concerned about her frequent headaches, pallid complexion and ongoing tiredness. He had insisted she 'get herself checked out' and they both went to see Dr Clohessy. Jenny thought that if anything she was just run-down.

She should have realised the timing though, of course she should have known. But there was so much happening back then. She and Mike had just begun planning the wedding, she'd got another promotion and was working flat out to justify it. Had she discovered the news by herself, Jenny was certain that she would have admitted her infidelity and made Mike aware of the possibility that he wasn't the dad.

Ironically she had never been a good liar, unable to sit comfortably with deception, partly because of her own experience of being lied to.

In different circumstances, Jenny would have told him the truth and faced the accusations and admonitions. At the very least, she would have let Mike be the one to decide whether he wished to continue with their relationship. And if he had left, then she would have dealt with the consequences and got on with raising the baby on her own.

It would have broken her heart, but over time Jenny convinced herself that she would have come clean, had she had the chance.

"Anyway," she told him then, "the odds felt that you might well indeed have been her dad." While she still couldn't see Mike's face, Jenny heard a quiet sob escape and she moved closer and laid a hand on his arm. "I'm so sorry love. I made some terrible choices that I can't take back, and you don't know how much I wish that I could. But please believe me when I tell you that none of this was intentional. Try to put yourself in my shoes back then. There was nothing else I could have done. I never, ever meant to hurt you or intended to deceive you. You have to believe me."

Mike said nothing; he just kept his gaze fixed on the bedroom carpet. "I was so happy," he croaked. "We were so happy."

"I know."

"No you don't know. You don't bloody know anything!" His entire body shook as he spoke. "You've made me look like a fool and all you can say is that you're sorry. Tell me this – why now after all this time, did you decide to tell me? Why turn what I thought was our happy little world upside down? Why rock the boat?"

"Because he's back," she whispered. "Plus I think I'd always known deep down that the truth would out eventually. When you said this morning that he was back on the scene, I figured that there was no hiding it. It was fate. Karma even. Somebody somewhere is making me pay for what I did to you – and Holly."

Mike wiped his eyes. "So the plan is to go off and play happy families with *him* now, is it?"

"Of course not. And I'm not sure whether he needs to know."

"Oh I see," he said, knuckles white. "You decide to turn *my* life upside down, but you're going to go easy on him, is it? Well, fuck that."

He stood up and angrily resumed flinging clothes into his suitcase. "He deserves to know the truth too, no? After all, he *is* Holly's father." And with that, unable to hold back any longer, Mike broke down.

Jenny went to him, desperate to hold him in her arms and try and make everything OK again. But when he recoiled at her touch, a look of disgust on his face, she knew that for Mike things would never be OK.

What she'd said was true: she *hadn't* decided about revealing anything to Roan. But that didn't matter. His return had been the catalyst to rid herself of the guilt that consumed her since Jenny discovered her worst fears had been realised.

It had hit her suddenly not long after Holly was born, when one day she noticed her daughter gazing at the baby-mobile dangling above her cot.

She was staring at it with the same intense expression Roan used when he was trying to figure out something.

And as she grew, Holly's complexion and hair colour darkened while both Mike and Jenny's colouring was fair. Though she had inherited Jenny's blue eyes, which seemed enough to deflect comment or suspicion from anyone, Mike included.

Oddly enough though, Holly possessed Mike's

temperament. She was rarely grumpy or troublesome and such a good-natured child, always smiling and laughing at everyone. Jenny had often been stopped on the street by strangers captivated by her daughter's beaming smile and happy giggle.

"She's got the cutest little dimples," an older woman had said to her one day.

Now, Jenny remained on the bed in silence, as Mike finished collecting his things.

Then, picking up his suitcase and refusing to look at her, he walked through the doorway and out into the hallway.

Hesitating a moment, he dropped his bags and went into Holly's room, planting a quiet kiss on her forehead as she lay sleeping. When he came back out and Jenny saw the pain etched on his face she thought her heart would break.

"I'll – I'll try and be out of here as soon as I can," she mumbled, afraid to look at him, aching to touch him.

Mike picked up his suitcase and headed downstairs.

"Take your time. I wouldn't want her ending up in some dingy flat," he said, his eyes hard as flints.

Jenny enquired as to where he'd go but he told her nothing other than she should notify him once she and the baby were settled elsewhere.

Then Mike walked out the front door without another word.

Jenny stood in the open doorway for a long time after, trying to pretend it wasn't real, hoping that it wasn't happening.

She hadn't heard a word from him since. It was over, and both of them knew it.

But had she truly expected anything else?

The scent of burning milk brought Jenny sharply back to the present. She looked at the cooker and saw to her dismay that the pot of milk she'd been warming for Holly's breakfast had boiled over and congealed all over the hob.

Feeling well and truly defeated, she slumped down at the kitchen table and put her head in her hands.

Mike was really gone. She had hoped initially that after he calmed down and had a chance to think, that they might talk everything through and figure out what to do next.

But now Jenny knew there was simply no hope to cling to.

She and Holly would be out of the house by the weekend. Despite her protests that her friend had enough to contend with, Karen had insisted they come live with her until Jenny found something else.

"Anyway," Karen added wickedly, "the more of us living there, the harder it is for a judge to kick us out."

Jenny had reluctantly agreed, if only to get away from Mike's. She felt bad enough that he was the one who'd left. Now she'd need a find a place of her own and begin a new life, just her and Holly.

But despite the pain of losing him, there was also a palpable sense of relief at the proverbial weight lifting from her shoulders that she no longer had to live a lie. While uncertain about what life had in store for her and her daughter, at least now Jenny could finally live with herself, and that alone brought her some comfort.

Across the room, little Holly watched ill-at-ease at her mum's melancholy demeanour and the tears streaming down her face.

"*Da-Da*?" she called out, banging her spoon, trying to cheer her up by reciting the only word her baby vocal chords had yet managed. "*Da-Da. Da-Da. Da-Da.*"

60

Karen looked around her beloved home and tried to view it through fresh eyes, prospective buyers' eyes. Inviting and homely, the warm gold walls, terracotta curtains and three-piece suite of her living room perfectly complemented the wooden floor.

Shane had been so proud of the house, but Karen knew that this room in particular had been his favourite. She remembered him cursing wildly the day he tried laying the wooden floor. It had taken him much longer than the 'couple of hours' the sales assistant had advised, not to mention the additional time sanding and varnishing.

But to Shane, it had all been worth the satisfaction of being able to tell everyone that he had done it all himself.

She had been surprised that he'd so easily taken to DIY. He had tackled the kitchen units with gusto too, albeit with help from Aidan, whose dad was a carpenter by trade. Between them, they had ripped down the tired formica doors and chipboard and completely modernised the space by replacing the units with bright maple doors, chrome handles and a solid granite worktop.

Room by room, and with infectious enthusiasm, Shane had transformed the dull outdated décor of 22a Harolds Cross Crescent. Gone was the jaded floral wall-paper, seventies swirling carpets and the ancient doors and skirting boards. Instead, he and Karen had opted for wooden fixtures, warm colours and textures.

She knew that if this house went on the market, it would be snapped up within days, if not hours. But the property would *not* be going on the market anytime soon, not if she could help it. No way the Quinns were getting their grubby, selfish little hands on her home, not without a fight to the death.

Or to put it less dramatically, a court battle at least. Her solicitor had phoned that morning to tell her that a hearing date had been agreed. She and Jack Quinn were to come before a judge early next year.

People she didn't even know very well; work colleagues, her boss, her next-door neighbour – a snob-bish woman who had never deigned to speak to either Karen or Shane before his death – had been telling her that she was coping well, that she was doing the right thing by going back to work so soon after the funeral, that she was managing 'admirably'. Even her mother had complimented her ability to 'bounce back', a few weeks after the funeral when she and her dad had finally been able to tear themselves away – the same weekend they had scheduled to come home for the wedding.

Karen had sent them back to Tenerife early, frustrated with her mother's incessant jabbering about how living in a sunny climate had done untold damage to her skin, and didn't she notice all her latest wrinkles?

Clara could never have been described as maternal, and Karen didn't expect her to be any different, but she wondered how any mother could be so self-absorbed and seemingly oblivious to her child's pain. After spending a couple of days with her mother, Karen had to stop herself from throwing her out, and would have had Aidan not been around to calm her.

He had been wonderful, especially in the time immediately after the funeral, when everyone else had left her alone and got on with their own lives. Aidan had been the one to cancel the wedding and honeymoon arrangements, ensuring Karen would not have to make the difficult calls to the registry office or the hotel.

Jenny and Mike had been there whenever she needed someone to talk to, or a shoulder to cry on and Tessa was always on the phone too.

On Karen and Shane's intended wedding day, both couples insisted that she pass the day with them, hoping to keep her mind occupied, but Karen knew she couldn't pretend. What should have been the happiest day of her life would forever be associated with grief and pain. She and Jenny had never made it to Belfast for their shopping trip, so at least she didn't have a wedding dress to remind her of everything she had lost.

Maybe it would get easier as time went by. People kept telling her it would, but how did they know?

Aidan was the only one who seemed to understand, the only one who didn't tell Karen that she would get over it, that it would get easier, that she had to get on with things. United in their mutual loss, each seemed to share the understanding that it would be a very long time before either of them managed to do that, if ever.

It was this shared pain and unified sorrow, that enabled them to lean on one another. For this, Karen was grateful, relieved that every time she rang him crying, lonely and vulnerable in the middle of the night, after waking up from a nightmare, Aidan understood. And that unlike everyone else, he had respected her wishes to be left alone on her wedding day, but had dropped everything when she phoned that evening and let her cry silently in his arms for hours. Karen knew that each would have been lost without the other's support.

However, Aidan was in serious disagreement about her decision to fight the Quinn family for possession of the house.

"Stuff like this, the law is clear cut. You are not Shane's next of kin; you never were. You can't fight reality," he argued after Karen had been turned down by yet another in a string of lawyers who refused to take on the case.

But now she had someone willing to fight her corner and nothing anyone else said would stop her.

Karen was fully prepared to take on Jack Quinn, and come hell or high water, she was going to win.

61

Later that evening Jenny arrived, tired and straining with the weight of her problems, and the bags containing her and Holly's stuff.

"I didn't want to leave anything behind," she explained, seeing Karen eyeing the Fiat Punto's open boot stacked with suitcases and refuse sacks, ostensibly containing everything they owned.

"Did you tell Mike you were coming here?" she enquired, trying to pretend she didn't see Holly holding her arms out, wanting to be released from her car seat. She was one of the few children that Karen wasn't afraid of, but she wouldn't go as far as picking her up and cuddling her. "Here, I'll get the stuff – why don't you organise herself first?" she offered.

"I left a message," Jenny replied. "I was kind of relieved that I didn't have to speak to him directly."

She handed Karen the luggage, mopped her sweating

brow and then went about the not-inconsiderable task of settling the baby.

Karen nodded sympathetically, appreciating that things were difficult for Jenny, but they must be equally difficult for Mike who knowing what he did, also now had to work side by side with Roan for his troubles.

Once Jenny had settled her things in the spare room and Holly was sleeping peacefully in her travel cot, Karen opened a bottle of wine and the two sat companionably in her living room.

"So, how are you feeling?" she asked, pouring Jenny a glass of chablis.

"At the moment, relieved. I needed to get away. Thanks so much for letting us stay here."

"Goes without saying that you're welcome, but unfortunately I can't add that you can stay as long as you like. I told you a court date's been set, didn't I?"

"You're definitely going through with this, then?"

"Absolutely," Karen said in a tone that brooked no argument. "I told you, even if I haven't a chance in hell I'm not letting the Quinns walk all over me."

Jenny shifted uncomfortably. They'd had this conversation many times before and she knew that Karen would never yield. She feared that her friend was making a big mistake taking on Shane's family over an already established point of law. She couldn't possibly win and the Quinns knew it, their solicitor knew it and Karen's solicitor surely knew it too. The only person who didn't – or at least wouldn't admit to knowing – was Karen.

Jenny believed that the entire situation would end not only in tears but also with fat legal bills on both sides. And Karen certainly couldn't afford that; as it was she could barely afford the mortgage.

"What does Aidan think?"

Karen sniffed. "He wants me to give up, and move on – same as you."

"It's not like that. You know that I'll support you, *we'll* support you every step of the way – I suppose we're just not as convinced as you seem to be that this is the best way forward."

"And what am I supposed to do?" Karen shot back, cheeks reddening. "Where am I supposed to go? This is my home, our home, Shane's and mine. He worked himself to the bone to get the deposit and sacrificed a lot. You know how tight things were for us. It can't be all for nothing." Her eyes flashed angrily as she spoke. "You saw it yourself that day when the estate agent turned up. Jack just wants to sell this place off – he doesn't care about me, doesn't care about Shane and what he might have wanted. He just wants to make a profit, another few quid to add to the loot he already has in the bank. He doesn't give a shit, Jenny." She wiped her eyes viciously.

Jenny knew better than to say any more. She had thought, *hoped* that just for a minute, she was getting through to her. But she had forgotten how solidly stubborn her friend could be.

The landline rang and Karen got up to answer it. Then raised an eyebrow as she listened to whatever the person on the other end was saying.

"Here she is now," she said, shrugging as she handed Jenny the handset.

"Hello?" she said tentatively.

"Jenny – hi, it's Rebecca. I hope you don't mind me calling. I got this number from Rachel."

"Rebecca ...um, hi," She was shocked. Why was Mike's ex phoning her at Karen's? And, more importantly, how did she even know she was here?

Her tone must have betrayed her because soon her unspoken questions were answered. "Mike told me what happened."

Mortification burned through Jenny like fire through crepe paper. "He told you?"

"Yes, but that's not the reason I called. I'm not going to judge, or take sides – believe me, I might've done the same thing in your position – after all, you weren't to know for sure, but –"

"You mean he told you *everything*?" Blood rushed to her head so fast Jenny thought she might faint. Betrayal, anger and disappointment coursed through her simultaneously. How *dare* he? How dare he humiliate her and Holly like that? She knew that he had been upset and betrayed, but did he have to exacerbate those feelings by telling everyone else?

That didn't sound like the Mike she knew.

Worst of all though was the realisation that he was evidently determined to cut – not just her, but Holly too – out of his life. As if she'd never existed.

And that hurt the most.

She'd hoped that maybe he might still want to be a

part of her daughter's life. After all, he had been Holly's dad since the day she was born, had been beside Jenny throughout all fifteen hours of labour and had even cut the umbilical cord. He adored her.

Maybe she was being selfish in hoping that he might be able to come to terms with everything, but Holly had been Mike's world. He couldn't have loved the baby any more than he did. Or so Jenny had thought.

But in revealing their personal issues, it showed a callous and unforgiving side of him that she hadn't thought existed.

"I only called because I figured you must be wondering where he is or whether he's OK. He's staying with Rachel at the moment. Don't worry," she added, correctly reading Jenny's thoughts, "he hasn't told her anything, but you know Rachel, she'll be digging and he's sworn me to secrecy. Anyway sweetheart, I just wanted to let you know that I'm thinking of you and don't worry – these things tend to work themselves out in the end."

"Um ... OK, thanks."

Jenny's head was spinning when put down the phone.

"What did she want?" Karen asked; intrigued by the side of the conversation she'd been privy to.

"I don't honestly know," Jenny said, wide-eyed with mystification. "Mike told Rebecca everything and she called to say that he's fine and all will surely work out."

Karen arched a dubious eyebrow.

"O.K. I know you said the ex is nice and all, but hearing that, she must also be a bit partial to the strong stuff."

62

The weather was mild, but the sun was nowhere to be seen. A dense blanket of angry clouds hid it well. As she walked, Karen felt the air become thicker as it passed through her lungs.

It was especially humid today, although perhaps it just felt that way because she was here. She didn't come very often, didn't feel the need to, because she knew that he was always with her.

But today, Karen needed to ask Shane something.

She noticed that the Quinns had since erected a black marble headstone at the head of the plot. Her beloved's name, date of birth and death had been etched in gold beneath a similar inscription bearing the name of Shane's father, Patrick.

She had only been at the graveside twice, once at the funeral and more recently for his first anniversary, but judging by the marble's pristine appearance and fresh etchings, it had been a recent addition.

Karen took out the gift she had brought him – a small teddy bear dressed in a miniature Liverpool football jersey – and sat it against the headstone. She smiled. He would get a laugh out of that.

"They still haven't won anything, love, not this year, but I hear they're getting better." She gave a little chuckle and then her tone grew serious. "So I'm in a bit of a quandary and I need your advice. Seems this court thing between your brother and me is really happening. I know I told you before that I was going to keep going, that I was going to fight to the end but, love, I honestly don't know if I'm doing the right thing any more." She bit her lip. "I'm tired. I mean, sometimes I can barely sleep at night for thinking about it. And I feel so angry all the time, not just at your mam and Jack, but angry at everyone. I get so wound up by the simplest little things. And I know that people think I'm obsessive too, to the point that they can't even mention it without me flying into a rage. They all think I'm going to lose, that I haven't a hope of winning but they don't understand that I have to – for your sake, I have to try, don't I?"

She tried to summon up Shane's face in her mind but as time went on, this was becoming more difficult. It wasn't as though Karen had forgotten him; it was just getting harder for her to picture him exactly how he had been. The thought terrified her.

"It's just – God this is hard – it's just ... I don't know if I'm doing the right thing anymore, love. I'm finding it so much harder to make ends meet too, and you know I've never been the best with money anyway. It's difficult to keep up the repayments on my own. I know how much you loved our home and I love it too but, Shane, I don't know if I have the strength left in me to fight for it."

She stooped low beside the grave and leaned her head on the headstone, fresh tears dropping onto the cold marble.

"If you were here, I know you'd encourage me to keep going, and I will if you want me to. But if you could just let me know somehow, give me a kind of sign or whatever, that I have your support. Please love, could you? Because I just don't know anymore. I'm doing my best to keep your dream alive but it's just so ... hard."

Hearing a sound from nearby, Karen swallowed the lump in her throat and stifled a sob. Her eyes widened for a moment until she looked behind to see someone standing at the next grave over.

The woman sneezed again, and head bent low, held a handkerchief up to her mouth. Karen exhaled a long breath, the unexpected interruption calming her a little, then turned back.

"I'd better go, love," she said softly. "Looks like it's about to rain." She gazed up at the clouds about to unleash a torrent.

Gathering her jacket tightly around her shoulders, Karen hurried back towards the car and had just reached it and was struggling to find her keys when she felt heavy raindrops on her head. She was soaked within seconds, unable to locate the offending keys, and then swore under her breath as she realised they'd been left in the ignition.

The car wasn't locked and a sodden Karen removed her drenched leather jacket and flung it onto the back seat. Luckily, there was a spare fleece in the car. In an attempt to get dry, she put it on, then looked miserably out the window up at the rain clouds. There wasn't a streak of blue in sight.

Despite herself, she chuckled.

If this is supposed to be a sign from Shane, Karen mused, starting the ignition, she was more confused than ever.

63

"Thanks, appreciate that – see you soon." Jenny hung up the phone. "She said I can take the exam some other time, thank goodness," she told Karen, who was trying her best to stay calm having been given the job of feeding Holly while Jenny called the bank HR department.

Clearly enjoying herself, the baby giggled and shook her head from side to side whenever a spoonful approached her mouth.

"Um, Jen – I don't think she's hungry," Karen said, hopeful of being relieved from her duties.

"What? Oh, she can be a bit fussy sometimes. Just keep trying, she'll eat it eventually."

Karen couldn't be sure, but she was almost positive that she saw Holly wink at her just then. Encouraged, she tried feeding her again but to no avail. Eventually, she put the food back down on the kitchen table and folded her arms across her chest. As soon as she did, the baby began to whine.

"Oh, I get it," she said with a sardonic smile, "you don't like it when the shoe's on the other foot, do you? Well, Missy, what's sauce for the goose is sauce for the gander and now you won't get it until I'm good and ready."

Holly gave her a look that conveyed utter disbelief.

"Karen, she's a baby!" Jenny tut-tutted. "She doesn't understand guile."

"Oh really? I reckon that wide-eyed innocence thing is all an act and they know well how to play the game. We're the fools."

"Give it here, you idiot," Jenny grabbed at the bowl, a smile playing about her lips. "God help us all if you ever have kids."

"If I do, they won't get much past me. And no, let her wait now," she refused, still locked in a showdown with the infant.

"Yes I'm sure they'll be perfectly behaved – model children even. Before the age of two, they'll be able hold full conversations, change their own nappies and feed themselves, because Mammy won't let them get away with 'the innocent act'. I really can't wait to meet these kids."

Karen laughed. "Well, you'll have a long wait since there isn't even a daddy on the horizon."

"What about Aidan?" Jenny asked carefully. "You two have become very close."

Karen felt herself flush. "He's been a great friend."

"And?"

"And what? It wouldn't be right. We'd feel as though we were betraying Shane."

Jenny was about to start a spiel about wanting her to be happy, but she had put her foot in it too many times before. She didn't want to risk upsetting her friend, who seemed in much better form since visiting Shane's grave this week.

"I know what you're thinking," Karen continued, "and there's a side of me that understands I should move on. But there's a lot that needs sorting out. I wouldn't be able to deal with seeing someone else and all the complications that entails."

"And what does Aidan think?"

She blushed again. "We'll see what happens. Maybe we've just become close because of everything we've gone through."

"It's as good a basis as any for a relationship," Jenny encouraged, thinking it would be wonderful to see those two get together. Her friend had grieved long enough. Karen would never stop loving Shane and she would never forget him, but that didn't mean that she should hide away from life or love forever.

Aidan was possibly the only one equipped to understand that while she would never quite let go, at least she could move on. Such a pity Jenny thought, that she couldn't move on from her obsession with keeping the house.

Karen resumed feeding Holly, who this time took the food from her without complaint.

"See? Told you I was onto her," she said triumphantly. "Girl's a fast learner. She knows that she can't mess with the likes of me."

"Right," Jenny said, tidying up. "I'm going to take her for a spin out to Dun Laoghaire to meet with the estate agent. It's the same guy that sold Mike the place in Blackrock, so I hope he doesn't recognise me. If all goes well we'll be out of your hair in no time."

"I told you before that it's not a problem," Karen assured her. "I like having you two around. After all, I wouldn't know myself if I didn't fall over one of Holly's toys on the stairs, and I *definitely* couldn't live without regular doses of *Bananas in Pyjamas* – hey, I'm joking." She ducked laughing as Jenny tried to shower her with washing-up suds while Holly let out a shriek of delight, pleased to see her mother being playful again. "Seriously, you can stay as long as you like – well for as long as I'm here anyway," she added with a shrug.

Jenny hugged her. "Thanks. I don't know what I would have done without you. Again."

"Likewise. So how do you feel about everything now?" Karen asked, picking up a bundle of cutlery and drying each piece before replacing it in the drawer.

Jenny shrugged. "It's strange but kind of ... liberated, I suppose? I couldn't ever say that I'm glad about what happened, but I'm relieved the truth is out at least."

"Have you decided about telling Roan?"

"No. I don't think I will tell him. It was never about him, after all."

Karen hesitated. "Perhaps it was a little unfair of you

to tell Mike then. I mean, why hurt him and deprive Holly of a father? Why say anything at all?"

"I had to. I couldn't continue living a lie."

"And none of this was about Roan at all? Not even a teeny-tiny bit?" Karen pressed.

"Not even a teeny-tiny bit," Jenny replied truthfully. "He means nothing to me now. And anything I felt for him doesn't even come close to my love for Mike. He is, well, he *was*, the only one for me. I don't think it's possible for me to love him any more than I do." Her eyes brimmed with unshed tears. "And it's for exactly that reason that I had to tell him. I know that he's hurting now but in the long run, he's better off knowing the truth. My relationship with Roan was built on lies and I know how devastating that can be."

"Maybe. I feel bad for him, though. He loves you two so much."

"Not any longer, but we'll have to live with it. And we'll be OK, won't we Hols?"

The baby responded by grinning and waving her hands in the air.

Karen went to refill the kettle, then stopped and turned back to Jenny. "Aidan's met with Roan a few times since he came back," she said, hesitantly.

"Oh?"

"Seems he got married. They have a baby now too, a boy I think."

"Wow," was all Jenny could say.

"Does that make you question whether you might've rushed into telling Mike?"

"Nope," she insisted, with a definite shake of the head.

"Nope?"

"I told you before – it was never about Roan, it was about being honest. He has his own family now and I'm sure they could do without any complications."

Karen shook her head. "I still don't fully understand, but there's no denying you seem all the better for it."

Jenny bit her lip. "I wouldn't say that exactly. But I'll get there."

64

Once Jenny had set off to see about a new place to live, Karen decided to make the most of a quiet afternoon to herself.

She was nestled comfortably on the couch with the latest John Grisham novel – legs sprawled across the coffee table and a packet of half-eaten biscuits alongside her – when she heard the doorbell ring.

Suspecting it was Jenny returning early from a cancelled appointment or an unsuccessful viewing, she let out a theatrical exaggerated sigh, expecting her friend to hear. But when Karen opened the door, she got a shock. Standing in her doorway and looking uncomfortable, was none other than Nellie Quinn.

"Hello," Shane's mother said quietly. "Can I come in for a minute?"

Karen was so surprised to see her that she forgot to engage the menacing manner she typically affected when dealing with any of the Quinn family. She and Nellie hadn't spoken face-to-face in over a year.

She stood back to let the older woman come inside and immediately wished she hadn't. As usual, whenever one of the Quinns came within ten yards, the house was like the aftermath of a hurricane.

Jenny had left a selection of clean babygros drying on one arm of the couch, a pair of used mugs sat on the coffee table and the floor was littered with toys – stuff that Jenny had insisted Karen leave for her to tidy once she got back.

Nellie for once didn't comment on the mess and seemed too preoccupied with whatever was on her mind to notice that the dust on top of the television was nearly an inch thick.

Now she turned to face her. "About this 'thing'," she began, obviously referring to the court case. "I'd like to talk to you about it."

Karen's instincts sharpened and her hackles rose. "Fire away," she said, folding her arms defensively across her chest.

"Do you mind if I sit down?" Nellie asked wearily.

Nodding, Karen perched across from her on the edge of Shane's armchair and waited, arms still folded.

"I don't know how to begin, really," the older woman said. "I suppose I just want to tell you that I'm sorry."

Sorry? The very last thing she expected to hear from Nellie was 'sorry'.

"Sorry for the way we've treated you since ...well, since we lost poor old Shane."

Karen's mind began to race and her brain clicked into overdrive. What was Nellie trying to do? Was this some kind of trick to get her to back down?

The older woman exhaled. "You see we didn't – well, I suppose *I* didn't truly appreciate what you were going through. I think it's fair to say that you and I never really saw eye to eye. Somehow I always saw you as a spoilt little rap trying to play house with my son."

"Now hold on a minute ... " Karen began, but Nellie interrupted her with a slow shake of the head.

"I'm sorry, that came out wrong. What I mean is that back then I saw only what I wanted to see. Shane was the baby of the house and – I suppose I might as well admit it – my favourite. Jack was and still is, very independent and the girls – well, you know yourself, girls are different." She removed her glasses and smiled then – a real smile that softened her features and displaced her typically brittle countenance. "It wasn't that Shane was a Mammy's boy," she continued. "It's just that I could never quite picture him all grown-up and with a wife too. I knew he had lots of girlfriends growing up, but when he met you, it was different. You were the one he wanted for the long haul and it broke my heart, to be honest."

She gave a short laugh and Karen didn't know whether to be insulted or touched.

"I know this will be hard for you to understand, but I would never have expected Shane taking up with a girl like you – now don't take that the wrong way," she added, putting a hand up. "What I mean is that I always imagined him with a quiet little thing, afraid to say boo to a goose – or more to the point, to me. But you were nothing like that. You were never afraid to speak your mind and you never left us in any doubt about your feelings on marriage, kids or otherwise. You had everything, a good education, your own career and a strong will, and to be perfectly honest, I felt ... threatened by you, I suppose. After a while, everything became a battle between us. It was always you versus ourselves – Shane's family. I've thought about it a lot and told myself that I don't know how it happened – but now I think I do. You won't like to hear this, but you remind me a lot of myself when I was a young one."

Without meaning to, Karen snorted.

"Oh I know what you're thinking," Nellie chuckled, "but I'm not wrong. You and I are so stubborn that between the two of us, we could torment the Dalai Llama." She laughed and this time Karen had to smile. "And I couldn't tolerate it. I couldn't stomach someone getting the better of me, particularly when it came to my boy. And I know I'm not the only mother who doesn't see eye-to-eye with her daughter-in-law – sure, there have been many tomes written about that very struggle." She paused. "But when Shane died, I didn't reach out to you and I should have. For some reason, I was never able to imagine that you were as bereft as I was, maybe even more so, since you lost the man you were supposed to marry. I never pictured you grieving for him the way I did and I was angry and upset when I heard you weren't going to the funeral. I wasn't able to put myself in your shoes, but I should've pet. Because I knew only too well what it was like to lose my Patrick." Her eyes glistened as she stared across the room at nothing in particular.

"When Shane's father passed, he took a big piece of me with him. If he were here now he'd probably tell you he wished the piece he had taken was my sharp tongue." Nellie chuckled softly. "Anyway over time you and I had built up this wall between us, and after Shane's death and all this business with this house, it became higher."

Karen nodded wordlessly, still wondering where this was going.

"Pet, I was at the cemetery the other day too," Nellie confessed. She saw the shadow cross Karen's face but continued when she said nothing. "I go up there a lot. It's a nice walk and very peaceful – a welcome break from the farmhouse, especially if Marie's youngsters are around," she chuckled. "Anyway, a good friend of mine is laid to rest across the way and I said I'd pay her a quick visit before heading over to Patrick and Shane. I was in the middle of a decade of the rosary when I saw you come up the hill. I knew you hadn't seen me and I was making my way over to you, fully intending to give you a piece of my mind for deigning to visit when I knew you rarely did."

"But it isn't that I don't care ..." Karen blurted, unable to hold her counsel any longer.

"I know that pet," Nellie soothed. "I discovered that when I overheard you chatting to him. I didn't intend to eavesdrop but I was glad I did because it was only then that I could get it into my thick skull that you loved Shane just as much as any of us." She removed her glasses again and dabbed her eyes with a handkerchief.

Karen fixed her with a look of utter disbelief.

"How could you *not* know that!" she cried. "How could you *not* know that I was as broken-hearted as the rest of you, that I still am?"

"Shush, child, let me finish, please."

Karen sat back rigidly in her seat.

"All this time, I thought that you were trying to keep this house to get the better of us – of me, even. That you were determined to fight to the death for it, just to prevent us from getting our hands on it. It was only when I heard you talking to Shane the other day that I realised exactly why you're doing this. You're trying to hold onto him, aren't you Karen? You're trying to preserve all that you have left of him– your memories."

Karen looked away; her eyes brimming with unshed tears as Nellie leant across the space between them for her hand. "But, pet, that won't work – Shane is gone. There's only one place you can keep those memories safe, and that's in your heart."

She squeezed her hand. "When Patrick died, at first I wouldn't let anyone near anything belonging to him. I wouldn't let them get rid of his things – you know the way people always make you do that? They tell you that it's for the best, that it'll be easier, but how do they know? How do they know that it'll be easier? They don't know how it feels – how you feel, when it's like someone has sliced you in two, taken away one half and told you to fend for yourself with the part that's left." Nellie's eyes now too brimmed with tears. "Love, I did you a great disservice when Shane died because I left *you* to fend for yourself. I'm sorry; I should have helped you, I should have known what you were going through. Because I went through it myself."

At this, Karen slumped heavily back on the chair; her body heaving with sobs that couldn't come. When they finally did, Nellie went to her and held her close and the two women wept together – at last sharing their mutual grief.

"I'm sorry too," Karen sniffed, after a little while. "What you said there was true for me also. When Shane died, I didn't give a toss about what you were feeling, I was too wrapped up in myself and so determined to keep you away from the house."

"There's two of us in it, and we're as bad as one another. At this stage, there's no point in going back over it. What's done is done, and we've both made mistakes."

They sat in silence for a bit longer, each comfortable in their shared truce, until eventually, Nellie patted her hand.

"Sure stick on the kettle now and the two of us will have a chat about the house and sort something out between us woman to woman." Wiping away tears, Karen duly stood up. But as she walked towards the kitchen, she heard Shane's mother give one of her trademark sniffs. “So are you going to tidy this place up,” she mumbled, “or will it be left to me, as usual?”

Karen looked back sharply and then let out a chuckle of relief when she saw the twinkle in Nellie’s eyes, and a devilish smile playing about her lips.

Shane would be so proud of them both.

65

Jenny struggled with directions while trying to block out the sound of Holly babbling along to a song on the car radio.

"King's Green, King's Lawn – where the bloody hell is King's Terrace?" she muttered impatiently and then instantly put a hand to her mouth.

She was a very bad mother. If Holly's next words were 'bloody' or 'feck' then she had only herself to blame.

She finally located the correct street to meet the agent about the two-bed townhouse that could well be their new home. The 'To Let' sign affixed to a wall at the end house confirmed that she was in the right place.

Jenny checked her watch. It was two-forty, she was ten minutes late and there was no sign of the agent. Had she missed him?

"Terrific," she grumbled out loud and Holly chuckled contentedly in the car seat. "Oh, you might think it's funny now Missy, but if Mummy doesn't find somewhere for us to live soon, we might have to donate all your toys."

The baby was silent on cue as Jenny rummaged for her phone to call the agent. She was certain she'd left in on the passenger seat. Or had she put it in the glove compartment?

"Da-Da. Da-Da," the baby continued singing giddily. "Da-Da."

"He's not here, hon," Jenny replied absentmindedly. Frustrated, she unfastened her seatbelt to search beneath the seat. When she heard a knock on the driver's window, she popped up with a start and bumped her head on the roof.

"Jesus*!*" she gasped, rolling down the driver's window.

"Not Jesus," Mike said. "Sorry to disappoint you." He shifted his gaze to the back seat. "Hello, honey."

Jenny's thoughts raced through her mind like a horse at Cheltenham. What was he doing here? And how did he know they were here?

For one terrible second, the thought crept into her mind that he might attempt to snatch Holly. Then she calmed herself. Mike wouldn't dream of doing anything like that.

Would he?

"This is a coincidence," she said as calmly as she could muster. "Are you meeting a client around this area or something?"

"No, I came here to see you two, actually," he said

resting one arm on the roof of the car. "I think we need to talk."

"Oh." Confused, Jenny couldn't think of anything in reply as he opened the passenger door and sat in beside her, then turned back again to Holly, cathcing the baby by the hand.

"Can we go somewhere else? Maybe take a walk on the pier – do you have the buggy?"

"I don't have it with me," Jenny lied, completely ill-at-ease. This was all so unexpected.

"What's wrong, Jenny – don't you trust me?" he asked in a menacing tone. Then his face changed and he laughed. "I'm sorry," he snorted, "but it's so obvious from your face what's going on in that imaginative little head of yours. You thought I was about to run off with her, didn't you?"

"No, I did not," she argued, her red cheeks betraying her. "I'm just trying to figure out what you're doing here, that's all. You have to admit, it's a bit strange bumping into you like this."

"Not strange at all. I arranged it."

"You what?"

"The estate agent had to cancel. He recognised you from that time he sold me our place, so he rang me instead. So here I am."

"You came all the way out here to pass on a message? Why didn't you just phone me?"

"Because I wanted to see you," he said seriously. "We have things to discuss. I thought this would be a good opportunity."

Jenny said nothing, still completely unsure as to what he wanted. This was surreal.

"Look, let's go for a walk somewhere, the three of us. Somewhere quiet," he urged gently.

She nodded her assent, wondering what was to come. Then drove away from the shabby street and continued on to the coast road, until reaching The People's Park on Dun Laoghaire waterfront.

With Holly strapped into her buggy and Jenny at the helm, they strolled through the park.

"When you first told me about Roan, I didn't understand," Mike began without preamble. "I didn't get why you lied to me for so long, and then shattered all we had built by admitting the truth. I don't know how many times I've repeated that conversation over and over in my head since." He paused for a moment. "But there was one thing you said that stuck out in my mind. '*I love you too much to lie to you any longer.*' At the time Jen, that didn't make any sense. I mean, how could you say you love me in one breath and destroy everything that was precious to me in the next?"

"I had to," she replied simply. "The guilt had been eating me up inside for so long that I knew I couldn't go on. I should've told you at the beginning I know that, but it just went on and on - to say nothing of the fact that I was never quite sure if he even was the father and – "

"There was never any question about that," Mike said, stopping and she frowned.

"What? What are you talking about?"

He sat down wearily on a nearby bench. "I could

have saved you all that worry, all that guilt and confusion if I'd been honest with you from the beginning."

"What do you mean?" she asked again, perplexed.

Mike exhaled. "That day, when we found out you were pregnant and I started jumping around like a demented kangaroo ... remember you asked why I was so happy when I'd never wanted kids with Rebecca?" He hung his head. "That wasn't it. It was never that I didn't want them, Jen. The simple truth is that I couldn't."

Her mouth dropped open.

"It was true that I wanted to wait until InTech was up and running and yes, Rebecca agreed that we should wait until I thought the time was right. Eventually, we decided to give it a go. We tried for over a year and when nothing was happening we both went for fertility testing. They told me that for various reasons, the chances of my fathering a child were extremely low, even with IVF. Rebecca was devastated. As you know she's older and the doctors told us that her age would probably work against us too if we tried IVF. We did anyway, and ... nothing." Mike paused for a moment and then continued, his voice hoarse. "At first she was OK, very supportive and we decided that we'd do whatever we could, try whatever we could. But eventually, the strain of it all got to both of us and she began to blame me for waiting so long. She would have been that bit younger so our chances would have been better. Eventually her resentment and my guilt, drove us apart."

Jenny listened numbly, her mind all over the place.

"If I'd told you that at the beginning, if I'd been

honest with you back then, the truth would have been obvious when you learned of your pregnancy. But I was just so overjoyed. I thought that by some miracle or freak of nature even, that I'd managed to do what the doctors said I never could."

"Oh, Mike ..."

"I'm sorry," he said, "I'm sorry that I didn't tell you. You deserved to know it, as much as I deserved to know about Roan. Becky was adamant from the very beginning that everything needed to be out in the open. You remember how she reacted a bit strangely when she heard about the pregnancy? She knew that something was amiss. But I foolishly believed that some kind of miracle had happened."

"So Becky suspected all along?"

Jenny felt her insides spin, felt as though the ground was rising up to meet her. Mike had been keeping secrets too.

"She wanted to speak to you then, to ask if there was anything funny going on but I wouldn't let her. I was furious with her for even thinking such a thing, plus I couldn't even consider the notion. As far as I was concerned, I was defying all the odds, a medical miracle." He gave a wry smile and looked out towards the sea.

Jenny stared at Holly, her thoughts going a mile a minute. She tried to comprehend what she was feeling – anger, hurt, disappointment ... what? And yet she couldn't deny that the dominant emotion was once again, relief.

They were both silent for what seemed like an age, until Mike tentatively took her hand.

From her buggy, Holly gurgled up at them both and he looked at the baby tenderly.

"We haven't given her a great start, have we?" he said softly. "The very foundation of our family was built on deceit."

"That's not true," Jenny shook her head. "We loved one another, didn't we? I made a stupid mistake and a bad call, and you wanted to believe something so much you were afraid to face the truth. There's nothing wrong with that either."

"Yes, there is," he argued. "I should never have asked you to marry me without telling you first. God knows I should have learnt how something like that can kill a marriage before it's even begun. And you'd already been lied to enough."

Again they grew quiet, while Holly kicked her legs out, evidently eager to get going again.

"What are we like – the two of us?" Jenny said, eventually.

Mike caressed her hand with his thumb. "I don't know how you feel about what I've told you just now, and I'm not asking you to make any snap decisions but – "

Her expression grew serious. "Mike, Holly needs people around her she can trust."

"Yes." He looked away, stung.

"People she can rely on."

"Of course." He took his hand away and hung his head.

"I suppose," she added, with a twinkle in her eye, "I suppose we could always put the word out, and see if we could find her better parents?"

His eyes widened and then his face broke into a wide smile. "You divil – you frightened me there for a minute."

"Ha. I couldn't frighten you."

"Come here."

"Where?"

"Here." Mike's arms encircled her waist and he pulled her close. "So what do you reckon? Can we start afresh? No more lies."

"No more lies." Jenny embraced him tightly, almost afraid to believe that she actually was in his arms again and she wasn't just dreaming.

"Yay!"

Startled, they both looked down at little Holly, and the baby giggled, thrilled to have had the final say.

MORE FROM MELISSA HILL

Read more unputdownable novels by Melissa Hill, available now.

ABOUT THE AUTHOR

International #1 and USA Today bestselling author Melissa Hill lives in County Wicklow, Ireland.

Her page-turning emotional stories of family, friendship and romance have been translated into 25 different languages and are regular chart-toppers internationally.

A Reese Witherspoon x Hello Sunshine adaptation of her worldwide bestseller SOMETHING FROM TIFFANY'S is streaming now on Amazon Prime Video worldwide.

THE CHARM BRACELET aired in 2020 as a holiday movie A Little Christmas Charm. A GIFT TO REMEMBER (and a sequel) was also adapted for screen by Hallmark Channel and multiple other titles by Melissa are currently in development for film and TV.

Visit her website at
www.melissahill.info
Or get in touch via social media links below.

Printed in Great Britain
by Amazon